Praise for *Nigerians in Space* by Deji Bryce Olukotun

"Olukotun reminds us of some of the most exciting pan-Africanist and anti-colonial futures of the twentieth century. Olukotun crafts a knowing, Afrofuturist pastiche of traditional pulp cliché — reproducing the cocksure attitude, over-the-top descriptions, and authoritative tone of the radio play, while inventing an alternate-history for a covert African space program launched in the 1960s and coming into its own at the cusp of the twenty-first century."

— *Los Angeles Review of Books*

"An exquisite blend of unpredictable twists and lightning-speed plot."

— *The Guardian*

"A madcap first novel that unravels like a spy thriller."

— *Flavorwire*

"Fast-paced, well-written and packed with insight and humor. Olukotun is a very talented storyteller. "

— **Charles Yu, author of** *How to Live Safely in a Science Fictional Universe*

"You can taste Cape Town, you can hear it in the dialogue, see its beauty in the descriptions. Deji Olukotun has my city's number: especially its nasty underbelly, the dangerous dealing of abalone poachers. "

— **Mike Nicol, author of the** *Revenge Trilogy*

"*Nigerians in Space* is one of the most entertaining novels about Africa to come out this year. It's a quirky, multi-city, fast-paced noir fiction piece about a Nigerian lunar geologist who dreams of leading a Nigerian space mission."

— *Brittle Paper*

"A crime thriller that is out of this world."

— *The Brooklyn Paper*

"A deft mingling of satirical humor, Noirish twists…and a keen-eyed yet accessible take on cultural displacement in contemporary times. "

— **Olufemi Terry, winner of the Caine Prize for African Writing**

AFTER

THE

FLARE

DEJI BRYCE OLUKOTUN

The Unnamed Press
Los Angeles, CA

The Unnamed Press
P.O. Box 411272
Los Angeles, CA 90041

Published in North America by The Unnamed Press.

1 3 5 7 9 10 8 6 4 2

ISBN: 9781944700188

Library of Congress Control Number: 2017949599

This book is distributed by Publishers Group West

Cover design & typeset by Jaya Nicely

AFTER

THE

FLARE

For Carolynn

PROLOGUE

That was the night the sun wrapped the Earth in colors like glowing sheets of cellophane. Masha Kornokova was peering through a porthole facing the dark side of the planet, Moscow and Berlin dotting the matte black surface as pinpricks of light. She had just finished a six-hour space walk with Stankov and had swiveled to look back, like she always did. It was her ritual—to remind herself that she had fulfilled her dream and that she was actually *here*, in space, floating above it all.

Through the porthole, intense light blinded her momentarily, and when she could see again, Earth was bathed in lime, purple, and tangerine light, the colors dancing like playful sprites along the crest of the globe. Almost as quickly, the light dissipated, and the entire hemisphere fell dark. Moscow and Berlin were gone, extinguished. The moon was the only source of illumination, reflecting onto carded-wool clouds as the Atlantic Ocean slid away beneath them.

"Did you see that?" Stankov whispered, having come alongside her.

"Kornokova! Stankov!" the comms erupted. "Get to the capsule!"

"Prepare for evacuation!"

"Get your suits on!"

The two astronauts hurtled through the station, clutching handhold after handhold, passing the mess room, then the Destiny module, control panels shorting out around them. The emergency lighting cast a washed-out pall over the place. Kornokova, just behind Stankov, saw a bright trail of sparks erupt above his helmet.

"Stankov! Watch out!"

But her comms were dead. She pulled him away by the arm, spotting a lick of flame shooting along his suit liner as he clutched his head. His oxygen line was torn. The gas was hissing out of it. If the flame touched it, he would go up in a fireball.

"Steady, Stankov. I've got you!"

She pushed off toward the opposite wall and wrested a canister from its Velcro strap, while Stankov swatted blindly at his head, trying to extinguish the source of the heat. With his own comms lost, he was shouting uselessly into his microphone. She pulled the pin from the canister and showered him with foam suppressant.

Immediately Stankov twisted off his helmet, and she saw that the skullcap of his suit liner was smoldering, so she doused that too. It looked bad. The cream-colored liner had melted onto his skin, and Stankov was already clutching at his scalp with his eyes shut tight. He was a tough man—trained in the Bulgarian Special Forces—who never complained. But he was in excruciating pain.

They tried to hail CapCom from within the JEM module but couldn't get a signal, and moved quickly to the Columbus, but still no one responded. Everyone seemed to have disappeared. They kept pulling themselves along toward the Russian end of the space station, where they found the rest of the crew sealed in the Soyuz escape capsule.

There were four astronauts on the station, including Masha and Stankov, and the other two, Jeppsen and Hiroyuki, were huddled inside the capsule. Kornokova rapped her glove on the hatch until someone opened the door.

"Everything's offline," Kornokova said.

"Battery power?" Jeppsen asked.

"Limited. Only emergency lighting."

"Are you injured?"

Kornokova noticed then the smeared blood on her suit. "No, it's Stankov."

"I'm fine," Stankov urged.

"What's our status over here?" Kornokova asked.

"This capsule was shielded and withstood the bulk of the flare," Hiroyuki explained. "We're talking to CapCom now."

On the comms, Kornokova could hear their mission director, Josephine Gauthier, barking information. "We're sending you an updated emergency plan. We weren't prepared for a coronal mass ejection of this intensity. Even radiation-hardened electronics have been pulverized by it. We'll be on generators down here within four hours." Then, noticing her for the first time: "Masha, you're okay?"

Josephine never called Kornokova "Masha" on an open channel. Kornokova could register the concern in her voice, the subtle uplift as she pronounced her name.

"I'm all right," Kornokova said. "What's the new plan?"

"We have detected that the Zarya module has adequate power to support a crew member for six months. There are enough supplies in the offline modules to last much longer, recoverable through EVAs. Our primary concern is orbital decay."

"Propulsion is out too?"

"Yes, both engines on the station have been damaged. The current plan is to evacuate."

"I don't understand," Kornokova said. "We can stay in orbit for three years, even without propulsion."

"Our projections show that the CME will cause the atmosphere to expand, increasing drag on the station. You'll fall out of orbit within twenty-four months, if not sooner. We expect to lose thousands of low Earth orbit satellites."

"All from a solar flare?"

"Listen to me, Masha. *Nothing is working.*"

She registered a hint of fear in Josephine's voice.

"We've got about two hours of emergency power left here in Paris. This is global. By our estimates, all electricity transformers have been destroyed in North America, Europe, and Asia. The Arianes were in the loading docks at Marseille. They're finished. All of the North American rockets are fried. No one else has one ready. Conservative estimates suggest an eighteen-month recovery time for basic infrastructure. For all intents and purposes, most of the world has gone dark. There is"—Josephine paused, trying to find the right words—"total chaos down here."

"What are our orders?" Kornokova said.

"Commander Kornokova, Rilke, and Kazuhito will take the Soyuz down using the instructions I'm uplinking to you now."

Calling me Kornokova again, Masha thought. *Back to work. That is good.*

"The capsule's designed for two," Josephine went on, "but it can accommodate a third passenger with some modifications. We can't guarantee an extraction if you land in the sea, so you'll have to guide it to land. Stankov will remain behind for a rescue mission."

"Stankov should get in the capsule," Kornokova said. "His suit caught fire."

"I am fine," Stankov intoned.

"No, you're not. It's a substantial burn."

Kornokova caught a furrow appear over Josephine's eyebrow.

"Hiroyuki, take a look," Josephine ordered.

The medic maneuvered out of the capsule to examine Stankov's scalp. He turned the astronaut's head this way and that, Stankov wincing from the pain.

"Masha's right, third-degree burn," Hiroyuki concluded. "He can't remain on board without being operated on—he'll need a skin graft. Antibiotics could stave off an infection for about six weeks."

On-screen, Josephine tied her dreadlocks into a ponytail. She couldn't bring herself to give the order, so Kornokova did it for her.

"I'll stay behind."

"The evacuation plan says that you should go, Masha."

"You wrote that plan, Josephine. The plan says that the most able-bodied crew members should always remain. I have no injuries. I've trained for this."

"You've been up there for six months already, Masha. You've lost a lot of bone mass."

It hurt to watch Josephine pleading with her in front of the crew, something she would never have done under normal circumstances. In fact, Josephine rarely acknowledged that they had known each other for more than the duration of the mission. Six months since they had last awoken in each other's arms, pushed together by gravity. Six months since feeling the slip of skin on skin. She missed Josephine more than she missed anything else on Earth.

"I choose to remain here," Stankov tried to insist. He had a strong machismo impulse.

"You're evacuating, Stankov," Josephine decided. "That's an order. You all will be. We'll come back for you, Masha. If this station falls out of orbit, there is an eighty-five percent chance it will strike land. Our current projections show a deorbital footprint landing on Mumbai, India. Most of the station will burn up, but some of it will certainly fall in a populated area. Let's get to work. There is no time for arguments. Follow the procedures." But she didn't sign off. Her face lingered on the screen, as if afraid to cut the connection. "I'll see you soon, Masha."

"I love you," Kornokova said out loud.

She didn't care anymore. The crew all knew anyway. They had kept their relationship off the air so that the media wouldn't cover it. Their love had always been tempestuous, passionate: two fiercely ambitious women who bowed before no one. Yet they were cautious when separated, cold even, repelling everyone around them and sometimes even each other.

Josephine touched her finger to her lips.

Later, as the rest of the crew finalized their evacuation procedures, Kornokova began her inventory of the items that would keep her alive. This cramped place, which she had shared with three other people for six months, would now be her own. Perhaps there would be comfort in that. No dependence. No passive-aggressive comments about escaped boluses, or body wipes, or rehydrated packets of soybeans. Then again: no conversations at all.

Everyone on Earth would soon be offline, Josephine had indicated. What did that mean? When Kornokova became homesick—which was rare—she could take solace in the fact that Josephine stood on firm ground. What would happen to Josephine now? Yesterday she had said she was going to drive to Montpellier for a holiday by the sea, her first day off in months. She would have to cancel that trip now. Maybe Josephine would sleep more soundly without the electric hum of the world. But she had always slept fitfully without Kornokova by her side, complaining when she slipped into bed late.

Kornokova pushed herself farther from the capsule. Time to focus. Time to get away from the cloying emotions. Get things started. This was temporary. This was just another assignment, one that they would finish together.

I am three hundred kilometers above you, Josephine, and falling all the time. I will be a streak in the night when I come to you.

CHAPTER 1

Kano, Nigeria—1 year later

The door to the office burst open, the hinge nearly ripping off, as a throng of workers surrounded Kwesi Bracket's desk.

"*Oyibo, oyibo*, we can't work anymore!"

They all seemed to be shouting at once. Bracket, by custom, was expected to respond with an equal amount of enthusiasm, but he preferred not to excite his crew even further. Instead, he calmly took a sip of water.

"Tell me what happened."

The workers' voices erupted again. They came mostly from the Fulani and Hausa ethnic groups, with a few Igbos sprinkled among them. Their skin ranged in color from rich loam to lighter walnut, all of them darker than Bracket himself.

"*Oyibo*, the dig is finished," one worker announced over the others, placing a ceramic knickknack on his desk. Bracket didn't pick up the thing as a hush came over the room.

"Is that right? I thought that was my call."

"Yes, call! Call the police. They should know about this."

"No, no, that's not what I meant." Bracket shook his head. Sarcasm wasn't their strong suit either. "I meant it's my decision. It's a sports term."

"Sports. There's no sports. Just this!" And everyone pointed at the little vessel.

"Never mind."

The police in Kano, in Bracket's experience, were completely unreliable, and they were the last people he would ever call. If anything, protocol demanded that he notify the spaceport's own security office, Op-Sec. But the strange lump of fired clay currently sitting on his desk didn't merit such a response, regardless of what the laborers thought. Their work stoppages for prayer he'd expected and even encouraged, thinking they were good for morale, in a way, but he was still trying to grasp the rhythmic subtleties of employment here. His crew worked hard but not when he expected them to.

"Everyone out but you two," he said, pointing at the man who had carried the thing in and another guy standing next to him. The rest shuffled out, though he was certain they wouldn't resume the dig until the matter was settled.

After the room cleared and the door was shut, he picked up the little mass of clay. It was encrusted with dirt, shaped like a teardrop, and about the size of an apple. He could tell it was made by hand, and it was surprisingly heavy. It reminded him of old Navajo pottery he'd once seen on a trip to Canyon de Chelly in Arizona when his marriage was dissolving (cottonwood pollen circling in the air; his daughter pointing at an ancient granary in a cliffside ruin; and he and his wife quietly bickering at each other). At the base of the teardrop he found a small crack, and through the crack he could see a dark rock like a lump of coal. The vessel, if that's what it was, was ringed by strange script.

"This Arabic?"

"No, *oyibo*, it's not."

"Can you read it?" He handed the vessel to the second man, a devout Muslim named Abdul from the city of Maiduguri.

"I can't read it, *oyibo*. It's very old."

"It's not Arabic, then?"

"I don't recognize this writing."

"If you don't know what it is, Abdul, then why should we stop digging?"

That was the only question that mattered, after all, but he should have paid closer attention to Abdul's posture. As soon as Bracket placed the relic in his hand, Abdul clutched it tightly and began twisting it about, trying hard, it seemed, not to look at it. Then he flung a stack of papers in Bracket's face and hurtled out the door.

"Wait!" Bracket yelled. He was around the desk in an instant, but the man caught everyone by surprise and slipped by before they could grab him, heading down the stairs, around the heavy machinery of the dig, and out into the blazing heat of the Sahel. Bracket knew there was no hope of returning to work now, not when one of his own crew had stolen from him. They would expect retribution—or justice. The other workers dropped what they were doing and joined the chase after Abdul without Bracket having to say a word, weaving among the bulldozers and excavators that were salting the air with dust.

Far beyond the work site, a rocket platform towered in the distance, draped in webs of scaffolding. A second platform had already been completed, hulking imperiously in green and white a kilometer away. Closer to the work site lay the prep rooms, the mission control tower, the long administrative buildings, the cafeteria, and the airstrip, all dotted with thorn shrubs and wild grasses. At the center of the complex stood a ten-meter-tall bronze spaceship, a stylized replica of the *Masquerade*—the ship being built to rescue Masha Kornokova—festooned with black-painted ziggurats and Gelede masks peering into new realms of time, the cultural heritage of Nigeria forged into a colossal sculptural vision of the future.

Bracket ran after the workers chasing Abdul, who were already cutting off Abdul's escape route, driving him toward a large array of white-painted radio antennae. This was good. There was nothing behind the antenna array but two electrified wire fences and stretches of scrubland. He'd have nowhere to go.

Bracket was a tall, fit man who cycled the twenty kilometers around the spaceport every morning, sometimes before the sun went up, so he quickly outpaced the others and closed the distance.

Abdul was tiring, his gait becoming disjointed and awkward as he was flanked by his pursuers. He tried to force open a door at the base of the biggest dish of the antenna array, but the door was double-locked and dead bolted.

"Hold on, Abdul!" Bracket shouted. "Just stop and nothing happens. Nobody gets hurt. There's no need to run."

Abdul paused, as if considering the offer. "I keep my job?"

"Sure, we can talk about that."

Then they heard the screech of metal grinding against metal. Above them, the massive antennae were beginning to pivot on their axes.

"Give that back to me, and calm down."

But Abdul was frightened off by the other workers encircling him. He leapt on to one of the access ladders to the antennae, pulling himself swiftly up.

"No, stop!"

Bracket had no desire to jump onto the twisting tons of metal, but he couldn't risk the alternative, that this man would somehow halt his project in its tracks with a suicidal leap. He climbed up rung after rung until he could set his feet on the mesh of the parabola. He steadied himself as the dish continued to pivot. Abdul was running along the face of an antenna as the dish began to dip. Before Bracket could reach him, Abdul swung his body over the lip of the antenna like a gymnast and dropped himself to the ground. The dish was at a steep angle now, and Bracket started sliding down its face. He desperately grabbed on to the feedhorn in the middle of the dish to stop himself from dropping. It was a good five-meter fall to the ground, enough to snap a leg or bust a tendon in his knee. He clutched the feedhorn, his legs dangling beneath him, until, thankfully—miraculously—the antenna flattened out again, and he ran back along the dish to the ladder.

He dropped to the ground, breathing hard. Shouts emerged in the distance. He started running again and scrambled over a waist-high berm of soil. On the other side, he saw a low, flat structure about ten meters long that was scarred with broken windows—an old building that was no longer in use, possibly a barracks. He followed the shouts around the corner of the building and nearly collided with several members of his crew, who had stopped and were staring at the ground.

"Where'd he go?" Bracket said.

A worker pointed at a patch of scratchy grass. On it was a spreading pool of dark liquid.

"What the hell is that?"

"Blood."

"What do you mean? Where did he go?" Bracket approached the puddle and stuck his finger into the liquid, disbelieving. It felt warm and viscous, and it stained red against his palm. Blood, to be sure. Human or animal, it was hard to say, but blood it was. The workers looked at him in fear.

"What happened to Abdul?"

"Taken inside."

"Inside the building? Then what are you waiting for? Get in there."

Still gasping for air, Bracket motioned for them to open one of the doors. One of them peeled off and could be heard kicking it open.

"No, *oyibo*, he's not in the building."

"Then where is he?"

"Inside the ground."

"What do you mean? What did you do to him?" He'd heard of mobs killing thieves in the local markets in Kano, but whatever Abdul may have done, he didn't deserve that.

"We chased him here."

They pointed again at the spot and watched as the blood spread out in the leached earth, bubbling like an oil seepage. There was a lot of it, a liter or two maybe. Bracket felt nauseated. "Will someone please tell me what happened?"

The laborers' Pidgin swarmed around him. "He vanished," they concluded. "Like smoke."

"Vanished? What do you mean, vanished?"

"He went away. He was here before, and then he disappeared."

"Did you kill him?"

"No, no, he went away. We didn't touch him."

"You're telling me that man up and vanished?"

"Yes, *oyibo*, that's what we said."

"A man doesn't just disappear. What about that thing he had with him? The pot?"

"It vanished too."

"Magic," someone whispered.

Bracket contemplated this. He hadn't seen Abdul carrying anything other than the artifact. Had he been carrying blood with him for some reason? Had one of the others?

Someone could have helped him escape. He looked closely at his crew, who were all sweating now in the sun. But he knew they were mostly good men who would do nothing to jeopardize a paycheck. Bracket had seen some strange things since arriving in northern Nigeria eight months ago—a thousand ornamented prancing horses during the Durbar festival, and, once, a woman whose limbs were stained deep blue from using indigo dye—but never earth that oozed blood like a fountain.

Either way, his crew was sufficiently disturbed to have calmed down. He went into the nearby building and searched around despite their insistence that he was looking in the wrong place. Inside there were overturned chairs—the type you might find in an elementary school—some file cabinets, and a tall machine lined with what looked like switches for a circuit breaker. On the machine's front panel he could make out the word BENDIX. The floor was coated with dust and he didn't see any footprints, much less any blood.

"Raise your hand," he yelled in exasperation, "if you saw what happened to him." Three men halfheartedly raised their hands, as if unsure what trouble the admission would cause them.

"I want you all to know there's a logical explanation for this. It's not magic. Don't be alarmed. We'll start normal operations shortly."

"What are you going to do, *oyibo*?"

Bracket had ripped his collared shirt when he was dangling from the feedhorn of the antenna. He tore off a sleeve and used it to tamp at the ground, searching for a sinkhole on the spot where they claimed Abdul had disappeared. But the ground was firm. And he realized he had soaked up some of the blood on the shirt. He snatched a plastic bag that was trapped on a shrub, and wrapped the grisly thing up.

"We'll keep this as evidence."

"Of what?"

"Of whatever this is!"

"You going to call the police, *oyibo*?"

"No police. I'm going to talk to Op-Sec and we'll let them take it from here. In the meantime, I want you three witnesses back at my office. Your jobs are safe. And everyone else—get back to your posts."

Bracket assigned a team of ten men to sweep the area one last time. Then, holding the bag in his hand, he walked around the old building. It wasn't on any of the maps of the spaceport complex, as far as he could remember, and it had been abandoned for some time. The machine he'd seen inside had a military feel to it, for what purpose he couldn't say.

The antennae were still moving in unison, screeching on their axes. Watching them rotate, Bracket shook his head, angry with himself for not remembering that there had been a planned telemetry test today. He could have electrocuted himself up there, or been ground to a pulp by the metal gears. He would have died over a piece of old pottery.

As the last of his men started moving out, he called after them: "And I want you all to quit calling me *oyibo*. I told you before, I'm not a white man."

"It's okay, Mr. Bracket," one of them said over his shoulder, laughing. "Everyone from America is called *oyibo*. Black, white. *Oyibo*."

CHAPTER 2

Kwesi Bracket had once believed that living in Africa would be like a homecoming, that the throngs would rise up in jubilation to celebrate his triumphant return. He would impart the wisdom that his people had gained during their centuries of surviving in the modern wilderness of America, and his long-lost brothers and sisters would instill sacred knowledge in him. His journey into adulthood would be marked by clear rites of passage that were as bright as beacons lining an airstrip, launching him across space-time to another plane of meaningful existence. The homecoming would allow him to make sense of his marriage and of his flatlining career at NASA. Bracket was a practical man—trained as an industrial engineer—but after his mother had layered him with batik dashikis, like a cake, somewhere he'd hidden the belief that what was lost would be once again found.

In Africa.

Then the Flare came. Everything changed. Bracket was working at NASA in Houston, and he watched as the United States buckled under an infrastructure collapse of such magnitude that people's lives were changed forever. Everyone thought the government would quickly restore electricity, but then someone—no one knew who—launched cyberattacks that crippled networks, disabling everything attached to them, from heart pumps to refrigerators and generators. At first people stayed put and hoped to ride out the aftermath, eking out simpler versions of their lives and helping their neighbors where they could. But when the White House didn't offer a timeline for recovery, the country began to splinter along ideological lines. Progressives flocked to the Southwest to establish what they called the Pueblo Confederacy, as citizens from all over the country migrated there from colder states where services and supplies grew scarce in less than two months. The affluent locked themselves down on the coasts, hiring private security firms to protect company campuses, neighborhoods, even whole towns; and the San Francisco Bay Area became an entire city-state nicknamed the Silicon Territories, where the tech titans tried to immunize themselves against the chaos. None of this was official, nor was it always real; these were often imagined geographies that people invented in the hopes of regaining control over their lives, which had grown paranoid with mistrust. The Wallers, by contrast, were very real, and some Americans became Wallers overnight no matter where they lived or how they identified. Wallers armed themselves to the teeth, preparing for a battle for survival they feared would happen if the government didn't repulse the cyberattacks and restore electricity. And yet Bracket knew that before the Flare most Wallers had hated the federal government for existing at all.

In Houston, Bracket watched as Texans trampled the border fences with their SUVs on their way toward the Yucatán. Because the reality was that the whole world wasn't offline. A narrow band along the equator—including West Africa and parts of South America—had been protected from the Flare by the magnetic fields of Earth, which had deflected the charged particles. These countries destroyed their international gateways to the Internet and sealed off their networks, with only limited, highly monitored exchange points that allowed information to move across borders. Mass migrations to Central America increased each week as families packed up their belongings in search of the modern way of life. They relied on battery-powered devices, until those ran out, and on modified ham radios that created localized mesh networks to painfully, slowly transmit data. But by then it seemed all everyone had was time.

When the Flare hit, Bracket was working at NASA's Neutral Buoyancy Laboratory, a 6.2-million-gallon water tank that allowed astronauts to run simulations of space walks underwater. First the utter silence awoke him in the night. Out his bedroom window, as if in a dream, the air was infused with rainbow sherbet. He saw swirls of magenta and vermillion, and bursts of green so bright that it was as if you could eat them with a spoon. And then the next day he realized how interconnected everything was. No electricity, no indoor plumbing. No air-conditioning.

No heat.

The Army Corps of Engineers requisitioned the NBL as an emergency reservoir and Bracket found himself unemployed like millions of other Americans, suddenly paralyzed by a lack of purpose. Einstein had failed to include employment in his theory of relativity, that time slows down when you're out of work, the job being the universal constant from which all things flow.

His daughter Sybil was safe at medical school, and he thought about heading north to join her, but she would need money from him, not the other way around. You needed a big bank account to enter the Silicon Territories, too, and their gated artificial intelligence enclaves with their raw computing power could not even begin to meet people's basic needs. The "cloud" had come tumbling down to Earth, fogging the world in confusion.

He was saved by an air-mail letter from Nigeria's National Space Research and Development Agency, inviting him to "design and operate a simulation tank." At first Bracket brushed off the letter as a cruel hoax, but when an old colleague managed to run a search for him on the military net—a sacrifice, given that military staff were allocated limited bandwidth per week—he learned that Nigeria operated the only remaining space program because it had been untouched by the Flare. He immediately applied for the position, including with his application a state-of-the-art design of a water tank that he drafted himself.

Nigeria! In Africa! It was the place his mother had told him so much about, the land from which many black traditions had been drawn. All he had to do was pass a DNA test to prove his African ancestry. One-eighth was the minimum required for a diasporic diplomatic visa to Nigeria. Bracket failed it. He scored one-sixteenth Igbo, which disappointed him after all the dashikis his mother had made him wear in his youth, but didn't surprise him either. When he looked in a full-length mirror, the most African parts of him were his navel and his penis, the dark melanin enrobing the skin. No matter that Bracket could pass for white, which he had never consciously done; his mother believed that he would give rise to the kings and queens of a new Nubian dynasty. The DNA test showed Bracket was also one-sixteenth Seminole, his great-great-grandfather having married an Indian after emancipation in Florida. This pushed his application over the line.

The next day—and not yet four months since the Flare had changed the world—Bracket boarded a C-5 military transport plane from Houston directly to Kano, along with a dozen other black engineers and scientists. It was his homecoming. Except when he arrived he realized that northern Nigeria had nothing to do with dashikis because people didn't wear them.

CHAPTER 3

In formation, the astronauts trotted past Bracket like a platoon of colorfully painted soldiers as he hurried back to his office. The Naijanauts were outfitted in green-and-white tracksuits, the colors of the Nigerian flag, while the Vyomanauts—those were the Indian astronauts—were wearing green, white, and saffron. India had been knocked offline by the Flare too, but when the country learned that the International Space Station was expected to fall onto its largest city, the government sent over its scientists to Nigeria to help build the rockets in a show of mutual cooperation. So now the astronauts wore the colors of their respective nation, like home and away jerseys for a sports team. Bracket kept his head down because the astronauts were waiting for him to finish the simulation tank, and they tended to pester him about its progress as if he had somehow forgotten about it.

Instead he pushed toward the Naijapool complex to debrief the three witnesses who had seen Abdul Haruna disappear. In the operations room, he oversaw every aspect of the project, literally, because the room was perched on the second floor, and it had a viewing window that looked down upon the enormous gulf of the concrete pool, which was as deep as a four-story building.

The mock-up of the International Space Station was already installed at the bottom of the pool. The NBL in Houston could fit only small sections of the station, so Bracket had designed Naijapool to accommodate all the modules that would affect the rescue of Masha Kornokova. This included the European lab and the Kibo module, and they were all built full scale. For now the astronauts busied themselves with walking inside the mock-up, but it couldn't compare with an actual underwater simulation in which their weighted suits behaved like they would in space.

From the operations room, Bracket could also observe the other facilities already built out and occupied by staff: the test conductor rooms, the control room, the locker rooms for the astronauts and scuba divers, the suit-donning room, the assembly area, and the hyperbaric and hypobaric chambers. Flags of supporting space agencies were draped from the ceiling between the overhead cranes: the Indian Space Research Organisation, the European Space Agency, NASA, JAXA, KARI, and others. The operations room itself was filled with banks of computers, video monitors, and large drafting desks to review blueprints or examine equipment as the need arose. Bracket compulsively kept the room neat and organized.

The workers were there when he arrived. One by one, he recorded their testimonies:

Witness 1: Sandton Magu, Kaduna State:

I was chasing the thief because he was a bad man. I did not know him. I came to the building and I was going to beat him with a stick. When I found him he was not there anymore. I didn't see what happened to the thing he stole. I swear I did not attack him. Just because I'm a big man, people think I attack everyone. It's not true. I'm a gentle man. I think he's still out there somewhere, and we should catch him, *inshallah*.

Witness 2: Billy Madueke, Bauchi State:

His name was Abdul. I did not like him very much because he didn't talk a lot. He was always watching, you know, like he might steal something. I am not surprised he was a thief. I like people who talk, not people who hold secrets. I'm a naturally outgoing person myself. I was close to him when he tried to run away. I thought I could catch him, but he fell down before he disappeared. He was low to the ground. His hand was pulled ahead of him, like a dog tugging on a leash. I didn't see what happened to the thing he stole. And then the blood appeared, like he had melted, or a cow's throat had been slit. Good riddance.

Witness 3: Handsome Amaechi, Kano State:
I'm a fast runner, so I was close to him when he disappeared. We came to the building and he looked sick. What do I mean by sick? Like when you are about to vomit. His body pulled forward like this. [He acts as if his body is lurching.] It looked like someone knocked him over onto his face. Maybe the blood is what he vomited. I don't know where he went after that. The little pot—he took it with him, I think. It was in his hand. Yes, Handsome is my given name.

The men left and Bracket was finally alone. He leaned back in his chair and closed his eyes, going through a breathing exercise his daughter had taught him.

Breathe in.

From the very beginning, there had been countless obstacles at the spaceport. He'd needed to find oversized earthmovers in Kano, and they weren't easy to locate, since they were mostly owned by Chinese parastatal companies; he'd also had to secure a large supply of diesel fuel on his own because the program hadn't allocated him enough fuel to power the generators, thinking that the pool would already be linked to the solar array.

Out.

That effort alone had been a logistical nightmare, more from the standpoint of figuring out how to bargain with local suppliers, who tried to fleece him, than installing the tank. The sheer size of Naijapool demanded extra grading of the earth, as well as reinforced rebar that was rare in this part of the country. On top of this, the electrical equipment ran on different voltages depending on their supplier, and the specifications could either be Imperial or metric.

In.

And then there had been the other things. The things that could not be described as the normal course of trying to launch a rocket from Africa. Many of his electronics spat out inaccurate or unreliable data. This wasn't because of the heat, but some kind of electric discharge that the on-site technicians couldn't explain. Bracket had since reinforced much of the hardware—at premium prices—and then placed the servers on rubber mats so that they were air-gapped from the wall. He'd also mandated regular data backups on numerous devices. And yet, the failure rate of his equipment seemed to increase the further they dug into the ground. And he wasn't alone either. His colleagues told him that they often received skewed data on routine technical tests. Not to mention that the political status of the project always seemed to be wavering, with many pundits and politicians wondering why Nigeria was wasting its resources and funds when the country faced so many other challenges.

Out.

And now this. He started composing an incident report for Op-Sec that included the testimonies, but found himself deleting it midway through. If he contacted Op-Sec, word would soon get to his boss, Josephine Gauthier, that something had gone wrong. And Josephine did not like surprises, especially not surprises that could lead to a police investigation. He was on bad enough terms with her already, as she'd attributed nearly every unforeseen setback at Naijapool to problems of his own making. And in truth, if he hadn't run out to the antenna array himself, he never would have believed the workers' stories. He needed to bring this to her in person.

Bracket searched for his Geckofone to reach out to her, but couldn't see the device anywhere. He called for it. It blinked green on the ceiling next to an overhanging lamp, where it was drawing solar power. He snapped his fingers twice, and the Geckofone obediently slithered along the ceiling and down the wall, allowing him to pluck it off with his hands. The G-fone flattened its body and retracted its legs once in his palm, so that it looked more like an ordinary phone. He could swipe through screens, use gestures, or give it commands through its microphone. Its legs, head, and tail—formed from interlocking graphene scales—could extend and scale up sheer walls like an actual lizard. Indeed, the effect was so convincing that real geckos would slither over to inspect the device and occasionally attack it. Most of the time Bracket kept it in his pocket, where it would draw energy from his body heat.

He logged on to the Loom, the spaceport's secure network, by wrapping all four fingers around the skin of the G-fone and saying a random passphrase aloud to gain access. He quickly fired off a note to Josephine Gauthier:

Need to meet. Important. KB

The Loom had originally been called the Akwete Network, after the exquisite cloth weavers from the town of Akwete, but the astronauts had christened it the Loom and the name had stuck, because people treated the astronauts like royalty, even if Bracket felt they didn't deserve it.

He checked his inbox.

Message 1: PRIORITY MESSAGE
Message 2: Weather Report—NIGMETSAT
Message 3: Consecration of the *Masquerade*

To read the priority message, he had to take out a key that looked like a straw from his desk and then check the calendar. The kola nut was designated for Tuesday. He opened up a small jar, extracted a kola nut, peeled it, and took a bite, feeling a sharp rush as the stimulant coursed through his taste buds and gums. Kola was still used in Nigeria as a traditional greeting, part of a ritual to begin conversation among a number of tribes, and this, along with many other traditions, had been integrated within the facility's security systems. The nut tasted of metal, like a cool can of Coke, and exhilaration at the same time. After chewing for a moment, he inserted the straw into his Geckofone and blew into it. The device analyzed the particles in his breath and opened the message.

A convoclip from Sybil.

"Hey, Dad! I'm doing good down here in Grenada. Second month of classes."

"How's the weather, baby?" he whispered to his daughter. The rest of the world seemed to dissolve around him.

"It's all right," she responded. "Hot all the time, but at least we can go swimming in the sea. Thurston bought me some snorkeling gear, and he said he's going to teach me how to dive next week. We might even see some sharks!"

"Who's Thurston?"

"I'm sorry, Dad. I don't know the answer to that. Have another question?"

"Is Thurston your boyfriend?"

"I'm sorry, Dad. I don't know the answer to that. Have another question?"

"Are you dating someone right now?"

"I'm sorry, Dad. I don't know the answer to that. Have another question?"

In.

Convoclips took up less data than video clips and could get through the Loom firewall, but they were frustrating, designed to make the messages more intimate by simulating a conversation. It didn't always work.

Out.

"How do you like Yale, Sybil?"

"I'm doing good down here in Grenada. Second month of classes."

Doing well, he thought. She'd picked that poor grammar up from his ex-wife, and she kept saying it much to his irritation.

Seeing that he wasn't going to get anything more out of her, probably on purpose, because Sybil was clever when it came to talking about her boyfriends, he said: "You got enough money, baby?"

"Thanks for asking, Dad. I received your cowrie transfer so I was able to pay this semester's tuition. It didn't leave a lot of money for living expenses, but it's all right, I'm going to get a job on campus somewhere. Hopefully Dr. Crother's lab. He's an expert on limb transplants."

The medical school in Grenada had officially been taken over by Yale when the Northeast went dark, and the Ivy League school now occupied the complex that had once been invaded by President Reagan in the 1980s. Many people had flocked to the south Caribbean, and Grenada was viewed as a safe haven from the Wallers. The libertarians preferred the Silicon Territories. It could be difficult to keep track of the isms—the Flare had rearranged the geography of political philosophies.

"You still doing your paintings, Sybil?"

"Mom made it to Santa Cruz with Ramsey. She said they found a house in one of the enclaves. They have a redwood in their back-yard! If I can save up enough, I'm going to go visit them at the end of the semester, since you said I can't come to Nigeria."

Now the convoclip felt positively toxic. Bracket didn't know his ex-wife's new husband, Ramsey, well, other than he lived beyond his means and had a daughter of his own from a previous marriage whom he lavished with gifts. He was a selfish prick. The visa into the Silicon Territories must have cost a fortune, a land-settlement claim even more so. Yet somehow Ramsey couldn't scrape together any cowries to send to Sybil for her studies. Bracket wanted his daughter to come visit him in Kano, he really did, but the spaceport was no place for a kid like her to live, not now at least.

"Tell your mom I said hi," he said, the words grating against his tongue.

"I'm doing good down here in Grenada. Second month of classes."

"Can you send me a photo?"

"Good-bye, Dad. Irie! Love you!"

"Love you too, babe."

He closed the message, thinking: *I need to send her more money.* Then: *Fuck Ramsey, I can't lose my job right now,* and: *Who the hell is Thurston?* He hoped he wasn't some local gangbanger. He hoped she was smarter than that.

Come see me at the Nest. JG

Josephine had written back. It was time to go.

Finally, he looked at the weather report:

NIGMETSAT-12 Report. Kano. Tuesday. High 35 degrees Celsius. Low pressure detected over the Gulf of Guinea, with accompanying high pressure over eastern Sahara and dust plumes rising to two kilometers above sea level. Harmattan may begin as many as four weeks early.

As if there wasn't enough trouble, Naijapool would be filled with sand from the Sahel if they didn't begin pouring the water soon.

CHAPTER 4

A muezzin sent out an amplified, wavering call from the space-port mosque as Bracket made his way toward mission control to meet with his boss. His crew began setting down their tools along the pool deck to pray. Outside in the half-light, the oblong angles of the mission control tower cut sharply against the sky. The building, which staff called the Nest, stood atop six enormous pylons of concrete and was ringed by giant windows of photosensitive glass. Thick conduits of fiber-optic cable pulsed with light from information networks extending along the equator to the spaceport. Crystalline antennae poked this way and that, transmitting wireless signals throughout the country, creating the feel of glowing twigs lining the top of a bird's nest.

Josephine Gauthier was the mission director of the Nigeria Rescue Venture, and she had already cleared Bracket to enter the Nest—but the steel door at the entrance remained closed as he approached it.

"Turn off your identity," Josephine announced over an intercom. "You're not cleared under Hausa."

"It's my default."

"Switch your tribe to American. That's what you are."

Bracket reluctantly switched from Hausa back to American, and the door slid open. The Geckofone allowed you to alternate rapidly between multiple ethnic identities—Yoruba, Igbo, Fulani, or even Ijaw and Ogoni—each isolated from the next identity at the root level, meaning that the tribes couldn't be compromised by malflies, dumb microdrones that hovered around electronics trying to inject malware. The identities were more than avatars, since they changed the inflections of your voice and exaggerated your physical gestures too. It allowed for security and anonymity and in theory served as a defense against violence caused by tribalism.

His identity switched, he climbed the stairs and emerged in the mission control room, a voluminous, domed structure packed with screens displaying locations all around the spaceport. One set of screens showed the interior of the International Space Station, where the astronaut Masha Kornokova was evidently asleep, strapped into a sleeping bag on a wall of the capsule, strands of her blond hair drifting above her brow. Through the exterior windows, which wrapped 360 degrees around the Nest, Bracket could see the lights of the airstrip illuminated in the distance. The building felt like a control tower at an airport because Josephine had designed it that way.

His boss sat within a circle of monitors at the very center of the control room. Her hair was tied into a ponytail, the tips of her dreadlocks dyed orange, like a tarantula. Josephine was of French-Guadeloupian descent, so in the United States people might have guessed she was Dominican or mixed race, or certainly a person of color. But her skin color didn't stop her from saying some of the most discriminatory things about Africans that Bracket had ever heard. On the console in front of her, Bracket could see a video of a crane lowering a strut into place, probably at the engine-testing facility run by the Indians.

"Controlled burn," Josephine explained. "Third test today." She spoke some commands to an on-site engineer, and data from the burn appeared on her screen.

"We're going to have to do better than that, Raj," she said. "I want another test tomorrow morning."

The engineer on the screen signed off. During a real mission, Josephine would be hooked into a heads-up display with haptic feedback, which would buzz based on the importance of any issues that might arise. For now, she appeared to be keeping an eye on things without hooking in.

"Have a look, Kwesi," she said. She swiped to a new screen. Bracket could now see a video of himself in his office at Naijapool: the black plastic glasses, the overhanging brow, the sharp-edged, wide-flared nose, and the light gray stubble poking around his thick jaw. The broad shoulders and muscular forearms. The circles under his hazel eyes blackened like a catfish. Standing next to Josephine, he rubbed at his eyes and felt dirt peel away.

I need coffee, he thought. *Or a drink.*

"You were at your desk and then you bolted, Kwesi," Josephine said. "Tell me what happened."

"How often do you look at that camera?" Bracket retorted.

"Don't flatter yourself. I'm not spying on you. I look when something happens. Your G-fone showed your pulse going through the roof."

He looked around the room to see who else was within earshot. Her staff all appeared to be deeply engaged in their tasks, but someone might be paying attention to their conversation. People gossiped at the spaceport as much as anywhere else.

"It's confidential," he said.

"All right," she said, and nodded. "Duck." She reached down to pull a lever at the base of her command chair. A yellow warning light spun around her desk as four milled alloy wedges emerged from the floor around them. Soon they were encapsulated in a metal shell lit by infrared lighting, and a manual keyboard popped up. A ventilation fan buzzed on, keeping the chamber cool.

"Nothing's getting in or out of here except through the keyboard," Josephine explained. "You can speak openly."

Bracket cleared his throat. "My workers found something at the site, a piece of old pottery. One of them took off with it, and we chased him down. But by the time we got there he had disappeared."

"Disappeared?"

"We couldn't find him anywhere. There was some blood, but we don't know if it was his. No one saw where he went."

She leaned back in her chair, thinking it through. "What do you think happened to him?"

"We searched everywhere for him and didn't turn up anything. He could have been working with someone else. I think it could have been a trick too, although I'm not sure why he'd trouble himself with it. The pottery looked old, I mean real old. Like an artifact of some kind. My workers dug it up near Naijapool."

"*Merde putain,*" Josephine swore. "You're sure they found it near the tank?"

"Yes."

"Did you tell Op-Sec?"

"I wanted to bring it to you first."

"Good. You'd better not tell them, Kwesi. Don't tell anyone. We're on federal territory, but Bello was only able to buy the land from the Emir of Kano by promising to turn over any cultural patrimony—anything with historical value. There are rigid protocols for that. We'll have to halt the mission, bring in an archaeologist, catalog the site, everything. We can't afford to do that right now, not on the schedule we're pushing. People have been living in Kano for a thousand years. I already warned Bello that we can't stop for every little calabash we find in the ground. What's the worker's name, the one who ran away?"

"Abdul Haruna. Quiet guy. No one expected it of him. All I know is he's not coming back here again."

"I'll delete his employment file. He'd better keep his mouth shut. You think he'll do that?"

"If you ask me there might have been someone else involved. I had three witnesses come forward and give me their testimonies, but they didn't see anyone besides Abdul."

"Give me their names," she said. "I'll delete their files too."

He shook his head. "I gave them my word their jobs would be safe if they came forward."

"You shouldn't have done that," she snapped. "Now you have to watch them too."

"They won't talk, Josephine," Bracket insisted. He wasn't sure of it, but he felt his crew was ultimately loyal to him.

"They'd better *not* talk. At least scrub their testimonies. And another thing," she went on, "you should never have left your G-fone unattended. That's a major security risk. If you had been injured, we would not have known how to respond. I can't find you if you don't take it with you."

"Won't happen again," he said. He didn't like bowing to her every criticism, but she seemed to be coming at him from every angle of attack today.

"Kwesi, I truly don't have time for this. We needed to begin filling Naijapool yesterday."

They glared at each other for a moment—he wasn't going to serve as her punching bag either.

"We're scheduled to begin pouring the water on Thursday, Josephine. I told you that the cabling isn't up to scratch. I want redundancy before we drop anyone in the water."

"It's not my fault you ordered inferior cable."

"I didn't order it. You made me go through the approved vendor list. I never know what I'm going to get from them, if they deliver at all. I needed a hundred millimeters and they brought me sixty. It's what showed up. Five hundred meters of it."

It had been five hundred yards, actually, which the vendor couldn't explain because Nigerians used the metric system.

"Okay, fine. On Thursday, you fill the pool. You'll be ready?"

"If I find the right cable."

"If you find the cable—do you know how unprofessional this is, Kwesi? This never would have happened in Paris. We always stayed on schedule. We can't launch a rescue mission without the astronauts running simulations. The pool is the only way to do this. Every day that you keep it dry we lose a day of practice. Do you know how many people I have breathing up my neck right now?"

Down your neck, he thought. *Breathing down your neck, not up it.*

"Kwesi, you need to stop running on Nigerian time. I thought you were from America. You're not acting like an American. Nigerians spend a fortune on fancy watches to tell time that they will never keep. You're acting like a Nigerian, like this is a sinecure. It's not a sinecure, Kwesi. There are actual lives in danger."

Bracket didn't know what *sinecure* meant, though he caught the gist of it. She was saying he was lazy.

"You're being unfair," he said. And he listed off a dozen obstacles he'd overcome that week alone.

"Look," Josephine admitted, softening for once. "Nurudeen Bello is coming back tonight."

"For the dedication ceremony? I thought that was a staff event."

"Not anymore. I tried to convince him we're not ready for him, but he didn't want to listen. He's going to be here in an hour with all his people. Don't you dare say a word of this to him."

Now Bracket understood why she was so irritable. Nurudeen Bello was the politician who had founded the entire spaceport, but he mostly spent his time raising funds for the project in the halls of power in Abuja, the capital of Nigeria, or regaling the glinting boardrooms of Lagos, the economic engine of the country. When he worked from the spaceport he tended to bring a coterie of hangers-on who interrupted everyone.

"I'll make sure my crew knows he's coming," Bracket said. "One more thing, Josephine. You ever heard of Bendix?"

"Bendix? It's a kind of chocolate mint. Haven't had one in years. Quite delicious." Then, as if he held some in his pocket: "Do you have some? The chocolate in this country is shit."

"You're saying Bendix is a chocolate company?"

"One of the best."

One more mystery of Kano, he thought.

"I didn't see any chocolates. All that I saw was an old machine in a building by the array."

He could register her disappointment as she turned back to the console before her. "What does this have to do with anything, Kwesi? *Rien!* I told them when we hired you that you didn't have enough experience. I was hoping you could prove you weren't just a handsome face. This is your last chance. Fill up the pool, or I'll have to put one of the Indians in charge."

She switched the lever in the command chair, and the alloy petals retracted, with thirty staff members now watching them curiously, trying to guess what they had been talking about. He wondered if she had made the same threat to them too, that she would outsource their jobs, if given the chance, and replace them with an Indian who was smarter and who could do the work at a lower cost. She never threatened to replace Bracket with a Nigerian.

He shouldn't have mentioned the chocolates.

Over the past few months, he'd seen Josephine dismiss people for minor mistakes, and she held it against him that NASA had fired him after the Flare, as if this were a stain he could never erase, a birthmark of indolence, even if ten thousand other workers had been fired at the same time.

Josephine had advanced her career at the European Space Agency in what Bracket called the slipstream: pulled along, like a crafty cyclist in the peloton, by mentors who recognized her intelligence and determination. And when her bosses left for another job, typically to the private space agencies, she slung forward in the draft to the top echelons of management. Like most people who glided along the slipstream, she had no patience for people who rode outside it, and she downplayed her own luck—that she happened to be at the agency when they were promoting women, or that she was hired because she had a business degree from INSEAD instead of the usual astrophysics degree. In Josephine's view, she had found the slipstream by herself and she didn't care whether she had made her own luck. People like Bracket weren't clever enough to join the peloton in the first place.

Now Josephine was always spinning around the next bend, threatening to leave him behind. She kept a calendar of the number of days since Masha Kornokova had been stranded in the International Space Station, which she would log with a red grease pen as thick as lipstick: 370.

CHAPTER 5

Later that night, spiritual leaders from all over the country began to appear, flown to Nigeria Spaceport at great expense for the consecration of the bronze replica of the *Masquerade*. Bracket marveled at the jingling dresses of Ijaw priestesses and the intricately carved masks of the Ogoni inside the spaceport's central auditorium.

Oh, Mom, if you could only see me now, Bracket thought. *The homecoming that you dreamed of for me.*

The Emir of Kano himself arrived on horseback from the city, with his cavalry and horses festooned with pomegranate-colored cloth, imparting an air of importance and dignity to the affair. He served as the spiritual leader of Kano and much of the Muslim north, but right now he also was the one who could close down Naijapool if he knew what Bracket had discovered there.

After cleaning himself up at his quarters that night, Bracket had thrown the bloody cloth in the wastebin, thinking if it was still there when he returned after the dedication ceremony, and the sanitation crew hadn't tossed it away, then he would do something more about Abdul Haruna. He walked only a couple of steps from his door before turning on his heel to stuff the cloth into a drawer. It felt cowardly to pretend it hadn't happened. He understood why Josephine wanted him to keep it quiet, but he had questions of his own. A man did not just disappear into thin air like that.

Mulling over these thoughts, Bracket filed into line with the rest of the spaceport staff to shake the hand of Nurudeen Bello, who insisted on receiving each of them as if they were at a wedding. Bello was a compact man whose head barely reached Bracket's chest, and yet he was rarely described as short. The politician possessed a natural charisma that made it seem like you were always looking up to him, and lucky to be shaking his hand. His reputation made him seem even larger: a whistleblower who had escaped imprisonment to reveal an entire secret counterterrorism organization that had once controlled Nigeria like a shadow government; a former bandleader who had once toured the country with his music; now, the head of Nigeria Spaceport. The list went on. He was wearing an airy indigo agbada covered with prints of rockets and sporting a *fila* cap on his head crooked to the left side.

"Nice to see you again, Mr. Bracket." He scrutinized Bracket with an intense gaze that caused him to lean back. "Any water in Naijapool yet?"

"It will be ready soon, sir. We're set to begin filling it before the end of the week."

"I look forward to seeing it. We can't afford any more delays."

"Thank you, sir. We'll do our best."

The next woman in line pressed forward, interrupting them, with Bracket thinking, *When was the last time I called someone "sir"?*

Bello soon took the podium and a hush descended over the audience. "There are seeds I've seen on the Jos Plateau," he began, "that can only propagate by means of fire. It takes a broiling, enraged inferno to crack the thick shell and release the seed, which will be carried by the wind over the charred, brittle earth. Only then does the seed enlodge itself in the soil and spread its tendrils to grow into a hearty plant. We too have been forged in the fire. We too required the cauldron of the sun to melt down our ambitions, our dreams, and our enmities to seek out a bold new direction. The Flare—the great cosmic intervention—has given us an opportunity to prove our ingenuity and to right the wrongs of the past. Before it, our program had a modest goal to send an astronaut to the moon, but now our aspirations are much higher, tied indeed to the very fate of space travel. Other countries shook their heads when we announced our intention to rescue Masha Kornokova. But we weren't dismayed.

"Nigeria has looked beyond our imaginary borders so that we could find you. You are the paragons of African ingenuity who are destined for the stars—the bones of our women are nearly twenty-five percent more dense than other people, making us perfect for long-term space exploration. We all must take our opportunities when they arise, and our moment is now."

A cheer rang out from the hall as he riled up the crowd, and Bracket too felt the excitement of his infectious vision. The politician led the notables outside with the help of his aides into a warm evening pillowed with clouds. Before them, the replica of the *Masquerade* shone under the spaceport's klieg lights. The actual spacecraft was sealed in a sterile hangar a kilometer away.

The replica was an impressive blend of artistry and engineering, designed by a sculptor from Ife who specialized in bronze who had pulled off a terrific feat: all the curvilinear surfaces—from the nose cone to the swell of the ram's-horn thrusters—incorporated the geometry of traditional masks from the country's numerous ethnic groups. The viewing windows opened like slits, and the hatches jutted out prominently. The slow curve of the hull resembled the canoes of the floating villages of Makoko. Instead of tiles, the underbelly of the real ship would be covered with heat-absorbent, lab-grown scales that the sculptor had interpreted as crocodile skin.

Each soothsayer took turns blessing the *Masquerade*, throwing rice, burning smudges, pounding drums, or clapping their hands in drawn-out ceremonies, which were cacophonous and chaotic and beautiful and long-winded, yet Nurudeen Bello insisted that no one could eat dinner until they were completed. The final ritual closed when an ancient, leather-skinned Tiv elder tooted on a mahogany horn until he collapsed, and Bracket was nearly trampled by the rush to the banquet table.

He tried to make conversation with the director of India's Liquid Propulsion Systems Centre, who politely asked what he did on the project.

"I'm the director of Naijapool," Bracket said.

"Ah, yes, the swimming pool. I've heard it has no water."

Before Bracket could retort, the man clutched at his chest as his Geckofone burst from his pocket.

"Catch it!" he shouted. But Bracket missed it as it scurried under the table.

And he wasn't alone. All around the room Geckofones were leaping out of purses and coats and pockets, as the banquet hall erupted in pandemonium. The escaped G-fones clustered together in the middle of the room to form the shape of a large arrow. Then the arrow illuminated in bright neon blue, and slid rapidly out of the room, their owners sheepishly running after it. Gradually, the banquet hall calmed down, and people sat back down to eat. Bracket clutched at his pocket but his Geckofone hadn't moved. The emergency signal wasn't meant for him.

Sitting by himself at a table, spooning *ewa agoyin* stew into his mouth and thinking, alternately, about what the emergency might be and what had happened to Abdul Haruna, he didn't notice at first when a woman sat beside him.

"You didn't get called into the Nest either?" she asked.

She had large brown eyes flecked with green and thick, luxurious black hair that fell to the small of her back. She was a full head shorter than him.

"No, I work on ground operations. You know what that was about?"

"Something about the Kibo module being damaged. Space debris."

"Kornokova?"

"She's alright."

"Good," Bracket said, relieved. "I'm sure Josephine will send out an alert soon."

"I feel bloody useless," the woman admitted. She pointed at his plate. "Especially since we're enjoying this feast while Kornokova's up there."

"We should eat while we can." This day had drained any desire to ingratiate himself. Besides, he had plenty to focus on. He'd have to drive into town bright and early to get cable for the pool.

"You sound like a good ol'-fashioned Waller, stuffin' your face fulla barbecue as the rest of the world starves."

"The Wallers ration like everyone else," he corrected, "and they kill anyone who tries to take theirs. They spare the children, mostly. I've seen them gun people down right in front of my eyes."

"I'm sorry," she apologized. "Shouldn't have said that. I know it's bad in America."

"Bad everywhere." He shoveled another bite of rice into his mouth as she extended her hand.

"I'm Seeta."

"Kwesi."

Just then, the loudspeakers erupted with highlife music, and everyone set down their plates to dance. The most sullen Nigerian astrophysicist was now sticking his rump into the air and twisting to the trumpets. Seeta pulled Bracket to the dance floor, twirling her hands about her face. She turned around, grinding her butt into his groin, then spun around to press her thighs against his hip. Her moves helped the other dancers. Freed from any awkwardness, they all slipped forward in the groove.

Much later, Bracket pulled two bottles of Guinness from an ice bucket and joined Seeta on a bench outside in the cool night air. They spotted a satellite falling from the sky, flaming across the darkness and disintegrating. She explained that she was a vibroacoustic engineer whose job was to ensure the integrity of the structures exposed to the tremendous pressures of rocket launch, when acoustic shock waves could exceed 180 decibels. The sounds were extremely random, meaning that both the amplitude and frequency of the energy changed continuously. A strong shock wave could dislodge parts of the structure or send a fissure through the rocket that could blow apart the entire spacecraft. He'd long since learned that a space program had many ultra-specific jobs that he'd never imagined before.

He watched her lips as she spoke, seeing the upper lip pucker with the vowels in a charming, fascinating way.

"You should have heard the sounds I measured on the Mangalyaan missions," she reminisced. "The wind pushing through the rubble-strewn valleys of Mars. It was haunting."

"Must have been a big change for you to come out here."

Anything to keep her lips moving.

"I signed up for the exchange program," she continued, "thinking I could do my part in the mission. But I was bored to tears when I got to Kano. The rocket platforms had not even been built yet, so I spent my time recording local musicians. I record all my own music, you see, but not like ethnomusicologists. It's important to me to record the ambient environment as well—the insects, the birds, street sellers, even the car horns. I went out to Lake Chad to record some musicians playing outside, and the biophony—that's the full range of sounds in an environment—is extraordinary. Around the lake, the insects time their vocalizations so that they don't sing at the same moment. This way they have a better chance of finding a mate. And if an insect has to vocalize at the same time as a bird, or a mouse, or a bat, it does it at a different frequency, so that the signal can still get through. You can find this all over the world in any rich habitat. But what I found out by Chad—listen to me, I'm making it sound like the lake is a person—the soundscape is so rich, and the musicians are part of it. I met this lute player who wasn't especially skillful, not in the way you find with kora players, but her music felt so right. She had good rhythm, I knew that much, but only when I listened to the recording later did I understand it wasn't the rhythm. She had tuned her lute a half step down so that it fit perfectly with the cicadas and other insects in the background. Her music fit the biophony. On its own, no one would have called the sound beautiful."

"That's all new to me," Bracket admitted. "When I listen to music, I like to hear the beat, the vocals." He wasn't sure what to think of this woman. He didn't have a high opinion of anthropologists as a rule, especially amateur ones. They seemed like pornographers of the authentic, leaching off other people's lives.

"I've tried to share the recordings with my girlfriend back in Delhi," Seeta added, "but I can't reach her. It's not a high enough fucking priority to leave the Loom."

Bracket unlocked his eyes from her alluring face, embarrassed. *Was she teasing me the whole time? What was the sexy dancing all about?*

"When was the last time you talked to her?"

She looked at him and laughed, as if surprised. She had meant to shock him.

"The bloody Loom won't let anything through. It rejects my messages."

"Rejects mine too. Sometimes a convoclip will slip through."

She threw her Guinness into a recycling bin and began walking away, but glanced over her shoulder as if to invite him along. He found himself falling into stride with her as the sounds of the dance party began to fade away. He didn't ask where they were walking, afraid it would break their flirtation. She had just talked about her girlfriend, but he still felt a thrill that there might be something more.

"Who are you trying to talk to?" she asked.

"My daughter, Sybil, mostly. Sometimes my ex to talk about my daughter. She's going into her second year at med school, and doing well too. But the Flare set her back awhile. At least I know the cowries get through to her. How about you—how'd you meet her?"

He wanted some finality around the situation, so that if she was closed to him tonight he could act accordingly.

"Before I went to graduate school, I worked as a Pyper. We'd communicate through the music, you know, make a game of it. I'd ask her at the end of the day, when we were lying in bed, which song I had chosen for her," Seeta said, peering up at the stars. "I feel cut off from her now. Really cut off. Sure, I was spinning for a lot of people, but every set had something for her in it."

What the hell, Bracket thought. "You still got your equipment?"

Soon, they were back at her trailer, and he could see that he had activated something joyful and liberating in Seeta as she set up her broadcast equipment.

Bracket had tried listening to Pyper DJs, who walked around spinning songs over a hyperlocal mesh network, and if you were tuned in, you could follow along. Some of them were famous and made money walking the streets or riding on bicycles. If you had the frequency and the passphrase, you could listen in. Now they were totally illegal because of the wireless spectrum they used, which was strictly controlled by governments after the Flare. But he was willing to hear her play if it meant he could keep talking to her.

"I call this one 'Aesop,'" Seeta said.

"Aysop?"

"Like the fables."

She gave him some earbuds and began spinning. At first he heard what he thought was a raven calling, or a crow. Then the throaty call seemed to get absorbed into the crow's chest. A slow beat like pebbles dropping into water carried the music forward with flutes fluttering over top, and the rhythm began to build into a subtle union of chords and water, all stitched together by filaments of soothing sound. Abdul's theft lost its grip on him, the empty depths of the still-empty Naijapool vanished, and Bracket drifted with the music.

When he awoke, Seeta was kissing his neck. She had stripped down and was rubbing her breasts against his chest. Her belly spilled over the line of the black string of her thong. She had changed the music now to something more primal with pulsating groans and a gritty, electronic beat. He opened his mouth and let her tongue in, feeling the fumes of the beer on his own breath as she pulled at him. The softness. He grew stiff under the weight of her body, and he could see her hand on her spin table, her belly ring gyrating, and her playing song after song and beat after beat until he couldn't stand it anymore. Her breasts gleamed with sweat from the exertion. But she wouldn't let him enter her and instead rubbed against his stiffness until she came, and he did too, grabbing her full buttocks in his hands. Afterward she was gentle again, and she played more songs that brought him down until he fell back to sleep.

CHAPTER 6

The spaceport was situated about ten kilometers outside Kano on a flat plain that soaked up the heat, with wilted bushes whose leaves seemed to curl into themselves, preserving whatever moisture they could. The engineers had built scintillating fields of solar arrays that tracked the sun. Kwesi Bracket biked along the entrance road and smelled the dank odor of the yellow-green neem trees as he passed security guards at their checkpoints. Max stood outside the gate in an old navy-blue Nissan pickup truck with the windows down.

"Hey, *oyibo*."

"Hey, Max." He realized there would be no shaking the moniker. In Max's eyes, just like the others, he was a white man. He locked his bike up and climbed into the cab of the truck.

"Where are we going today, *oyibo*?"

"Two stops, Max. We need to find some cable."

"What kind?"

"One-hundred-millimeter cable. Threaded rubber."

"All right, no problem. I'll fix it for you."

Max started the ignition and rolled up the windows to flip on the air-conditioning. The natural gas engine sputtered alive.

"Let's leave the windows open, Max. It's still cool this morning."

He shoved the plastic bag with the bloody cloth in the glove compartment.

"What's that, *oyibo*?"

"It's for the second stop."

"And where is the second stop?"

"Not sure yet, Max. That'll be decided at the first stop."

"All right, you tell me when you want to," Max said, and shrugged. "I'll fix it."

"Can't fix this one, Max."

They drove straight along the access road to the spaceport until they merged with traffic headed into the city. The cars ignored the lane markers, and the relentless blaring of car horns had no apparent purpose. Bracket felt the wind push against his brow through the open window, appreciating the cool energy of the morning before the heat blanketed the Sahel into idleness. They followed the crest of a hill until the corrugated rooftop expanse of Greater Kano spread out before them, the sun steaming its presence over the land in searching tendrils of pink and cream.

The engine of the pickup suddenly chortled and bucked, and Max pulled over to the side of the road.

"We running out of gas?" Bracket said.

"No, it's something else." Max was looking around the cab of the truck. "Where is that thing of yours?"

"What thing?"

"Your G-fone."

"My Geckofone? It was right here in my pocket." But he pressed against his shirt pocket and didn't feel anything.

"Hold on," Max said. He opened up the fuse box beneath the steering column, and sure enough, the Geckofone was sucking on the power cables. "These things use too much energy, man. You have to turn it off. It's draining my battery."

"I could put it on the roof to catch the solar power."

"No, we don't want people to see it. Only big men carry G-fones."

"All right, I'll turn it off."

"Don't worry, I'll find you a battery, *oyibo*. That will keep it happy."

Without the Geckofone's navigation and communication systems, Bracket felt vulnerable—if something went wrong he wouldn't be able to deal with the situation appropriately. But it also meant that Josephine wouldn't know where he was going, and this thought was mildly liberating.

Bracket had first met Max during a tour of Kano for managers at the spaceport, and they had visited the Kofar Mata dye pits to watch the artisans dip cords of cotton into potash and water in deep concrete wells. Max was waiting outside the gate in his pickup truck, holding a bottle of Blanton's, a fine single malt bourbon that Bracket hadn't even realized he'd missed until that moment. Bracket had never liked how the black official SUVs attracted attention, with the slow, self-driving vehicles running their sirens like a presidential motorcade. Now when he needed to go into Kano, he told Max to drive him around, preferring the anonymity of the humble pickup, which allowed him to move about the city without drawing attention to himself—at least until people noticed his light skin through the window.

They drove through the ancient wall that surrounded old Kano, ten thick, ponderous meters of fortifications that had been erected a thousand years ago, which formerly surrounded the city for twenty-five kilometers with fifteen imposing gates. The older buildings in the city were one-story dwellings crowned with cupolas and low-flung arched roofs opening onto interior courtyards and winding streets. There were numerous houses designed in the Hausa style, with walls the color of river silt and small turrets and thick wooden doors studded with silver and tin. These were eclipsed by new construction sites that broke ground after the Flare, when the spaceport made the city into a boomtown—already the first garish behemoths of glass and steel were rising above the city. Women carrying calabashes of fruit and vegetables sauntered past on the side of the narrow road, while goatherds swished their bleating animals to graze on weedy ditches along the roadside. He saw young men fanning burning coals to cook *suya*, a seasoned meat delicacy like a kebab. They were watching a soccer game on the screen of a tablet with malflies buzzing around it.

Digital technologies had flooded Nigeria, which could still use them, and the tech had found eager consumers in a country with a high degree of education. But as the goods flowed in, the borders were shut to non-Africans by the government, goaded on by Bello, who feared losing the chance for the country to press its temporary advantage. So instead of hordes of American and European immigrants, malflies came in, which tried to turn the cheap devices into botnets. Mostly the botnets were used by jobless American coders to peddle medicines to rich northerners who were starved for prescription drugs. That's why a scientist at the University of Nigeria at Nsukka had invented the G-fone, to secure devices against malflies—wedding artificial intelligence to the most advanced antivirus programs—but only the rich could afford G-fones, which fetched what was considered a princely sum even in the Silicon Territories. Indeed, Bracket's ex-wife had been begging for him to send one to her for months, as if it would ever make it there.

As if he owed her anything.

Once Max veered the pickup onto the main highway, traffic slowed to a crawl. Max talked them through a checkpoint, chatting cordially with a heavily armed police detail. Then came another checkpoint. And another.

"What's going on, Max?"

"Boko Haram. The police think an attack is coming."

Bracket had heard the muttering at the spaceport about the rising tide of violence. He tried to ignore the rumors because they distracted him from his work and he couldn't do anything about the situation.

"Jarumi," he said. He'd seen this all before.

Max nodded, gripping the wheel tighter. "That's right. They're called the Jarumi now. They go away for a while and then come back with another label. It means 'the courageous warriors.' 'The heroes.' Last week, a bomber attacked the market in Maiduguri."

They drove through the Kurmi market, a sprawling center of commerce where people sold everything from fresh fish pulled from Lake Chad to strings of handmade beads, fuel cells, leather sandals, soccer jerseys, and car parts. The truck inched its wheels through the throngs until they passed some women sitting on woven *karauno* mats.

"Stop here for a moment?" Max asked, as though remembering something.

"What about the Jarumi?"

"Sure, sure, *oyibo*. I'll be quick."

Max swung open the door and got down from the pickup before Bracket could protest. He picked through the crowd and approached the women, who were tall and thin and had bronzed skin with narrow, almost aquiline noses. They had rows of hoop rings pierced through their ears and alluring brown eyes lined lightly with kohl. One of the women had laid out a half dozen cracked calabashes and was drawing a string through the broken pieces. Another with a scarlet head wrap had set down several herbs in front of her. Max spoke briefly with her, and the woman mixed up the herbs before pouring them into packets of folded newspaper. The women weren't as aggressive as the other market sellers, and everything about them made them stand out. They wore clothing from a different time, the kind of garb you saw in documentaries of Africans living in huts.

"Who are these women?" Bracket said, as Max stepped back into the pickup. "They look different."

"They're nomads." Max chuckled. "Herders who only come to the city to make money during the dry season. They're from an old clan in the north called the Wodaabe."

"So they're not Fulani?"

Fulani was one of the major ethnic groups in the Kano region, along with the Hausa. Many others, like Max, came from other tribes in different regions of the country.

"They're Fulani," Max explained. "But the Wodaabe are a sub-clan that keeps their old traditions. You don't see them much because they spend most of their time in Niger. It's a bad sign that they're this far south. But they sell excellent medicines from the bush." He held up one of the packets. "This is for my son. He suffers from congestion. The other one's for me." Max patted his groin. "After a long day, I can't always get my pecker to work in bed. This will help me get it up."

"Ha! Well, those women turn some heads. That should give you some inspiration."

"No, no! I don't touch them. They're Wodaabe. I stick to Igbo girls."

Bracket considered this insight, thinking that tribalism in this country was as much an affliction as any other illness. Except there seemed to be no cure for it, and certainly no medicine woman from the Sahel would be solving its virulence. You could switch your tribal identity online—if you could get online—but you couldn't forget your own history.

Max swung the pickup into the industrial district, where auto mechanics raised ancient, rusted-out *danfo* minibus taxis from the dead and reassembled electric *okada* scooters with parts sourced from all over the world. Technicians resurrected modded tablets to control drip irrigation systems or to serve as unregistered nodes on Naijaweb, Nigeria's national Internet. Bracket checked first with a Chinese supplier named Xiao he'd dealt with before, but the man didn't have the right kind of cable. Max, meanwhile, used his time to find an extra battery for Bracket's Geckofone, a gummy polymer that wrapped itself around the device like a second skin.

"Let's try Musa," Max advised. "I heard he has cable now."

"Last time he charged way too much for my rebar," Bracket said.

Ibrahim Musa's compound was three blocks away. At the front gate, an armed guard carrying a machine gun patted them down and the trader accepted them into his dirt courtyard, which sat in the middle of three one-story buildings with arched doorways. Bracket caught a glimpse of a large swimming pool in the rear of the compound through the windows of one of the buildings, a luxury by any standard. Musa was a portly man whose flowing white gown opened wide at the neck, revealing a mass of black chest hair. He was doted on by three slim young women: one was his daughter by his first wife, while the other two were his second and third wives.

Bracket was thrilled to learn that Musa had enough quality cable to ship, but the price was ridiculous as usual.

"Fifteen per meter is way too much, Mr. Musa."

They haggled for a short while, but Bracket couldn't make any headway.

"I can give you what you need, my friend," Musa finally said. "But for that I need groundnuts."

"Groundnuts?"

"I understand that you are growing them at your facility."

"We have some greenhouses that provide food for the staff. I'm not sure about groundnuts."

"You have them. I've tasted them. And they're delicious. It so happens that the groundnut supply has dwindled this year because of the drought. I would be willing to sell you the cable for eight cowries per meter and one hundred kilos of your groundnuts."

Bracket looked over at Max. He had no idea if that amount was a lot of groundnuts or not, or if the greenhouse even grew many groundnuts. Max just stared ahead, fulfilling his duty as a fixer. He didn't negotiate, he arranged.

"I'd be happy to promise you one hundred kilos of groundnuts," Bracket said. "Except I don't know how many we have."

"That's no problem, I'm willing to accept future crops as well. You can provide me with thirty-five percent of your yield until it measures one hundred kilograms. I don't charge interest, as it is against my principles."

"That sounds fine to me."

"That weight does not include the stems. I would also like the first option to buy the supply from your next crop."

"Sure, we can do that. Only problem is I don't have any cowries. I've only got Naira."

"Not to worry. I have an imprinter."

"Here? In your house?"

Imprinters were extremely valuable and rare. The entire rocket site had only one imprinter and it was closely guarded by Nurudeen Bello, who kept it under lock and key in a vault. Musa was living humbly if he had such means at his disposal.

"I can offer you a rate of one to four-point-one."

"Last week it was one to three-point-eight."

"We do not trust Naira. We want to feel something in our hands, Mr. Bracket. Naira is our old currency and its value used to disappear overnight from inflation. Cowries are valuable by themselves."

Bracket went through the calculations in his head. He had about forty thousand Naira stored in his Geckofone, which should be enough.

"Okay, it's a deal."

Ibrahim had his first wife draw up a contract in Arabic. As they waited and sipped tea, Bracket asked the trader about the Jarumi and the police checkpoints.

"It's best not to talk about such matters," Musa said curtly.

"But, I mean, is this something we should be concerned about at the spaceport? I thought the terrorists were all gone."

"They are never truly gone, Mr. Bracket. The way to destroy Boko Haram is to destroy the mentality. But the conditions are the same as before. Poverty and shame. Nothing has changed. The army claims to be monitoring them with drones, but the Jarumi can hijack the cameras of the drones so they know when they're coming."

"If they've got that kind of technical knowledge, the government should give them jobs instead."

"The emir has tried. But it's hard to overcome their ignorance. There are generations of people here in Kano whose parents mistrusted schools—any schools—as promoting colonialist thought. Technology does not solve every problem. I remember when some foreigners—from Germany, I think—came to Kano promising thousands of free solar lamps. It was a logical idea because there is plenty of sun in northern Nigeria, and they trained people how to fix them. Today most of those solar cells, if they work at all, are used by the Jarumi to charge their mobile phones in the bush. These men are ignorant but not stupid. Their struggle has made them inventive."

Musa took a sip of tea, his eyes on one of his wives, who slipped past them in an aquamarine wrapper into a different building. Bracket noticed dozens of cowrie shells woven into the fabric of her clothing.

"My advice to you, Mr. Bracket, is not to discuss them. I have counseled young men to stay away from the Jarumi, and Boko Haram before them. Their thoughts about modernization are incoherent and based on a corruption of the Koran. I've seen Igbos from the south—like your driver here—get murdered before my very eyes in Kano, and I wholeheartedly condemn those attacks. My father was a member of the Izala reform movement, and he taught me that there are problems with graft, and that a lack of education is the real cause of our troubles in the north. Abandoning education just because some of the ideas are from the West is foolhardy. Algebra was invented by us Muslims, *inshallah*, and it's the foundation of modern mathematics. But I won't deny that these fanatics are observing truths about our poor leadership.

"They attacked Maiduguri last week, and my sources expect they'll be coming to Kano soon. If you see any Jarumi coming, run, Mr. Bracket. They don't negotiate. If they catch you, they will rob you and they'll rape your women. If you have nothing of value, they'll kill you because you obstruct their way. There's only one way to survive, Mr. Bracket."

"What is that?"

"If you yourself are worth something. Then they won't kill you. They'll kidnap you for ransom."

Bracket thought about this as Musa's wife scrawled slowly on the paper, the trader giving her commands. What conditions did the trader mean when he said they were the same as before? Musa had three wives, an enormous house with a pool, and a prosperous business. Would he give up a wife to make another man happy? Give up some profit to improve conditions for a stranger? Bracket had rarely seen a man do that willingly. And when he did so it was usually the tax collector who forced him.

"One more thing, Mr. Musa. Do you ever trade old artifacts? Like historical pieces?"

"I stay away from them. It's not worth the trouble. The emir will claim them, and if he does not want them, the state will take them. The emir holds as much authority here as the governor. It's best not to cause trouble with them."

So what Josephine said was true. The emir held enough power to shut down the spaceport if he learned of an artifact. Musa seemed to go to great lengths to avoid causing trouble with anyone, and his approach must have worked, judging from the opulence of his household.

Once the contract was completed, the trader's second wife wheeled over the cowrie imprinter, a cart containing forty parallel GPUs that could connect to Naijaweb and link it to the cowrie blockchain by a networked high-altitude drone. Cowries were nickel-sized white shells that looked like folded gnocchi pasta and had been traded all over Africa for centuries before European conquest. After the Flare, they had made a resurgence in a different and more powerful form. Musa's wife poured a sack of unmarked cowrie shells into a funnel like that on a coffee grinder. Each unique shell was naturally grown by a gastropod mollusk in the Persian Gulf before being harvested, making it impossible to fake them. The machine quickly stamped a substrate into the interior of each cowrie shell, and then laser cut the unique keys from the conversion from Bracket's account. The cowries were now embedded into the substrate of each shell. They would later be sorted into random groupings chosen by Ibrahim, so that they would be valid only when in proximity to one another. When you used a cowrie, the other cowries immediately knew and adjusted their collective value. This lessened the chance of theft. Cowries could be reused an infinite number of times because the substrate could simply be superheated and then imprinted with a new key. Only the owner knew which cowries were of value, so they could be worn openly like those on the trader's wife.

Bracket grew alarmed when he saw a fee hidden in the ledger. "That's not a straight conversion."

"I have waived it. We charge the fee when converting from cowries back to Naira. The fee goes to the Emir of Kano. He uses it to support the emirate by maintaining the marketplace and roads, repairing mosques, or giving alms to the poor. It's how we discourage financiers from taking money out of the local economy."

Ibrahim committed to delivering the cable the following morning after prayer, but something about the deal with the groundnuts, and the man's disturbing warnings about the Jarumi, made Bracket feel like an ignoramus who had signed away his own future. Nothing came easily to him in Nigeria. For that, he could blame the Flare.

What once was, is no more.

Before Bracket stood to leave, he had one more question for Musa that he didn't want Max overhearing. They spoke after his fixer left the compound, and then Bracket continued on his way.

Three short steps led to the entrance of the police station, a flat-roofed structure that was longer than its width. Thick iron bars crisscrossed the windows, and the pink paint flecked off into the dirt. Bracket hopped out of the truck and tried to enter through the front door, but an officer drew a pistol.

"You must clear the area!" he shouted. "This is off-limits!"

"Take it easy," Bracket said.

This only infuriated the officer more. "This area is off-limits! Leave here now!"

Max yelled something from the truck, arguing confidently as the pistol waved in Bracket's face, and soon the officer was laughing for some reason—most likely, Bracket suspected, at his own expense—and gave him a friendly pat-down before waving him through, while Max stayed behind in the pickup. Inside the station, it was all frantic motion, cops rushing through with machine guns and desk clerks fielding calls on the emergency circuit.

Bracket finally tracked down Idriss, the detective whom Musa had described as a competent and principled man with a talent for discretion, exactly what he needed. Idriss had a long, thin caramel face, with a body that didn't seem to match it: stocky arms and legs and a round belly. His horn-rimmed glasses were poised to fall off the tip of his nose.

"We have no time today," he said, tilting his head back to peer through the glasses. "Come back tomorrow."

"Musa said you would give me a moment. As a favor."

A Hummingfone was perched on the detective's shoulder. It was the preferred device for detectives, because its propellers and ability to hover allowed it to efficiently snap high-quality images of crime scenes. The device briefly took off to flutter about Bracket's pocket before landing on the detective's shoulder again. The detective lifted an eyebrow.

"So you're from the spaceport," Idriss commented.

"How did you know that?" Bracket asked.

Idriss tapped the little drone with a finger: "It found your G-fone in your pocket. Normally it can download your identification but the spaceport G-fones are well protected."

"I found something that I wanted to ask you about," Bracket said.

"Ah, what's that?"

"A humble discovery," he said. These were the words that Musa had told him.

The detective stood, the two men shook hands, and Bracket took the opportunity to slip him a piece of paper with Musa's personal stamp. The detective glanced at the paper: "Go ahead, then."

Bracket handed the detective the bag with the bloody shirt-sleeve inside.

"We found this at the spaceport," he said. "I suspect it's blood."

Detective Idriss looked inside the plastic bag, frowning. "Blood? You don't know?"

Bracket kept his mouth shut, trying to get a read of the man. He became afraid that Idriss was going to draw this out and make it difficult for him.

"I'd like to know if you could have it analyzed," Bracket said.

"All right, give me your key."

Bracket set his Geckofone down, and the Hummingfone hovered over it, setting down for a moment on the G-fone's back as they exchanged their encrypted keys through the G-fone's tongue and the Hummingfone's beak.

"This may be connected," Bracket explained, "to a missing spaceport worker called Abdul Haruna."

"So you *do* know whose blood it is?"

"No, it's just a guess. In fact, I suspect it isn't. But he's disappeared, and I thought you might let us know if he turns up again."

"That's quite a guess, Mr. Bracket. Do you have any personal effects for Mr. Haruna where we could find some DNA?"

Bracket shook his head.

"Any reason why you haven't reported this to your own internal security? You've got your own laboratories there."

"And we've got a lot of people who are better off not knowing about it."

"Like Nurudeen Bello?" Idriss asked.

Bracket tried to conceal his surprise. He wasn't so much concerned about Bello as Idriss seemingly knowing about the goings-on at the spaceport.

"Everyone knows Bello's there, Mr. Bracket. There's no sense in pretending. He talks about his spaceport all over Naijaweb."

"Bello has nothing to do with any of this. Look, it's a sensitive time for the mission. We're getting close to launch, and we need someone discreet to look into this. Op-Sec is not known for that. Musa said you were the guy I should talk to."

An officer ran up to the detective and spoke to him in Hausa. Idriss turned to Bracket and said, "Okay, fine. Another day. Today is not good. I'll call you."

On the way out the door, Bracket caught Idriss tossing the plastic bag under his desk, where it landed beside a garbage can and piles of manila folders. Bracket hoped he had done the right thing. To be sure, it was a risk, and he had no idea what Musa's message had told the man, since it was written in cursive Arabic, which his G-fone hadn't been able to translate.

They hit another traffic jam—or 'go-slow' as they called it Pidgin—leaving the city, this one outside the soccer stadium, where a stream of bright yellow-and-green jerseys engulfed the truck. The Kano Pillars, the local team, had evidently won, and faces appeared in the truck's windows, chanting victoriously.

"I can also call you Yankee," Max volunteered suddenly.

"What are you talking about?"

"Instead of *oyibo*. I know you don't like it. I can call you Yankee. It has the same meaning."

Bracket sighed and slumped down as they approached yet another checkpoint, where the police were aggressively inspecting each car now, tossing baggage and suitcases in the road. The soccer celebration continued behind them, while a few cars ahead of them, the police officers seemed to be frustrated with searching the instruments of a drum troupe, who responded by pounding on their drums even louder, irritating everyone enough to begin honking through the dust.

"You don't need to be offended by the term," Max said. "Yankee is for all Americans."

"That's what people say about *oyibo*."

"Yes, but *oyibo* means 'white man.'"

"I get it. I'm light skinned. You're not the first person to notice that."

A guard gestured for them to climb out of the pickup, waving away Max's bribe with annoyance as he rifled through the glove compartment, ordered them to lift up the seats, and stooped down to look at the undercarriage of the pickup. Finally, he motioned them forward, but Max had nowhere to go, because the car in front of them was stopped, flanked by two police officers.

"Your problem," Max picked up, as though there had been no interruption, "is that you take offense easily. Most Americans do."

"You're not offending me, you're offending four hundred years of exclusion and oppression."

"What were you excluded from?"

"Opportunities. Families. Love. Pride."

"Does that not happen to everybody?"

"I don't think everyone was beaten, whipped, and lynched. I had relatives strung up from trees, ancestors who were drowned in rivers as babies."

Max tsked as the policemen angrily berated a teenage girl who appeared to be refusing to get out of the car in front of them. "That's over now, isn't it? If you still have all this exclusion and this suffering, then why am I working for you?"

Bracket's gaze shifted to a tall woman who walked right past his window, her hoop earrings shimmering in the late-afternoon sun. He tracked her until she melted slowly into the crowd, entranced by her features. One of the Wodaabe women they'd seen earlier. Up close, he realized now how young she looked, barely out of her teens, if he had to guess. "How about this, Max: I don't want you to call me either of those things. First of all, I'm a Rangers fan, not a Yankees fan. And I don't like baseball if I'm being honest. My family's from Boston, so I'm no Yankee." He knew all of that was wasted on Max, but he said it anyway.

Max shrugged: "What should I call you?"

Ahead of them, the cops were trying to yank open the driver's side door, which the girl in the car would pull shut again.

"Call me what it says on my name tag: Kwesi."

"Kwesi is an Ashanti name. You're not from Ghana."

"It's my name."

One of the police officers was reaching inside the car, and they heard the girl yell fiercely. Bracket stiffened as the cop recoiled from the car window, a look of horror crossing his face as he held up his hand. The flesh was oddly bright white on his dark skin, before the blood began to drip. His palm had been slashed straight through with a knife.

The young woman was now getting out of the car. She was grasping for something dangling from her dress. It had a red tag on it. Now Bracket saw the Wodaabe woman breaking through the crowd, running toward the girl, singing something in the wind, an old song borrowed from another time, that lilted and leapt in Bracket's memory, and the cops were raising their guns. The girl screamed out as she pulled the red tag, and all Bracket had time to do was close his eyes.

CHAPTER 7

During the day, Balewa would lead the women in collecting medicines in the scrubland outside Kano, relying on the knowledge she'd learned from her husband before he was murdered. Sometimes she would encounter goatherds in the open plains and ask them for help.

"Have you seen any leaves veined with white and green?" she might ask.

"About a two-hour walk from here," one would reply.

The boys, and they were always boys, had a keen eye for the flora of the Sahel, since their herds survived on it. They were entrusted by their parents to watch over the goats so their families could tend to shops in the city, and they spoke a different dialect of Fulfulde from having grown up in Kano. Still, she trusted them more than she trusted the other townspeople, who looked down upon nomads like Balewa as backward simpletons from a bygone era.

Balewa's husband had been the lead scout for her Wodaabe subclan before his death, and whenever he would ride his camel searching for watering holes, he would collect herbs along the way. He'd return with his pack full of medicines and a boyish smile on his face, as if he'd found a new and exciting treasure. He thought he kept the herbs safely sealed away from Balewa's prying eyes, but she would notice certain things. Here, a chip of *badaadi* bark would poke out of his satchel. There, the pointed tip of a *gajaali* leaf. After two years of marriage, she had figured out some of the remedies and had been able to identify the plants by sight as she walked alongside her donkey during the clan's migrations. She never told her husband, of course, because medicines were gathered by men and it might have wounded his pride. And she knew how much he loved his secrets. Now he was long dead, and Balewa herself was far away from home.

When she gathered enough herbs with the four other women outside Kano, she would prepare the medicines by boiling root bark or chopping leaves into a fine dust, and together they would journey into the city to lay down their mats in the marketplace. They could earn enough money to buy food after a couple of days of busy selling, their remedies treating everything from colds and indigestion to warts and eczema. The richer residents in the city preferred to go to a modern doctor, but others sought out the more affordable traditional remedies, which had been developed over generations of grazing the wilderness of the Sahel. Balewa could not always find the herbs she needed for each medicine, yet her customers were so desperate, she found, that they would buy whatever she dropped in her packets of newspaper—especially the men. They would return to buy more, believing that the herbs had cured them of their impotence. She felt no guilt at this deception. After her husband's death, she had vowed that she would save her honesty only for women. Men would get what they deserved.

One day, while assembling a packet for a woman to cure her dyspepsia, Balewa started to hear whispers in the market stalls, and a word that seemed to touch everyone's lips: *Jarumi*. She eavesdropped on the merchants to find out what she could—you could learn a lot, she discovered, by having a sharp ear in the city.

Jarumi, went the refrain. *The Jarumi are coming.*

The police officers too increased their visits to the area, and she was able to learn from their conversations that they expected the militants to arrive soon. The news frightened the other women but sent a thrill through Balewa's heart, that she could finally stop running and do something.

"We can stop them this time," Balewa announced to the others while she was organizing her herbs on her mat. The five women were seated around their medicines in the marketplace, waiting for customers.

"How?" one of the other women responded.

"We've got nothing to stop them with," another added.

"We've got the stones," Balewa insisted.

"You can't control the stones," Durel, the eldest, argued. "None of us can, Balewa. We have to wait until we're stronger."

Few people understood their Wodaabe dialect, so the women could speak candidly without worrying about eavesdropping.

"I can control them," Balewa said. "Yesterday I surrounded Abir with a stone, didn't I, Abir?"

"She did," Abir admitted.

"That was when you were safe, Balewa," Durel retorted. "You won't be able to do it again when the Jarumi are shooting guns at you."

"I won't be afraid."

"That's easy to say now, Balewa, but you won't be so clearheaded when they attack."

"Let them come," Balewa said defiantly, wondering if she believed her own words.

"No," Durel declared. "We won't confront them. We'll go home instead. Do you all agree with me?"

"Yes," the others said. They didn't mean their real home, the swath of green pastures and watering holes their clan used to follow from Niger into Nigeria and Benin. She meant their new home, and it was hardly a home at all, a dark, foreboding place where the women did not like to sleep.

Since Balewa, at twenty, was the youngest among them, she had to defer to the judgment of the others, at least in their presence, but it did not stop her from continuing to eavesdrop in the marketplace. She paid close attention to the peddlers of charred goat meat, lithium batteries, indigo-blue and green cloth wrappers, boiled cashew nuts, painted calabashes, mobile phone chargers, and woven mats. She determined that the Jarumi were expected to arrive very soon, although no one knew how they would travel to the city or what shape their attack would take. The police stepped up their inspections at the market, which mostly involved hassling sellers when it suited them, often demanding bribes in return for protection.

She felt the coming of the Jarumi with a dread of the inevitable, felt that she was drawn to them now and that they would be drawn to her, as if they knew what she carried inside her. The other women avoided mentioning what was happening to Balewa's body, the nausea that plagued her from morning to night, the malevolent energy swirling within her that enveloped her whole being, turned even sweet scents against themselves. Pure-smelling herbs made her want to retch; the wispy scent of wild blossoms disgusted her no end. In the marketplace, she fled the smell of porridge boiling in a pot, yet became ravenous for grilling *suya* meat.

In the end, it was revulsion she felt, nearly always.

If the child was born it would be a hellspawn of a jiini who would sully the world. She couldn't allow it to live. But the herbs she needed to suffocate the thing in her womb did not grow near Kano.

She would bring the child back to the Jarumi, she decided, make them kill the very thing they had created.

One afternoon, she heard her customers mention the words again, *the Jarumi, the Jarumi are coming today*. The other sellers packed up their wares and went home early for the day. When the police shifted their checkpoints to the soccer stadium, Balewa knew she would have to move quickly.

"They aren't coming to the marketplace," she said to the others.

"We should get away from here to be safe," Durel said. "Let's stay out of sight. Everyone agree?"

"Yes," the others said.

Balewa did not argue with them this time because she didn't think they could possibly understand, but she didn't acquiesce either, a form of resistance she'd learned from growing up in a clan in which most decisions about her life had been made by other people.

She was tired of running away. With the stone, she could stop the Jarumi from harming anyone and kill the child too, a valiant act of sacrifice that would end her suffering. She let the other women walk ahead of her, then ducked down an alley. Clutching the stone close to her chest, she paced quickly to the soccer stadium, scanning the crowds.

She began softly singing the notes she'd learned. The stone warmed to the touch.

She paused to watch the police checkpoints from a distance, observing the officers as they inspected each vehicle. She looked for cruel faces in the crowd to see if she recognized any of them. But the Jarumi were nowhere to be found. She was hoping, she realized, for something terrible.

Then she heard the yelling at one of the police checkpoints. There! Her heart began thudding against her chest.

She moved through the crowd as people parted for her, chanting the notes to the stone more loudly, building the field, and soon she could see it surround her, glistening in the late-afternoon sun. A merchant was grazed by the field and cried out as if he had been bitten. Another shouted out in fear. Her voice rose, making the stone grow hot now, the energy building upon itself. When she saw the attacker, she would expand the field around him as she had practiced, enveloping them both within it. They would die together.

She saw blood pouring from a police officer's hand and raced faster. But she stopped cold just before reaching them, when a girl stepped out of the car. It was all wrong. Balewa had expected a man, a monster from the Jarumi. Not a girl. And not one who was younger even than Balewa herself. She looked terrified, her eyes darting around her like a frightened animal.

I've made a mistake, Balewa thought. *It's only a girl.*

She stopped singing to the stone, and the field dissipated into thin air. The stone grew cold in her palm. She was starting to turn away when she noticed a red tag dangling from the girl's clothing and a bulge around her midsection.

Now she watched everything as if from a great remove. She could see the officers lunging for the girl. The horrified look on the girl's face.

If I die, Balewa realized, *they'll take both of our lives. They'll get what they want.*

And Balewa hummed the notes again, welling up from a place in the back of her neck. The song! She raised the stone before her. She pushed out the melody from within her belly, faster than she ever had before.

The girl was pulling the red tag. The girl was coming apart.

I will stop this, Balewa thought, as the stone burned her palm. *I will stop it all.*

CHAPTER 8

The glass lodged itself into every crevice of the pickup, into Bracket's clothing, into his shoes. And the larger shards—they broke into splinters, the sharpness branching endlessly in a cruel fractal of pain.

Something dangled from the roof outside the window, something that should not be there. In a haze, Bracket opened the door to pull it down: a strip of brown flesh seared into the paint. He ripped it off and threw it onto the ground.

The terrified look in the young woman's eyes as she detonated herself and then, as Bracket ducked his head beneath the dashboard, the final glimpse of the explosion tearing the young woman apart, the chest-heaving force of it. Her torso splitting open in an orgy of grime, where it had stopped suddenly, as if captured in the air in front of him before falling to the ground. The stench of carbide and the sound of the screams.

Bracket and Max stumbled into the road, where they discovered a woman trapped beneath an overturned fruit cart. A small brushfire had started behind her and it was spreading in her direction. Max dug up a thin berm of dirt as a makeshift fire break, while Bracket lifted the cart off her legs. The woman thanked him, dusted off her wrapper, and stacked the fruit back on the cart before pushing it away, disappearing in the smoky haze. Outside the car, Bracket saw that only the cars behind Max's pickup were still intact. The rest—in every other direction of the blast radius—had been utterly destroyed. Some force of luck had saved them, protected them from the explosion as if by a miracle.

Another hour passed before the fire department doused the rest of the flames. They cleared the way for police officers to interrogate witnesses who had been near the blast, and eventually they ambled over to Max's pickup truck as they were waiting for the traffic to clear. A Hummingfone circled about the truck, its mini propellers pivoting this way and that, snapping photos.

"Did you see what happened here, sir?" the officer asked.

"I saw a girl arguing with the police."

"Did you see her face?"

"We were far away. She was wearing a hijab."

"Would you recognize her if I showed you a picture?"

"I don't know. Maybe."

The Hummingfone buzzed in close to Bracket's face.

"Anything else?"

"She pulled on a string to detonate the bomb," Bracket said. "It had a red tag."

"How do you know she detonated the bomb?"

"What do you mean? Look around you. What else could have happened?"

"The tag could have been attached to a radio," the officer explained. "The bomb could have been triggered remotely. That's often the case when they use children."

It was a point Bracket hadn't thought of. He had assumed the girl had decided on her own death.

"One more thing," Bracket added. "I'm not sure if this is important. We saw another woman running toward her."

"What did she look like?"

"Tall, thin. I believe she was Wodaabe."

"What makes you say that?"

"We bought something from her earlier in the market."

"And what did she do?"

Bracket paused, considering how to answer. The woman had begun to sing as she rushed forward, and something seemed to expand around her—a presence? an emptiness?—and then there was the blast. He shook his head. "I'm not sure."

Bracket realized it sounded specious even to himself.

The officer examined the herbs that Max had bought and then ordered them to hand over their passports. Max argued with the officer for a while before eventually producing his national ID, since he didn't carry a passport.

"I've got diplomatic protection," Bracket insisted.

"If I could have a cowrie for every time a Yankee told me that, I'd be a rich man." The officer laughed. "Don't leave the space-port. If all is well, we'll return them to you in a few days."

Bracket smoldered in his seat as the officer walked away, trying to remember the song the woman had been singing, the music that had touched him in all of that chaos. Two hours later, the police removed the fence and allowed Max to drive through the wreckage. All that remained of the woman's car was a burned, crumpled chassis with the steering wheel still attached. The police had removed most of the bodies, and Bracket could see blood splattered on windshields and coagulating in the dirt. As they drove past, the same officer was bagging a severed foot, the toes callused and the toenails cracked.

Bracket returned to his quarters to find the interior of his trailer coated in a fine layer of silt. He had left the window open again. The Harmattan winds began offshore and chilled a belt of West Africa for a thousand kilometers, causing tornadoes and violent rainstorms throughout the region, which Josephine Gauthier had long warned might delay the rocket launch. One more reason she insisted they stay on schedule. His quarters were generous compared with those of the astronauts, with a double bed, a broad desk, and a bathroom with a steam shower. He had rigged his bike on a pulley from the ceiling, and he had enough room—bare-ly—for a small raffia armchair with an indigo cushion.

He picked the glass from his skin piece by piece and poured a bottle of rubbing alcohol over his body in the shower, his skin flaming so hot that he thought he would pass out from the pain.

After toweling off, he collapsed on his bed and surfed around on the Loom for a Nigerian show. He had been put off by the poor production quality of Nigerian movies—called Nolly-wood—when he arrived eight months ago, as scenes would cut in the middle of dialogue or the music would repeat the same electronic keyboard melody again and again, regardless of the emotional content. But eventually, the melodramatic story lines began capturing his attention and distracting him from the day's pressures, and the programs had become a critical sleep aid.

He sought out his favorite, *Mrs. N Hires the Help*, which followed a wealthy, strong-willed, and fiercely intimidating wom-an, Mrs. N, as she manages the domestic servants in her opulent home on the Calabar coast. She was constantly receiving visit-ing dignitaries and pop stars from around the country, and she expected the hired help to fulfill their duties, but if she caught you sleeping—*wham!*—she would fire you with her catchphrase: "You're terminated." The phrase must have been cribbed from Arnold Schwarzenegger in *Terminator*, yet Mrs. N had made it her own, adding a layer of frightening vindictiveness. When she said "You're terminated," you felt as if she were talking directly to you and you had to quit whatever you were doing. She had a Pythonfone that she kept curled around her right arm, and she allowed it to slither into the servants' quarters to monitor their business. Bracket found it fascinating to watch how she treated her servants—more cruelly, it seemed, than the rich in America—and while he'd never enjoyed reality television back home, Mrs. N was so menacing and vicious that he anticipated her confron-tations with her staff as if he were about to watch a track sprint in a velodrome. But Mrs. N always won. Her Pythonfone would record some offense, the staff would be held to account, the party would go off without a hitch, and her guests would enjoy her sumptuous meals while she observed them from the head of the table with a look of quiet conspiratorial pleasure.

After the day he'd had, Bracket could have used a new episode of *Mrs. N Hires the Help*, but he couldn't find one to download. He swiped through films of priests praying and young men dancing to hip-hop with auto-tuned singers and an evil archbishop from Lagos, and it all blended together until the buzzing in his ears from the explosion rippled through his mind.

Where was the reality show about the poor, uneducated girl from the northeast of Nigeria who blew herself to pieces in Kano? Where was the episode that explained why she did it? Or why she was forced to do it?

He thought he heard otherworldly sounds in the wind of the Sahel as it buffeted his trailer, but when he popped his head outside he just saw an Op-Sec guard making the rounds in the occluded night as a minor storm swept in, maybe the first one of the season.

The drums. They were pounding in his ears as if the music troupe was walking past the pickup outside the stadium. What had become of the musicians? Had they survived? Surely the bomber would have waited before blowing up some drummers. What about that Wodaabe woman? The one who had run toward the suicide bomber? Why would she sacrifice herself like that? To what end?

He messaged Seeta Chandrasekhan on his Geckofone:

Hey Seeta. Can you play me something nice?

She ignored him or she didn't see the message. He actually wanted to talk to her right now, to tell her about what had happened, but he didn't know if she would respond to that kind of honesty. He'd left that morning with her scowling at him like he had stolen something from her, her pride maybe. He didn't know.

He thought about what the trader Ibrahim Musa had said, that the Jarumi would spare only the lives of people who were worth something. If they were to come to the spaceport, who would they come for? Bello? Maybe.

Then it struck him. Of course. They would come for the very people who were being trumpeted all around the world: the Naijanauts. The true heroes. If the Jarumi came, they would come for the Naijanauts.

CHAPTER 9

Bracket awoke feeling he needed to find the peloton, to reach the slipstream after the chaos of the last few days had sheared away his momentum. So he went riding around the spaceport before dawn, looking for the slip, and when he couldn't find it, he pedaled until his lungs felt like they would burst. The wind from the previous night's storm had swept the landscape bare. The sun was yawning rays of denim blue and gold over the bronze statue of the *Masquerade* as he cleaned the dust from his bike's gears with an old toothbrush on his doorstep. He schemed how to improve the bike, whether he could upgrade the shifters to give him more speed. Speed could get him there, where he needed to be, back on track. Gliding again.

His Geckofone slid along the wall outside his quarters, lifting itself up and down to attract his attention. He grabbed it.

"Mr. Bracket, it's Detective Idriss. I've finished looking into the matter we discussed."

"Detective." In the background, Bracket heard a bird squawking, a parrot maybe.

"Next time, Mr. Bracket, I suggest you use something other than your own clothing when you want to preserve evidence from a crime scene. It will keep matters from becoming confused."

"I'll bear that in mind."

"We ran a DNA test on the blood, but we don't have other samples to compare it to, so it does not help us very much. The man was not in our database. But what we did find, Mr. Bracket, is that the blood most likely came from the Kanuri ethnic group."

"So it was human blood?"

"Yes, Kanuri are very much human. They are mostly located in the northeast of the country."

"Well, that's where we are right now. That shouldn't be a surprise."

There it was again, the bird cry, but this time the call was drawn out, attenuated. More of a screech than a squawk. Detective Idriss didn't seem bothered by it. He wondered if Idriss would object if he placed him on speakerphone, so he could finish cleaning his bike. He picked up a rag.

"Most members of the Jarumi also tend to come from the Kanuri tribe."

Bracket set the rag down again. "You're saying Abdul Haruna was a member of Boko Haram?"

"It's possible. If he was, then he was on the base for one of two reasons: either theft or sabotage."

"Theft?" Bracket blurted out.

"The Jarumi need money to operate. Money to buy food, weapons, explosives, and whatever else they need. They don't have a functioning economy of their own, so they prey on others. Maybe there was something there that they hoped to sell on the black market."

It added up: Abdul had taken off with the pottery after one look. There was little chance the emir would find out about it—unless, that is, Abdul planned to tell the emir to sabotage the project.

"So you are saying there could be Jarumi at the spaceport?"

"It's only a suspicion. But don't jump to conclusions yet, Mr. Bracket."

"Why not?"

"My cousins are Kanuri. And they are not members of Boko Haram. If you could provide me with more information about your employee, we may be able to learn more. Right now it's a suspicion. Anything is possible. He could be a common criminal."

"Thank you, Detective. I'll do what I can."

But he already knew that Josephine had deleted Abdul Haruna's employment files. It was a dead end.

"Your passport will be ready in a week, I should add. And you can tell Mr. Obinna to fetch his identification as well."

"I'll get word to Max."

"Now I've done you a favor. I'd like to ask the same of you. You said you saw a Wodaabe woman at the explosion. Would you be able to identify her in a lineup?"

"Surely she was killed."

"And if she wasn't? Your car was right next to the explosion, yet somehow you escaped with your lives. Everyone else within the blast radius died."

It seemed impossible, but Bracket told him he could, thinking it wasn't exactly a fair request. The man had his passport, and Yankees without papers, he knew, did not fare well in Nigeria.

Bracket found Seeta Chandrasekhan scrutinizing a rocket thruster that was bolted into a lattice of struts. Nearby, Indian engineers were scrambling to prepare for the first launch test. Her Nigerian apprentice was eagerly awaiting instructions beside her. They were both wearing white medical scrubs to avoid contaminating the machine, and throughout the gigantic hangar Bracket could see various parts of the *Masquerade* being carefully assembled— in one corner an air tank was being tested to help the spacecraft navigate in orbit.

"Morning, Seeta," Bracket said.

"I'm busy," Seeta snapped, without looking up.

"I need a sec."

"I don't have a sec. I don't have a micro-sec. I don't have anything."

She was examining the rocket thruster assiduously and ignoring him. Bracket remembered the feel of her hair slipping between his fingers.

"At least tell me what you're working on," he asked.

"I'm trying to see if a thruster designed for launch over the Andaman Sea will melt a launch platform for thrusters made for launch over the Atlantic. What could possibly go wrong?"

"I thought the platform was all-Indian. That's Bello's plan, right? Indian rockets, African ingenuity."

"It might have been Bello's plan, but it's not Josephine's plan. She said that the platform specifications were wrong, so it now meets ESA specifications. ESA specifications using Nigerian concrete, which is different than concrete in French Guiana. The humidity is different, the density is different, and they don't add gunite to the mixture. And then we're going to blast the bloody hell out of it with an experimental thruster that has never before been launched into space. Do you have any idea how different the engine is for the *Masquerade*? It's a Frankenstein's monster of the Space Shuttle and the Russian Buran. Now she wants it ready two weeks early." Seeta glanced at her apprentice. "Simon, you don't need to hear all this chatter. Why don't you take a break?"

"Are you sure, Dr. Chandrasekhan?" her apprentice replied. "I'm here to help."

"Give me ten minutes. And bring some coffee if you can."

"Two sugars?"

"Make it three. Or I don't know, bring the bloody bowl."

The apprentice walked away, disappearing behind a hail of sparks and heavy machinery.

"Difficult man," Seeta muttered. "It's easier when he's not around asking me so many questions. Sometimes you just need to watch, you know? Watch and learn." She grabbed a clipboard dangling from a truss and marked off a box with a grease pen, finally looking at Bracket. "Bloody hell, what the devil happened to you?"

"I was in town when the Jarumi set off a bomb."

She stepped toward him, her face softening with concern. "Jesus, you were there? We felt the explosion all the way over here." Now she was running her fingers along the cuts on his face, almost tenderly.

He bristled at the pain. "I went into town to get some supplies for the pool, and they set it off on our way back."

"I heard it was a slaughter," Seeta said. "Some suicidal maniac."

"It was a girl," Bracket corrected.

She recoiled. "A girl?"

"Yeah, we were close. We saw her blow herself up right in front of us. That's why I'm here, Seeta. We're about to finish the pool, and I need to know that the walls will hold up to any sabotage. Do you think you can scan it? It's going to be holding thirty-one million liters of water."

"After all you've been through, *that's* why you're here? For a scan? Don't ask me to look at it, ask the structural engineers."

"I've got their reports and they look good. We've been cleared. But that was before the explosion."

She sighed, as if she had been waiting for him to say more, and turned back to the clipboard with a humph. "Christ, Kwesi. You can't just go back to work after seeing something like that. Take a break."

"I don't have time for a break. We're already behind. We've encountered any number of strange things around the pool."

"What kinds of things are you talking about?"

He told her about the electronics that kept shorting out.

"That's been happening to all of us," she said. "Did you find anything else around the site?"

"Some old pottery," he said evenly.

"Like an artifact?"

"Yeah. One of my crew ran off with it. He got away."

She shook her head. "I suppose we should all be more careful around here. Anyway, that wouldn't affect my instruments. My readings have been unusual. Inconsistent. It's hard to get a proper fix on anything." Then she leaned toward him and whispered: "Is that really the reason you want me to come help you?"

"I value your opinion."

"You value me or you want me?"

"Come look at the pool for me. No one can scan it the way you can."

"We made a mistake, Kwesi. I was drunk. You should forget about it. If you want to see me, then I need you to say it. I don't chase men. I don't even chase women. They chase me."

"You've got a girlfriend."

She ignored this and tapped her pen on her checklist. "If you need me to examine your pool, make sure it gets on this list. If it's not there, it doesn't exist."

"I'll make sure it gets there."

"You should go see a medic," she said coldly. "You look like shit."

Of course, Josephine would almost certainly not allow Seeta to spend her day conducting acoustic readings of Naijapool. Seeta was right, all the structural engineers had signed off, and the electrical engineers would too, once he installed the new cable. But they hadn't been planning for an explosion. Had he gone to see Seeta to woo her back to him? Maybe he had. The bomb had rattled him more than he realized, his emotions feeling viscous and distended. When he looked over his shoulder, she was wearing her headphones and taking readings of the cone of the thruster, her apprentice peppering her with questions to her obvious annoyance.

He cringed at the thought of returning to an empty pool again, almost expecting to find Josephine glowering at him, but when he arrived he was happily surprised that the trader Ibrahim Musa had fulfilled his end of the bargain and delivered five hundred meters of high-grade cable, spooled perfectly on evenly spaced pallets on the pool deck. He looked over the lip of the tank below, realizing that this might be the last time he saw it without water.

Naijapool was larger than the Neutral Buoyancy Laboratory in Houston, at about seventy meters by thirty meters, and fifteen meters deep instead of thirteen. Unlike the NBL, though, the pool had been built from scratch instead of being retrofitted inside an existing building. So thirteen of the fifteen meters extended deep into the ground, with only two meters above ground level, mostly to protect against flash floods, which could hit Kano at the tail end of Harmattan season. Nigeria made some of the best concrete in the world, even if Seeta didn't like that it had a different composition. The richest man in the country had built his fortune on concrete, and Nurudeen Bello had convinced him to donate all the concrete the pool required, not to mention the equipment. In just four weeks they poured enough concrete to build a twenty-story building. Once they completed the pool, Bracket looked forward to watching the Naijanauts move slowly in their weighted EVA suits with the divers affixed to them like remoras, an underwater symbiosis that had always moved him back in Houston.

He merely had to approve the other tasks for the day, which were managed by highly skilled staff: the installation of the gas lines, so the safety divers could breathe Nitrox; the heating system; and the air-conditioning units for the suit-donning room, where the astronauts were in most danger of overheating as they spent fifteen minutes wriggling into their suits.

By evening, he should be able to make the order everyone was waiting for: open the taps. So why was he so uneasy? He trusted his designs, and yet he feared that the pool might not be strong enough, that another girl could walk right in and blow herself up and the Naijanauts with her.

Josephine still refused his request for more time to double-check the integrity of the structure.

"I've already ordered more perimeter security," she snapped over her G-fone. "And you should never have gone into town without an official escort. You're lucky you weren't killed."

She relented when he told her about the cable and, like Seeta, recommended that he report to the infirmary, seemingly unaware of the fact that she had also just told him to finish the project at the same time.

Bracket was used to mercurial demands anyway. He had never been totally in charge back at the NBL in NASA. His colleagues had always wanted Bracket on their team, but they'd never wanted him to lead it—or at least the management hadn't, as his ex-wife, Lorraine, had said. He thought there might be more to it than that, though. Maybe his being black, which Lorraine always brushed off as an excuse. After the Flare, citing his lack of initiative, among a list of other faults, she left him for Ramsey, a lover whom she had barely deigned to keep secret. Bracket had replayed horror movies in his head of stabbing Lorraine's lover through the heart and then turning himself in to the police, so he was shocked by how little he felt toward the man when he finally met him. That even though Ramsey used to drive a Tesla sports car, before the Flare fried its motherboard, he wasn't worth the trouble. Ramsey had preyed on another man's wife and had to look himself in the mirror and say: "I'm a man who breaks apart families. I'm the one who drives in the wedge."

Only later when he arrived in Kano did Bracket hear that Ramsey refused to offer a single cowrie toward Sybil's education. Then he did want to thump the man. Then he did want to plunge a knife into his chest. But it was too late, and they were homesteading in the Silicon Territories, sipping wine or shooting baby fawns or whatever it was the libertarians did.

He was startled out of his reverie when Josephine's face suddenly appeared on the security camera of the operations room—and she wasn't alone. Nurudeen Bello was with her, speaking about something intently, as they prepared to enter Naijapool. Bracket cursed under his breath—there was nothing to show them. He hadn't prepared for a visit, and ran down the stairs to intercept them before they saw the empty tank.

Josephine looked attentive and restrained, a sharp contrast from how she had berated him only hours before. She raised her eyebrows at him over a warning glance: *Don't screw this up, Kwesi.* Bello stood patiently beside her, inspecting everything with a proprietary gaze. Bello rarely visited Naijapool in person, so Bracket was used to dealing with him through the Loom when he used an ebony-skinned Yoruba avatar. Instead of a traditional agbada gown, he was wearing a heather-gray Western-style suit with tan calfskin oxfords that matched his belt. At the crown of his head Bracket could discern a bald patch.

"Good to see you, Mr. Bracket," Bello said.

"Welcome back, Mr. Bello."

"It's good to *be* back," Bello agreed, pumping his hand. "I spent the day courting investors, and I'll confess I'm glad to get another look at what they're investing in. The way they talk, you'd think that it was all a pipe dream!" Now he was looking over Bracket's shoulder at the pool. "We've built some of the best facilities in the world at the spaceport, bar none. I've assured them that when NASA and the ESA come back online that they'll still look to us for guidance. This pool is one of the reasons why."

Together they walked along the pool deck, until they arrived at the lip of the tank. Bello frowned and looked at Josephine. "You told me that you had started filling the pool today."

"We installed the cable today, Mr. Bello," Bracket interjected. "I had to find a new supplier after we received a bad shipment."

"You should have gone through the approved vendor list," Bello said. "When you go off the books, it makes our auditors nervous. I choose our vendors very carefully, Mr. Bracket. I don't want the anticorruption auditors taking down our project. Besides, the sister of our cable supplier just won a seat in the House of Representatives. She's a very important ally of our space program."

"It won't happen again," Josephine said, before Bracket could argue with his logic. The man clearly had no idea how bad his vendors really were—and how was a supplier with political ties above suspicion?

They continued along until they stopped at an open space the size of a basketball court that was overhung with cranes.

"This is where the real money will be made," Bello observed, his mood brightening again. "Where the contractors will be able to put their equipment before taking it into the pool." He folded his arms, admiring the empty space. "You know, those contracts will pay for this facility within five years. I've already rented out three years to the oil rigs, so their welders can practice deep-sea repairs."

"We did the same thing in Houston when Congress cut our budgets," Bracket reminded Bello. "That's why I designed this extra space." If anyone was familiar with the long-term plans for the pool, it was him.

"But in Houston they never could contain their costs, could they?" Bello corrected. "That's what I've been trying to tell the National Assembly in Abuja, that we'll soon be financially viable. The government has not provided us with all the funds we need. Nor should it. But we need more funds before we reach sustainability, like any successful start-up. I'm being dogged by an especially greedy senator who wants to line his pockets with our money. You see, the only way to overcome someone hell-bent on corruption is through political strategy. Alliances. Hence the reason why you need to respect our vendors—every action turns upon the next. The opposition is looking for any excuse to shut us down."

Bracket looked at Josephine for guidance, but she pretended to be engrossed in her G-fone. He marveled at how drastically she could adjust her personality to suit the audience—in Bello's case she was all humility and silence. Bracket cleared his throat, eager to usher them out the door. There was no sense in arguing with the man if he labeled everything a strategy. "Anything else I can help you with?"

"Well, yes. We have some visitors coming here, special guests of mine, and I'd like you to accommodate them here at Naijapool. Actors, to be precise. Some of Nollywood's most popular thespians."

A vision of Bracket's favorite program, *Mrs. N Hires the Help*, flashed through his mind. "I'd be more than happy to offer a tour."

"Ah, that's just it, Mr. Bracket. They don't want to sightsee; they want to film a movie."

"At Naijapool?"

"Yes, it's a promotional film that will celebrate the achievements we are making here and will generate interest in our work for our investors."

"Are they good swimmers?" Bracket asked.

"Oh, don't worry about that. Just put them in a space suit. They won't do any swimming at all. They can come in, film a scene or two, and that will be that."

"We'll find a way," Josephine intervened before Bracket could object. "We'll make sure we take excellent care of them."

Bello turned between the two of them, a clear look of amusement on his face. But it was unclear what aspect of it amused him exactly.

"Mr. Bracket, it may seem insulting for you to host entertainers, but we all have to do our part. This film, and others like it, will help convince people to invest in Nigeria's future. It can make a major impact for the space program. I never would have invited the actors if it wasn't absolutely essential to this enterprise."

"And for saving Masha Kornokova," Josephine added.

"Of course! That's why we hired you, Ms. Gauthier, because of your laser-like focus on our objectives. Masha Kornokova is the beacon that will guide Nigeria to our ambitions."

Bracket thought, *What ambitions? What ambitions are there besides rescuing Kornokova?* He could sense Bello stumbling for once, caught off guard. But he didn't volunteer more.

"When are the actors coming?" Bracket asked.

"They'll be here in two weeks. I'd count yourself fortunate. I had to twist some arms to get them to come at all. I'll be in Lagos, but I trust you will show them our greatest hospitality."

Josephine held the door open for Bello as they exited the building. "I'll join you in a moment, Mr. Bello." Then she hissed at Bracket: "Start filling the pool now."

"That will take more than two weeks at the pressure we can get from the well."

"Get it started. I've seen your reports, and you've been cleared. Why haven't you turned it on?"

"I was at the explosion in town. A bomb like that could rip this facility apart."

"You survived it, didn't you? This structure is a thousand times stronger than a car. He's talking about Omotola Taiwo."

"The movie star?" Bracket had watched her in what seemed like countless programs on the Loom: period dramas, fantasies, slapstick comedies, and even a zombie film based on Ogoni burial rites.

"Yes, they're an item now. She's his fiancée, so you'd better keep her happy. *Putain!*

"The Indians are even slower than you are. They want everything checked and double-checked. Fill the pool! Act like the white man you have inside you."

He didn't know why Josephine ended her angry rants at him with an epithet, a sort of racial digestif she liked to inject at the end of every disagreement, a reminder of where he stood in the order of things. It's true he was lighter skinned than Josephine, but he hadn't waltzed through life by passing as a white man. People always knew. From how he talked, how he dressed, the women he was drawn to. With him, the black boxes always seemed to be ticked. He was never confused for white—especially not by the Wallers—at least not until he came to Nigeria.

Outside, the sky was rapidly shifting from purple to navy blue, the quick dusk that flitted through this part of the world nearly finished already. A moment later and he would have missed it.

Seeing that he had no choice, Bracket called his full-time crew back to the pool on an emergency frequency. They would demand overtime—and he'd have to pay it—but there was no other way. They would have to open the taps as soon as possible, at pressures that he would normally never tamper with, for fear of bursting the pipes.

"We've got two more rounds of testing scheduled, *oyibo*," one of them objected.

"We're done with testing," Bracket declared. "Turn on the pipes. We'll work in shifts and start slow. It's time to fill up this damn tank."

He stood at the edge of the pool as the first tap opened up, watching the liquid spurt out brown, then yellow, then foamy white and plunge fifteen meters down, splattering on the concrete. The water slowly began to form a puddle that stretched and coiled, slithering along the walls. It took an hour before the liquid coated the bottom and another hour before the thinnest film glistened along the surface. Eddies of air rippled over the water like a pond.

But the walls held. Bracket didn't hear any creaking. He didn't spot any cracks in the edifice. The water was buttressed by steel and rebar and the careful design of some of the world's best structural engineers. He went inside to check the monitors, then ordered the other three pipes opened to full capacity. What started as a trickle became a torrent of rushing liquid.

Lorraine would never have believed the sight of it, a major structure designed by Kwesi Bracket from scratch. A facility he was in charge of. Him, the underachiever, whose own loyalty, she believed, had wrecked his career and their marriage. He stuck out his hand and the Geckofone dropped into his palm. He took a picture. Then another. Maybe he would send one to Lorraine.

He realized, then, listening to the sloshing of the water, that he had nothing to be afraid of. Josephine had done this for him. She had believed in him, in her way. It wasn't a soft touch. But it was a touch.

CHAPTER 10

On the doorstep to his trailer, Bracket found a weathered soccer ball with the panels scratched soft from being kicked along the dirt soccer field. One of the Nigerians must have lost it during a pickup game, boisterous matches with swift passing and plenty of showboating. He picked the ball up and was about to press his hand to the door panel when he heard someone behind him.

"*As-salaam alaikum,*" a voice said.

He turned to see Walid, a member of his crew. Al Walid had changed from his work uniform into traditional Hausa pantaloons and slippers.

"*Amin. Alaikum salaam,*" Bracket replied. "Your shift isn't until tomorrow morning, Walid. You should get some rest."

"Please. For you." He handed Bracket something wrapped in a gold-colored handkerchief, tied at the top in a knot.

"You know our policy. I can't accept gifts for doing my job."

His crew often gave him presents or invited him into their homes. He had obliged them when he first came to Kano, feeling honored, but he'd learned it was better to refuse everything or it seemed as if he were playing favorites. Walid waved his hands, not allowing Bracket to give it back.

"Please, it's for you," he said. "May God be with you."

"And with you. Get some sleep."

The man walked quietly away between the barracks. Bracket dropped the gift next to several others in the drawer of his desk, then poured himself two fingers of whiskey in a highball glass.

He swished the spirit through his teeth, marveling to himself over the memory of the water cascading into the pool.

That was me, he thought. *I did that.*

But he had no one to celebrate with. Seeta had a girlfriend back in India and seemed to be feeling troubled enough by that to stay away. The Loom had no pornography on it, as far as he knew. He hadn't indulged in augmented sex videos back in Houston because he wasn't single until after the Flare, and then there was no pornography to watch. He'd heard that Côte d'Ivoire was more permissive than Nigeria when it came to sex entertainment, and that you could mod your Geckofone in downtown Kano to stream the French-language videos and pretend someone was in the room having sex with you with vibrating haptic nodes attached to your penis. Seemed like too much trouble.

He heard a knock on the door.

"I brought you some palm wine," Seeta singsonged. "Beats bloody Guinness."

He let her in, amazed at his luck, and she brushed past him to settle down on his bed as if it was the most natural place for her.

"I don't agree with you about palm wine. I'd take Guinness over that any day. But this," he said, holding up his whiskey glass, "beats them both."

"Pour me one. You're going to need another too. I've got some bad news."

Earlier she might have sent him into a panic, but the thought of the pool filling with water had calmed him. He could handle this. He could handle anything. He sat down on a chair and saw she had tied her hair back in a bun. If he wasn't mistaken, she was wearing makeup. The rouge was awkwardly applied, but it was charming that she had tried.

"Go on then."

"I went down to your kiddie pool, Kwesi, and ran some acoustical tests. The entire structure is excellent. It's even better than the rocket platforms. You have done a superb job. Damn, this is good." She swigged the whole glass down.

"I've got a good team," he said, relieved.

"The quiet American. That's a first. Well, there's one thing you might not know. My readings picked up something else. Not in your pool. But very close by."

"You mean a fault line? A sinkhole?"

"No, not a sinkhole. It's—can you pour me another?"

Bracket refilled her glass, but a little less this time. He didn't want to get drunk tonight.

"Let me back up a little. My instruments use sound waves to test for anomalies that could threaten structural viability. Cracks, breakages, whatever. I can run the test at multiple frequencies, and the resulting image gives me an overall picture of what's there. I've detected all kinds of strange things before. Once, in Sriharikota, I came across an entire fossilized skeleton of an ancient deer. It was as if the creature was about to leap right out of the soil from twenty thousand years ago and start scampering about. When I found it, the government stopped the launch for two weeks so the archaeologists could dig out the bones. My boss cut me out of the publication credits, but I was happy to have contributed to the history of my culture. Anyway, fuck him."

Bracket sipped.

"What I found near your pool is different. It's not a fossil, and I'm not even quite sure where it is exactly. The readings were completely haywire. All I know is that whatever is down there under the ground is very large. And it's alive."

Bracket coughed up a swallow as the whiskey went down his windpipe. "You think something is alive in the ground?"

"Yes, but I'm not even sure what to call 'it.' It's like a field or an entity, maybe. It's very large, at least as big as your pool, and it seems to move in all different directions at once. Don't look at me like that—I've checked the instruments. They are working one hundred percent accurately. I have never heard anything like that before, Kwesi. Here—you don't have to take my word for it. Listen."

She removed her equipment from her backpack, an omnidirectional microphone and two much smaller shotgun mics that she could use to laser in on a sound source. He warily took the headphones.

"This is the recording from your site," she said. Bracket heard a low pitch for about ten seconds, which began to grow higher and higher until he could hear it no longer. "That's an A tone."

"What's an A tone?"

"It's the note that orchestras tune to. Shorthand for four-forty hertz. I was cycling through the frequencies when I realized something was projecting sound, not just responding to the acoustic imaging." She pressed a button on her recording device. "Now listen to this."

He heard an undulation, the wet pounding of a heartbeat moving at regular intervals, the firing of a fleshy valve pushing liquid along a channel. The sounds did not repeat, though; instead they oscillated with an eerie, deep resonance. It reminded him of a humpback whale record that his mother used to play when she was meditating.

"So why do you assume it's alive?" he asked.

"I've never heard anything like that in the soil. It's normally a much more subtle soundscape."

"Not a bird or an elephant or something aboveground?"

"What elephant? When did you see an elephant in Kano?"

"I don't know, we're in Africa, right?"

"This non-native elephant would live underground. It would swim through the earth, like a mole, with the rest of its herd."

"Do you think it's a threat to the pool? Is it coming closer?"

"I don't know. I don't think so. I heard movement, but it wasn't directional. It's hard to pinpoint exactly."

"Thanks for checking it out," he said quietly. "That's good to hear you think it's safe. I think we should keep this to ourselves for now. I'm on thin ice with Josephine as it is."

The image of Abdul's body, sinking into the earth and disappearing, flashed before him. But it was too much to think about an underground monster right now. Detective Idriss had suggested there might be someone sabotaging the project, and Bracket had considered a suicide bomber, but he hadn't prepared for this. He needed to focus on getting the pool filled.

"Listen, Kwesi, I know I was acting strange earlier."

"We're all acting strange these days, Seeta."

"No, I mean, I ignored you. I was mean to you. I haven't done that in years. I never even did that to Malavika."

"Don't worry about it."

"I was ashamed of myself for sleeping with you. It felt like I'd cheated on her, you know."

"No one should be ashamed of wanting companionship."

"See, that's what I mean. I haven't dated a man since I went to university. After I met Malavika, I never wanted to touch one again, much less sleep with one. But you know, the Flare wasn't good for us. She didn't handle it well. Neither did I. And some of the things we said to each other, I regret them."

"There's no need to apologize to me—"

"Look, what I'm saying is that we broke up. Malavika and I broke up. Before I was even called to join this mission. I didn't realize how long it had been until you talked with me. I've pushed everyone away for long enough. I don't need you to be my lover or anything. You are not conquering me. This isn't a conversion. Please."

He could feel it happening again, the tears wetting his shoulder, her fingers on his belt. Their bourbon tongues were meeting in the middle. He'd fallen for his wife like this, attracted by her sharp reversals of affection, and he knew the tenderness would be gone in the morning. The family split asunder. Now Seeta's hand was on his groin and she had pulled it out. Freed. The warmth of her mouth, him drawing her hips to his face. *Stop it, Kwesi. This will do you no good in the end.*

He heard the sound again in his dreams, an electric buzz, sand grinding on sand, then turning fluid. Seeta was spinning music for him, filling Naijapool with liquid sound, the acoustic waves spilling over the concrete walls in a torrent. Then a crash at the front of his trailer woke him up. *There was someone else inside.*

"Kwesi!" Seeta whispered.

He put his finger to his lips in the dark. "Don't move."

"That sound," Seeta said. "Do you hear that?"

"I can hear it." He got up slowly. "Turn on the light when I say. Quiet now."

Bracket slipped from the covers and moved toward his desk at the front of the trailer, maybe ten steps away. He could hear someone clumsily pushing around things on his desk and opening drawers. In the thin light of the window he could make out a silhouette. He paused, holding his breath. If he was lucky he could catch the man off-balance. Seeta would turn on the light, and then Bracket would tackle the intruder at the hips.

He crept another step forward and shouted: "Go!"

Instead of the lights coming on, three blasts of piercing sound slammed into him, dazing him. He felt an enormous weight shift on the floor before him. Something knocked him hard in his chest, hurling him to the ground with impossible force. "Light, Seeta!" he screamed.

"I can't find the switch!"

He scrambled back to his feet. The attacker was huge. He leapt forward to try to tangle up his legs, but his hand burned with pain. It felt as if he'd grabbed on to an electric wire. Something wasn't right. That thing—what he had grabbed, the energy of it—it made him feel a strange longing. The intruder staggered backward before steadying himself. Then Bracket felt himself lifted up by the force of a wave and tossed toward the bed. His back smashed into the corner and he crumpled across Seeta's legs.

"Ugh!"

The lights finally snapped on. Something towered over them. A presence of shifting light, a being so large it reached the ceiling. He couldn't get a fix on it, its outline rapidly spurting in and out of focus. Bracket thought he could see long, sinuous, bipedal limbs and they disappeared, and the head seemed to be covered by a tufted crown of electric wires, and then these too blurred out of sight. He couldn't see any eyes or find a head.

Bracket could sense the thing observing him, the light shifting to and fro, trying to decide what to do. He didn't dare attack it again. He didn't even know if it could bleed. With each movement the thing hummed.

"Go on!" Bracket shouted at it, as if it were a stray dog. "Get out of here!"

The beast floated across the trailer and flung the bed end over end toward them, so that Bracket and Seeta tumbled back against the wall. Then it ripped the front door from its hinge and leapt high into the night air. It glided on its own energy, landed in a cloud of dust, and hurtled away in a whir of deep, reverberating sound that he could feel in his chest.

CHAPTER 11

There was water in the rock, pressed from the sediment by the sheer force of the sand and the wind. The moisture made your wrapper cloy at your skin, the dirt cling to your kneecaps. This room could have served as a watering hole during the great drought, Balewa thought, if her clan had only known about it, and nurtured herds of zebu cattle fleeing the scorched earth of the Sahel. Instead, thousands had migrated to the cities, where they had picked garbage to survive, and never returned to the proper life again.

She watched the liquid trickle down the wall into a stone basin adorned with strange writings that she had yet to decipher. Like the mystery of the water, she still had much to learn about this cold place.

"Do you want something to drink?" Abir asked.

Abir had intricate, looping patterns of scarification on her cheeks that twisted below her ears, carved by her mother when she was a toddler from rubbing charcoal into the slashes of a razor blade. Balewa had a cluster of four tiny dots that ran from her nostrils to the top of her high cheekbones like a birthmark.

"I'm not thirsty, Abir."

"You should eat something, Balewa."

"I don't want to eat."

"You'll get sick if you don't eat."

"Maybe that's what I want."

"Don't talk nonsense. No one wants to get sick."

Balewa was curled on a mat, still troubled by the explosion. In her mind's eye she could see the young girl's body coming apart before her eyes, as if in slow motion, the limbs and the blood enveloping her. She could feel the terrifying power of the blast that had screamed at her like an evil spirit. She could still smell the burnt flesh.

She hadn't gone back to the market in Kano since it happened, partly because she felt so sick and partly because the other women wouldn't allow it, not since they'd learned that the police were looking for her, suspecting that she had been involved with the suicide bombing somehow. No Wodaabe girl would ever blow herself up like that, the women had insisted to the detective, who had arrived at their mats at the marketplace peering suspiciously through his glasses. The detective didn't reveal anything—he only asked questions.

Balewa had hoped to stop the Jarumi from harming anyone by surrounding the attacker in the field of her Songstone like a cocoon, but she'd become distracted when she'd seen the young girl, and she had mustered enough strength, at the last moment, to protect only herself. The blast from the suicide vest flung her five meters away. She landed largely unharmed, save for a ringing in her bones, as if the notes on her lips had penetrated her very blood and infused it with nitrite and carbon and burnt flesh. The Songstone had saved Balewa.

"You really need to eat something," Abir insisted. She was three years older than Balewa and had been a constant presence by her side since the attack.

"I told you, Abir, I'm not hungry."

"Starving yourself to death won't help anyone."

"I'd rather practice with the stones."

"Fine. After that, you have to eat your *nyiiri*."

The other three women had already left for the marketplace, leaving Abir to look after Balewa. They feared, perhaps rightly, that Balewa might try to harm herself through some drastic measure. For her part, Balewa didn't mind spending time with Abir, who was the most gentle and understanding among the women from her clan. Abir had suffered at the hands of the Jarumi too, but she still managed to draw from some source of resilience she'd secreted within herself.

Balewa grabbed her favorite Songstone from its perch on the wall, where it had been ensconced when they first discovered this room. It was heavier than any small stone she'd ever picked up, weighed down by some mysterious force. There were several other stones on the wall to choose from, but Balewa had been able to provoke a response only from the one she had used in the marketplace. Abir had managed to awaken two of the other Songstones—there were about a dozen—but the rest of them remained inanimate, their powers, whatever they were, locked within.

Balewa began to sing the same melody she'd used in Kano to build the field around her, warming the stone with a couple of bars of music. The black thing slowly responded to her voice and vibrated with an energy that at once thrilled and frightened her. She kept at it, adjusting notes here or there, changing pitch or octave as best she could. Before long, the stone began to heat up, enchanted by her music.

Abir stepped back as Balewa expanded the field, which dazzled a hazy electric blue. The field disappeared when you looked at it directly, but would tug at your vision, like a distant star, if you looked slightly away from it. On the inside she was surrounded by translucent bands of orange color that leapt and swirled inside. Each stone seemed to play with a different color of light. She repeated the sequence of notes until she no longer felt her lips moving, the sounds coming from within her throat. And in the melody she began to hear gaps, places where more notes could be layered on top. She tried clucking out another note with her tongue, continuing the humming all the while, and the field changed from the shape of a sphere to taking on a more organic form. She added yet another note, and the field seemed to draw in closer to her body. But she lost her focus and the field dissipated again.

"That was great!" Abir said. "You found something new."

"I couldn't sustain it. I ran out of breath."

"That's why we practice. It looked like you, when you made those other sounds."

"Like me?"

"Like a scary jiini! I didn't know you were so frightening."

Balewa chuckled, despite herself. She was thin and short, by the standards of her clan, and no one had ever called her frightening. Abir was always good-natured. They were friends now, after Abir had given her a small bracelet for her wrist, woven from palm fiber, as a token of her friendship, an act of kindness that none of the other women had ever offered.

Abir brought her a calabash full of cold millet porridge. This time Balewa slurped it down without protest.

She had only reluctantly tried the Songstones at first, because she had never felt like singing after the rape—for that's what it was, even if the other women wouldn't call it that, or mention it at all—feeling that no sound was worth uttering again, not when the child of her rapist could be growing inside her. She remembered the crushing weight of the man, the disgusting stench of his breath, and the helplessness as he pinned her arms behind her, the excruciating blows to her head, chest, and eyes. How he had choked her until she passed out and she awoke bleeding, as if she had been pierced by a knife and not his sex. He hadn't uttered a word to her or looked her in the eyes, and in failing to do so he'd robbed her of whatever modicum of dignity she had left. His indifference made her feel like an animal, or, worse, like nothing at all, a thing to be spat upon, a bug to be squashed.

Abir could awaken the Songstones with her lilting, resonant voice, and she'd already shown that the stones responded to dissonance and half steps in the octave nearly as well as tonal purity.

Balewa's stone was ovoid in shape and had a ring etched around the middle, while Abir's stone had sharp, crystalline structures that jutted out in three places.

"I don't feel well." Balewa moved to the corner, where she vomited up the porridge. She tried mopping up the mess as best she could.

"The nausea should be over soon," Abir said hopefully.

"Only when I kill it."

"We don't have the right medicines for that. There aren't any *badaadi* trees around here."

"I won't bear this child! Let me go to a doctor in the town. I won't tell anyone anything."

"We can't let you go. You were seen at the explosion. If they find you, they'll lock you away in jail."

"Please, we've saved enough money for a doctor. You have to let me go."

"The others don't trust you anymore, Balewa. Not after you disobeyed our agreement. We were all supposed to return back here, and you ignored them. You could have been killed in the explosion."

"I wish I had been."

"Don't say that." Abir frowned, which caused the scars to bunch up on her cheeks, re-forming the patterns. It made her look angrier than she really was. "Besides," she added, "it could be your husband's child. You might be killing his only offspring."

"It's not his child."

"How can you be so sure? Didn't you sleep with him?"

"It's a bastard."

"If it dies, there won't be any children left from our lineage at all."

"I'm telling you, Abir, it's not his child."

Balewa had contemplated taking matters into her own hands by using a Songstone to kill the fetus, but she didn't know the limits of the stones. The other day she'd seen Abir crush a calabash into fine powder after humming to herself.

Every time they experimented with the Songstones they learned something new, but the secrets were only slowly revealing themselves. There was no instruction manual, no shepherd to lead them to a wellspring of knowledge. They did not know who had made the stones, or why, only that they were extraordinarily precious and special. Instead, they would look at the impenetrable inscriptions and scour their own memories for melodies and harmonies long since forgotten, hoping that a new song could reveal a new power.

Music had opened this place to them, enormous caverns hewn into the rock that were adorned with exquisite markings, and several snaking tunnels that ran into the darkness. One chamber had vaulted ceilings buttressed by carved ribs of stone, which had once been painted with an ancient red dye. The dye on the stone had flecked off onto the dirt floor, melding with the dark earth, so that the caverns felt viscous, sprinkled with long-dried blood. On one wall, you could see images of cattle, crocodiles, antelopes, snakes, lions, and tall, tufted birds, as if all the creatures of the Sahel had once visited the walls. Some of the beasts—like the elephants—Balewa had heard about only in stories and had never seen in person during their migrations. Interspersed with the images of the animals were glyphs that looped in curlicues.

They had all been afraid to enter the biggest chamber, since it was filled not with images of animals, but with terrifying humanoid forms carved from the rock that towered above them. The heads all had curving beaks that ran from their faces down around their breasts, over their swollen bellies, before erupting again outward, swirling around the legs and plunging between their stone thighs. The other women found them revolting, but Balewa was drawn to these carvings. She felt that the people who had carved the grotesque figures had also known suffering. In the middle of the chamber was a circle of large, rough stones that had once served as a fire pit. The women gathered bramble and tried to use the pit, but once they lit a fire, the smoke soon filled the chamber. If there had once been ventilation, it had since been blocked by the rubble or the passage of time. They snuffed the fire out. On cool, frigid mornings they would burn a few hot coals and warm a pot of tea and drink together before leaving for the marketplace.

The other women weren't as interested in the Songstones as Balewa and Abir. When the women returned from the market, Durel announced that she wanted to leave the stones behind and to quit the chambers entirely.

"These rooms must be from the jiini," Durel warned, sipping tea. "We shouldn't touch anything here. Evil spirits will make us attached to such things."

The taboos in their clan mostly focused on relations between men and women and between parents and their children—namely, not to develop too much attachment in the face of desert hardship or it would rob you of your fortitude, hurting the entire clan. Attachment led to shame, which had to be shunned at all costs. It was Durel's constant refrain.

"Our own people may have created this place," Balewa argued. "Then it would be all right for us to use the stones."

"We have no record of such a place or thing."

"They're very old," Abir chimed in. "Maybe they were forgotten."

"Our written language is Arabic, not these symbols."

"Then someone left them for us as a gift."

Durel was unconvinced. "A gift from whom? Why would anyone know about us? We're far away from our home, and no one knew we would be here. I think we should leave them be and leave this strange place too."

"We could ask our Fulani neighbors for help," Abir suggested.

"They aren't Wodaabe. We know what happened after the drought. Our people left for the cities and never returned to our way of life again. Only the Wodaabe look after the Wodaabe."

The drought was always on their minds. Even though most of the women hadn't experienced it themselves, because it had come before their lifetimes, they'd learned about the drought in stories and how it had scarred their clan. People had vivid memories of watching their cattle die and spoke wistfully of the animals' passing as if their own children had perished. Some Wodaabe had fled for the cities and never returned again, the men stuck in debt bondage to traders, and the women enslaved as sex workers. Balewa's clan had somehow survived with just five head of cattle, and when the rains returned they were able to rejuvenate their herds. That was before the Jarumi found them.

"We need to return home," Durel insisted, "and pick up our lives again. Then we can find our children."

She was too old to have a child of her own—she was a grandmother now—but the others understood her point and let her thoughts hang in the air. It had been the cruelest blow after they had been assaulted, watching the militants hoist their children, screaming and kicking, into the backs of their trucks and drive off.

"This is not the same as the drought," Balewa argued. "The drought came from God. Those were men who attacked us."

"But they also claimed to come from God. They stole all our cattle, killed our husbands, and kidnapped our children. After the drought, our people survived. This is like the drought whether it is caused by men or by God. We have to do what we can to get our children back."

"During the drought," Balewa insisted, "our people went to our secret watering holes to keep our cattle alive."

The other women bristled at seeing Balewa, who was the youngest, argue with Durel, who was the eldest. Even if they agreed with her, they were afraid to intervene.

"That is what I'm saying. We shouldn't stay here. We should go to our meeting places."

"The routes are all blocked. And our watering holes are known by the one who betrayed us."

They argued some more about whether the Jarumi would know about all the watering holes.

"We should stay here and grow stronger," Balewa insisted. "This can be our watering hole. Once we practice enough with the stones, we can go get our children back."

Durel saw her chance to put Balewa in her place. "How dare you speak of children! You never had a child. Not like us. Besides, you're trying to get rid of the one child that is left to us."

Balewa sank before the accusation, too stunned to reply.

"You can't blame her for being raped," Abir objected. The word hung in the air shamefully.

"I can blame her for not wanting to keep our clan alive! She should have had a child before the Jarumi came."

"If she'd had a child," Abir said, "then the child would have been stolen too. All of our children are gone."

The others grew animated, turning on Balewa cruelly.

"Yes! She should keep the clan alive!"

"She can't kill the child!"

"It's selfish! She doesn't understand our pain."

"She still wears ankle bracelets like a little girl!"

Balewa sank to her knees, feeling the nausea erupt again in her belly.

Why? she thought. *Why are they doing this to me?*

There had always been jealousies among Wodaabe women, but never so sustained or bitter as this. And they were usually resolved at the Geerewol festival, when husbands and wives could pick out new lovers or reaffirm their love for their marriage.

She heard Abir come feebly to her defense as the other women used the opportunity to pounce on her, to pile on her misdeeds and her insolence for having tried to stop the suicide bomber. What's worse, she felt that all of their accusations were true. It would be wrong to kill the child in their eyes. And perhaps they were right, that Balewa didn't want to return to the migration routes, since her husband was now dead and she had no child to rescue. She would have to find a new husband who was generous enough to raise a bastard child whom he hadn't fathered himself.

She found herself reaching for her Songstone as the women continued to berate her, placing it in her palm. She began humming notes softly to herself, allowing them to hold in her throat, so that she was inhaling and exhaling in equilibrium.

"Listen to her shrill voice!" Durel huffed. "Like a whiny desert fox."

Breathe. The secret was in the breathing. She could hear the women murmuring around her and Abir's voice: "Be careful, Balewa!" The stone grew warm, hot even, as the field expanded around her. Breathe.

She began a second melody and the field drew close. She snapped her fingers with her free hand, and the field moved beyond her. She shifted the field to surround the burning coals and the kettle. She felt that the room itself was listening somehow, echoing and amplifying her voice, as the field merged with the wall, shooting out sparks and strengthening in intensity.

"Where did the kettle go?"

"What did you do with it?"

"Bring it back!"

She sang more loudly as the field compressed inward. She wanted to draw the sounds toward the center. Breathe. But she couldn't tolerate the pain any longer.

She screamed out, and the stone dropped from her palm into the dirt. It had burned her hand. She waved aside Abir's help and plunged her hand into the stone fountain.

When she turned back, the others were looking at her in fear.

"That's what we can do to them!" she declared, pointing to the coals. The teakettle had been compressed into a glob of silver metal. "That is how we'll get your children back. Now, do you still want to leave this place?"

CHAPTER 12

At the break of dawn, Bracket would have normally been grabbing his bike from its hook by now and lacing up his clipless shoes to go for a vigorous ride around the spaceport. He would have watched an episode of *Mrs. N Hires the Help* and enjoyed a full night of sleep. But this early morning he was still wide-awake, even after Op-Sec had repaired his mangled front door and left him alone with Seeta. Each ray of sunlight pierced into his eyes, as if scouring the back of his skull.

He swallowed an aspirin.

Seeta was busy locking and unlocking the door, reassuring herself that they would be safe if the creature returned again.

"They said only a petty thief would have waited until we were inside," she said, speaking quietly, "because that meant he couldn't bypass the security codes."

"That thing was not petty," Bracket said.

"No, it wasn't. But it did seem to be looking around in here."

The security guards were alarmed, but they were also convinced the attack had been an attempted robbery, even after Bracket had showed them the door that had been utterly destroyed. And they kept implying, indirectly, that it had been Bracket's fault for becoming a target of robbery in the first place because he hadn't properly locked his door. They had left promising to review the security tapes and to inform the two scientists if they found anything. That was an hour ago.

Bracket righted a chair and assessed the damage throughout the rest of the trailer. His drawers and files had been ripped open. "I've never seen anything like that," he said. "The skin—it was electric. Like a battery."

Seeta leaned against the wall, thinking now. "Is there something you have here that's secret, Kwesi? Something special?"

"I've got the same security clearance as all the project directors. Most of that is on the Loom."

"They did seem convinced of a break-in. Maybe they were right — that thing reminded me of what I recorded."

"At the pool?"

"The sounds weren't exactly the same. But there was . . . a feeling, mostly. Has anything else happened here lately? Anything that could have attracted it?" She began riffling through his belongings. "What's this?" She was holding the gold handkerchief that Walid had given him earlier.

"Gift from a guy on my crew. Walid."

"Why didn't you open it?"

"I get them all the time. I try not to show favoritism. Anyway, it's usually tea, which I don't drink."

"Mind if I look?"

"Go ahead."

She untied the knot of the handkerchief. "There's something wrapped in paper. It's heavy." She pulled out the crumpled form. "Look at that."

It was a terra-cotta vessel shaped like a teardrop, only this one was mostly intact.

"Any ideas?" Seeta said.

"That's like the artifact we found before! The one Abdul Haruna ran off with. But I didn't get a good look at it last time."

She handed it to him, and he saw that it still had dirt caked on the outside, as if it had recently been excavated. Walid must not have told anyone, or someone on his crew would have made a fuss about it.

Like the first artifact, the little piece of crockery was extremely heavy for its weight, almost unnaturally so. It was ringed with some sort of script. On the underside, through a crack, he could see a dark black stone.

"There was something inside the last one we found too."

"What?"

"A rock."

Seeta's index finger traced the images: "The writing might be a script or it could merely be ornamental. And these drawings, they seem to represent something. This is a scorpion, this one a dog."

"Detective Idriss thinks that Abdul Haruna may have been a member of the Jarumi, and that he was going to sell it on the black market. You think that thing was coming after this?"

"I don't think it was looking for the palm wine."

Bracket had a dim memory of looking at another stone like the one he could see inside the artifact. Where? At college? On the job somewhere? The heft of it was strange, the stone unnaturally dense. He tried to get a better look through the crack.

"Looks like a piece of coal. Or not coal—a rock with lots of folds in it."

"You, Kwesi, do not make a convincing geologist."

"No, that's who we need — a geologist. That's where I've held something like this before. A meteorite. I had a buddy at the Lunar Geology Lab back in Houston. He took me into the lab and let me hold a rock like this."

She grabbed the artifact from him and peered inside. "If it's a meteorite, that would certainly make it special. But why would an alien want a meteorite?"

"I am not willing to call it an alien."

"We've got to call it something."

"His name is Onur."

"You've named it Onur?" Seeta shook her head and laughed. "This is all too much."

"No, not that. Onur's my friend, he's a geologist. I will reach out to him."

"Then we can know for sure."

"Know what?"

"That we're not crazy, Kwesi."

Seeta peered up at him as she said this, fright shining through her brown-green eyes, and he knew what she was thinking, that they were scientists who thrived on the empirical and tested it through the hypothetical, and whatever had attacked them in the trailer and what they had heard earlier in her acoustic recording had no theory to bind them. They were flailing.

"We should get the artifact out of here," Seeta suggested, "or it might come back again for it. I can lock it in the engine-testing lab until you hear back from your friend. No one's getting in or out of those vaults, not even that alien. The doors are a meter thick."

Quickly Bracket snapped images of the new artifact on his Geckofone, and then Seeta put the artifact into her backpack and left. He fired off a note to Onur, knowing the message would be screened before exiting the Loom, but if he was lucky it might slip through the deep packet inspection on the way to the Texarkana Web.

As he dressed for work, he kept thinking about the blood that had bubbled up from the ground, and that sensation of grabbing the electric flesh on that creature, and then running his fingers between Seeta's thighs, as if his reckless passion had unleashed phantasmagoric monsters from his subconscious. Monsters that he feared would soon be coming for them again.

CHAPTER 13

Operational Security visited once after the break-in—to remind Bracket to lock his door properly—and no one else reported a robbery over the following weeks as the spaceport shifted its focus to the coming test launch. Conditions aboard the International Space Station were deteriorating rapidly for Masha Kornokova. A container of food had been contaminated unexpectedly, and the astronaut was forced to lower her rations to subsistence levels. Mission control's advice was now for Kornokova to sleep as much as possible. When she wasn't sleeping, she was encouraged to exercise to preserve her muscle mass—a fragile balance between inactivity and vigorous movement that must have been taxing for her. The only one who spoke to the astronaut directly, to Bracket's knowledge, was Josephine Gauthier, and she insisted on speaking within her privacy cone in the Nest.

The trusses of the mock-up of the International Space Station poked through the surface of Naijapool like the roots of white-painted mangroves. The water level had passed three meters, but it was still not enough for them to begin their simulations, which required the filter systems to be active. Bracket had done everything in his power to fill the tank, even forbidding staff from using showers inside the facility, and now all there was left to do was wait.

He was still haunted by the creature he had seen, the memory of the electric, burning sensation of grabbing the beast, and the feeling that whatever was watching him was intelligent. Seeta had called it an alien, but he couldn't bring himself to believe that. Physics and biology told him that alien life would look nothing like we expected—and wouldn't be bipedal or communicate in any recognizable form. It could be a three-kilometer-long slime mold from a 10-G planet or a being of light that oscillated across the higher dimensions. But he'd never seen anything like that creature before either. He had felt a primordial connection in its vibrations, a harkening back. When it decided to leave, it left abruptly. In his mind's eye he could still see it leaping into the moonlit night with speed and grace.

A member of his crew poked her head through the door as Bracket considered the possibilities, none of which boded well for the spaceport: "Mr. Bracket, there are some people here to see you."

"Who is it?"

The woman paused. "Lots of big men."

Bracket found Josephine waiting with a group very fashionable people, the men in tailored suits and the women in expensive dresses with head wraps. Three Naijanauts were also milling about, awed by whoever these people were. A drone circled the group recording video.

"What is all this?" he asked.

"What is all this, indeed!" replied a handsome smiling man with a hunter-green suit and a richly patterned lavender tie. His short pants revealed cherry-red socks, and he had glinting silver Reebok sneakers.

Looking at the man's shoes, Bracket realized who he was looking at. *He had completely forgotten about the actors.*

"And you must be the dashing man in charge," intoned a gracious, amber-skinned woman. Her face seemed to have been powdered. Her hair had a thick central braid that trailed down her back, and several tresses crowned her brow like a laurel wreath, fixed in place by some hair product. He had never seen a hairdo like it before, but he also knew not to comment on it.

"And you are?"

"Omotola Taiwo, of course." She held out her hand for Bracket to shake, but when he took it she recoiled her palm, as if he had sullied it. He forced himself to keep his face steady. Of course he knew her. He'd seen her in numerous programs on the Loom, but she had changed her costumes so often that he hadn't recognized her. So this was Nurudeen Bello's fiancée, he realized. She must have been thirty years younger than the politician.

"And I'm Baba George," said the man in the hunter-green suit.

"Pleased to meet you, Mr. George."

"Baba."

"Oh, let's get going, Kwesi," Josephine said. "Our special guests want to see our pool."

"We don't want to *see* your pool," Omotola Taiwo intoned. "We want to film inside it, to feel it. We need to be the Naijanauts, to live out their mission exactly like they would. We must feel the fabric of the space suits on our fingertips."

"You can feel *my* space suit," one of the Naijanauts volunteered.

Omotola Taiwo moved toward the pool deck, the film crew trailing behind her. Bracket told the drone operator to land the craft and shut off the cameras as they climbed to the pool deck. He heard a deep-throated yell.

"Whaaaat? But where is the water?"

He found Baba George looking over the edge of the pool.

"In three more days," Bracket said, "the water will be there."

"We thought the pool was completed," Omotola Taiwo whined. "A completed pool includes water."

"We just opened the taps two weeks ago," Bracket tried explaining. "I can't work miracles here."

"What's the estimate?" Josephine crossed her arms, trying to take charge.

"We've got it down to seventy-two hours. Then we have to run the filter for twelve hours to purify the water."

"Three days!" Baba George exclaimed.

"Yes."

"We will all shrivel up and die here in three days without water," Baba said dramatically. "It's as dry as a fart." He somehow made his words sound dry as he said this, the way he allowed his shoulders to droop.

Omotola Taiwo gave Bracket a winning smile. "Tut, tut. Let's not dwell on details. You might be aware that I run a profitable cosmetics company."

"Is that right?" Bracket asked.

"It's called Omotola's Magical Skin-Whitening Cream."

"Skin whitening? In Nigeria?"

"It's about discovering your inner beauty."

"And your inner beauty is white?"

"When you toil in the sun, your skin becomes leathery and dark as the night. It's your body's defense mechanism against the sun: your melanin protecting you from a life of labor. But this is the modern age, Kwesi." She draped her fingers over his shoulder. "We ladies no longer toil in the fields. We should restore our visages to their God-given beauty."

"Praise the Lord," a Naijanaut chimed in.

Josephine pulled Bracket aside by his arm and whispered, "What are you going to do about all this?"

"I can't help her with the skin thing."

"No, the pool."

"I can get more water for the pool if you get me more cowries."

"Talk to Bello."

"If you approve it now, I can have the pool ready by tomorrow afternoon."

"You do not realize how difficult it is to deal with Bello."

"Oh, I understand very well. That's why I need you to talk to him."

"All right. I'll talk to him this time, but next time I won't be around to help you. Get it done."

Bracket frowned. "Who's helping who here, Josephine? Looking after movie stars isn't part of my job description. One more thing. I can't put these people in space suits. Baba might squeeze into one, but Ms. Taiwo is not going to fit."

"Don't you dare say that to her face," Josephine whispered. "She has been a nightmare to deal with. She's a queen to Bello. Royalty! Do whatever it takes to make them happy. This is part of Bello's grand propaganda piece. I do not understand it and I do not care to understand it. Find me a solution."

Only now did he see a bandage peek out from beneath the sleeve of Josephine's dress.

"You injured?"

She hurriedly pulled the sleeve over the bandage. "I'm all right."

"Looks like you hurt your arm."

"Just focus on the job," she snarled, but he caught something— maybe embarassment—cloud her face. "There is a telemetry test in twenty minutes, which we'll fail. The Indians are complaining about the rice, the Nigerians about not enough fatty meat in the stew. I don't care. I don't care. I don't care . . ."

She left with Omotola Taiwo batting her eyelids at him as Baba George stomped about.

"It's impossible for me to stay in character," he was saying to someone, "with so little water. I can't pretend to be immersed. It's not right. It's unprofessional."

"Who is in charge here?" Bracket asked.

One of the men stepped forward wearing enormous wrap-around sunglasses. A wonder he didn't trip into the pool. "My name is Godwin. I produce all of Baba's films."

"Not anymore, you won't!"

"Oh, calm down, Baba!"

"You calm down, Godwin! This is unprofessional."

The producer nodded for one of his handlers to look after the actor, while Bracket pulled him aside. "Bello will not like this."

"What do you need to happen here?"

"They are supposed to be filmed in space suits in the pool. Show him, Sylvan." The man named Sylvan trotted over with two "space suits": elaborately festooned costumes with green feathers and sparkling sequins.

"That's not going to happen today. What were you trying to do?"

"I told you, film them in their suits in the pool."

"I don't think you get me," Bracket said. "This is a propaganda piece, right?"

"No, it's filmic history we are making here. We're capturing the courageous and bold risks that the Naijanauts are taking to rescue their suffering comrades. The perseverance of their training, when much greater odds face them. The lived experience. All for their country and the cultural patrimony of mankind. So, no, it's not a propaganda piece."

"All right. Get your photographer to take some establishing shots. I'll let you shoot wherever you want in here."

"But it doesn't matter if we can't—"

"After that, I can take you to a pool where you can get the actors in the water."

The producer looked dismayed at Bracket's suggestion, shifting a nervous glance now and then at Baba, who was now sipping coconut water as a handler mopped his brow with a napkin. "Baba doesn't like surprises. What are you proposing, exactly?"

CHAPTER 14

This time, with the actors, Bracket didn't try to sneak off the space-port, and instead he booked a caravan of three SUVs for an escort. The SUVs were powerful trucks, but they were also self-driving, which was one of the main reasons Bracket preferred not to use them. Imported from Germany, the trucks expected a certain order on the roads that the local drivers did not provide. Electric *okada* motorcycles swarmed past at high speeds, and cars regularly ignored traffic signs. Besides that, pedestrians walked along the sides of the road carrying their loads or swiftly crossed into oncoming traffic. The SUVs, which were programmed to protect human life, constantly stopped and started so that it took a long time to navigate the route to Kano.

They arrived at Ibrahim Musa's gate, and the trader warily admitted Bracket into his courtyard, but he made the rest of the caravan wait in their vehicles.

"Why did you bring so many people?" Musa said. "I do not like to attract attention."

"I brought your first load of groundnuts," Bracket said, pointing back at the trucks. "Twenty kilos fresh from the greenhouse."

"It does not take three trucks to transport twenty kilos of groundnuts."

One of Ibrahim's young wives noticed the commotion and peered out through the gate.

"I wanted to ask you for a favor, Mr. Musa."

"I am a trader, not a philanthropist."

"You'll be paid. I need to know if we can use your swimming pool."

"My understanding is that you have a very large pool at the facility. Much larger than my own. So big that it is lowering the water pressure throughout the city."

"That's an exaggeration."

"It's not an exaggeration. Your engineers are siphoning off water from the River Kano, the lifeblood of this city."

"We negotiated with the emir himself."

In fact, Nurudeen Bello had negotiated the deal, but Bracket saw no reason to explain that.

"Turn off your faucets."

Behind them, Musa's wife began chittering in Hausa, hopping around excitedly. She tore past them without saying a word. Ibrahim called after the young woman, who had collected the other two wives in an equal state of excitement. They ignored their husband as they peered out the front gate.

"Who did you bring with you?" Musa asked nervously.

"They are film actors."

"I will not have actors in my house!"

But even as he said this, the youngest wife was opening the gate to the compound and eagerly motioning for the entourage to enter. Baba George immediately recognized he had found an audience and strutted into the facility with a confident swagger, generously offering his hand to the women in greeting. Omotola Taiwo serenely entered as well, adding to the regal affair. Musa grabbed one of his wives by the arm and tried to admonish her, but she shrugged him off and invited the movie stars into their home.

"Where is the pool?" the producer, Godwin, asked Bracket.

"It's in back."

"Excellent. But where are you going?"

"I've got some errands to run. How long do you expect the shoot to take?"

They both looked over at Baba, who was already regaling the household with tales of his grandeur.

"At least a couple of hours."

As promised, Max was waiting outside Musa's compound in his pickup truck, looking thinner than before, his cheeks sunken and his eyes red. He had an altogether sickly appearance.

"You feeling all right?" Bracket asked, as Max started up the car.

"My son isn't well."

"What's wrong with him?"

"Congestion. I'm worried about our neighbor too. His daughter has polio. I don't want my son to catch it too."

"They've still got polio here?"

"Yes." Max swerved between a minibus and a bicycle cart overloaded with plastic bottles.

"You should vaccinate him."

"I won't give that stuff to him."

"Why not?"

"Vaccinations are the poisons of Western corporations. They are made to make money off us. The more we use them, the sicker we get."

"You're joking."

"No."

"What about chicken pox? Mumps?"

"There are many illnesses. Only Allah can protect you from them all."

"Didn't Allah create vaccines too?"

"No. Those were created by man."

"But Allah created the things that allowed men to make vaccines."

"I believe there are simply some things men should not do, *oyibo*."

"I've got a daughter. I would never want anything to happen to her. I bet you feel the same way."

Max nodded. "I am his father."

"As his father, you should look after him. When my daughter couldn't keep up in school, the teachers told me she was just developmentally slow and that she'd always be behind. It turned out to be dyslexia, so I got her special lessons. Now she's in medical school. You've got to do what a father should do—keep your boy healthy. Don't be silly. Life is hard enough as it is. Take your son to the hospital and get him vaccinated."

Max slowed the car down and looked angrily at Bracket, bracing his arms on the steering wheel. "I won't do it. It is the will of Allah. Look at what happened to your science—all wiped clean by the Flare. That was the will of Allah too. That's what your arrogance brought you. You big men all think you can tell a father how to raise his son."

"Doesn't the village raise the child?"

"You aren't from my village."

They drove in silence the rest of the way to Xiao's, Bracket angry at Max's ignorance but also angry at himself for indulging it. He knew it was a lost cause, so why had he even bothered? His fixer moved seamlessly across so many cultures and languages and could find Bracket any technology he wanted in Kano, yet he wouldn't even treat his son to a basic vaccine.

Xiao seemed unusually eager to make a deal to find Bracket more water for his pool at a fair price. "Slow week," he explained. "Slow week."

That piece of negotiating done, they headed to the police station, Bracket glancing over occasionally to see if Max was still upset with him. He couldn't tell if Max's mind was on his son or on their argument.

He found Detective Idriss at his desk, combing over a newspaper. He was wearing a blood-orange Hausa cap embroidered with an image of a race car. He sported a matching orange, full-length kaftani that was tight around the ankles. Bracket had at first found reading a newspaper trite or even nostalgic when he'd arrived in Kano, because like most people before the Flare he was used to pulling news off the Web, which would be updated by the second. Now he enjoyed the look of the ink on the paper, the finality of the conclusions affixed to the page. Naijaweb was crawling with malnews, fake news articles created to entice you to buy something frivolous or that could infect your device with spyware. Entire crime syndicates had profited from malnews.

"Sit," Detective Idriss said.

Bracket sat, as the detective finished reading the article before him.

"Ah, Mr. Kwesi Bracket."

"Yes. I've come to get my passport, Detective."

Idriss fished about in his desk and plopped the passport in front of Bracket. "There. You have it now. Is that all?"

Bracket pointed to Max. "He needs his too."

Idriss held Max's national ID in his hand. "You're not registered to operate a business here in Kano."

"No," Max said.

"Then what services do you provide for this man?"

Max appeared to be weighing whether to turn on the charm for Detective Idriss, but didn't say anything.

"He's a friend of mine, Detective," Bracket said, thinking: *I doubt Max would call me that right now.*

Idriss might have held out for a bribe if Bracket wasn't there, and the detective slowly handed the ID back to Max, making a show of it, as if he were doing him a favor.

In the back of the station, Bracket heard a high-pitched shriek and then coughing, or perhaps whimpering. The detective did not seem to notice.

"There's something else you should know, Detective. A few weeks ago we were attacked by something in our lodgings."

"I'm not allowed to conduct an investigation on your base without a formal invitation. Even if I discovered a crime, I couldn't detain anyone. You should refer the matter to your security to investigate it properly."

"I did, and they did nothing useful. This is beyond their abilities. They're not capable of handling a complex investigation like you are."

"I see." Idriss smiled, flattered. "Well, who else was with you? Mr. Obinna here?"

"No, it was a colleague of mine. The intruder came into my quarters looking for something. Only, it wasn't normal. Not human, I mean. It had a presence—a kind of shifting space—with electric skin. I think it was looking for this." Bracket showed him a photo of the artifact on his Geckofone.

The detective peered through his glasses dangling on the tip of his nose.

"What is it?"

"It's an artifact. We found it in the ground."

"You didn't bring it with you?"

"No."

The artifact was still safe in the engine-testing lab with Seeta, who had been slammed, like everyone else, with preparation for the test launch. Besides, Bracket didn't want Detective Idriss to pester her, not after the way he had treated Max. No one seemed to rise above his suspicion.

"I'm not an expert on these matters," Idriss said. "I suggest you try the department of archaeology at Bayero University." Bracket made a note of it as he put the Geckofone in his pocket. "This person that you say attacked you. Did he have red eyes, light skin?"

"Red eyes? Like an albino?"

"Yes, we're investigating some child abductions. We've been tracking reports of an albino man who people claim has been stealing children."

"You mean kidnapping them?"

"No, there is no claim for ransom."

"But an albino—"

"Is often more than they first appear. They are held in deep suspicion in this part of the country. People trade their body parts for medicine, believing that they are imbued with magical powers."

Bracket reasoned through it, trying to understand why albinos were feared, yet killed for their body parts. "Do you think that an albino could have taken Abdul?"

"It's possible, of course. But so far only children have been disappearing, and we rarely find any evidence like you did. It wouldn't fit the pattern."

"Well, I didn't see any red eyes. I'm not sure what it was, exactly. I didn't get an image of it."

Idriss sat back in his chair, pensive. "Well, as I said, I'm not allowed to come near your rockets. It's quite strange to me, because I went to the site many times as a child when my father used to work for Bendix Corporation."

The name struck Bracket like a spoonful of hot pepper soup. The name on the old machine! The one in the old building where Abdul Haruna had disappeared in the pool of blood.

"You mean your father worked for the chocolate company?"

For once, Idriss softened a little. "Chocolates, no. What gave you that idea?"

"Bendix makes chocolates. They're popular in Europe."

"No." He smiled, trying to contain a laugh. "Those are Bendicks, with a *ck*, not an *x*. Bendix Field Engineering Corporation was the contractor for the flight tracking project here in Kano. Chocolates." He looked at Max. "He said chocolates!" He put his hand over his mouth and gave a laugh that was almost a snort. He called over another officer and explained it to him, and he guffawed much more loudly.

"All right, my mistake," Bracket said.

"Chocolates! I mean, Mr. Bracket."

"Enough already."

"Okay, all right, I'll tell you."

Idriss explained that the project was part of NASA's Mercury Space Flight Network, which tracked the orbit of John Glenn, the first American to orbit Earth. The Kano station shortened the communications blackout period as Glenn's capsule hurtled across the Atlantic. Idriss's father had been one of about twenty-five locals hired to staff the facility, who had all received training in advanced telemetry and computers. NASA chose Kano because it was free of light and signal pollution, and the emir at the time found the site made for poor pastureland. Nothing grew there.

"The Americans shut it down after Glenn's first flight. They never explained why. One day my father was contributing to the space age and the next day they said they couldn't use the tracking station anymore. He was devastated. There was no local use for the skills my father acquired except for the military. To give you an idea, people still used camels to get around in those days. My father worked on radar tracking for the Nigerian Air Force during the Biafran War. It bothered him until he died. He joined Bendix to support peaceful space exploration, and instead he ended up aiming ballistic missiles at his own countrymen."

"They didn't take everything," Bracket corrected. "I saw a Bendix machine in one of the old buildings on the site."

"I'm sure it's worthless, Mr. Bracket. I have met many expatriates, and I have noticed that their eyes often play tricks on them. I've seen men go mad when they have strayed too long from their homelands. As a man of science, I suggest you trust in that instead."

"Sound advice," Bracket said, confused by the detective's logic. He had just asked him about albinos as if they were warlocks. Now he was telling him to trust in science. Bracket rose to leave, tucking his passport into his back pocket. "Did you ever find out who the bomber was?"

"All we know is that she was from Borno State. Poor, fifteen years old, and pregnant."

"Pregnant?"

"We collected what body parts we could after the explosion, and we found a fetus among her remains."

Bracket's first thought was *Where—where did they find the macabre thing?* Then he wanted to know how many months pregnant she was. Was it big? Little? A boy or a girl? Did it have features? Who had collected it? Who had disposed of it?

"We suspect she volunteered," Idriss went on, "with full knowledge that she was pregnant. Likely to protect someone else in her family. The Wodaabe woman you described may have been trying to stop her. We're not sure why."

"You mean you didn't find her either?"

"She hasn't been seen again. But one witness said the explosion did not touch her."

"That's impossible. She was right next to the girl when she blew herself up."

"Could be. But then so were you, and you survived." He tapped on the newspaper. "They'll be coming again. I don't know when, but I suspect soon. I admire Nurudeen Bello for gaining the world's respect. But Mr. Bello focuses too much on what is happening in the sky above us, and he seems to have missed what is happening on the ground. The Senate is deadlocked and still has not voted to send the armed forces here. Look."

Bracket saw an image of a bearded man pointing accusingly at another legislator. The caption read: *Senator Kidibe accuses space program of cost overruns.*

"A shipment of AR-15 rifles was captured near Maiduguri," Idriss added, tapping the paper again. "Yes, I expect the Jarumi will be back in Kano very soon. Now I'd like to show you something, Mr. Bracket. Mr. Obinna will have to wait outside."

"He comes too," Bracket said, thinking he might be belaboring the point.

"It's okay, *oyibo*. I'll wait in the truck."

"Fine."

Idriss set down his newspaper and led Bracket through a long hallway to the rear of the station. They passed a door where Bracket heard a resigned whimper and someone speaking angrily in Pidgin. The detective fumbled with his keys before turning the lock, then entered a code on a keypad. It was a large, windowless room about six meters wide. Two dozen rifles lined the walls in a locked cage. Behind that, something was inside.

"Is that a hawk?" Bracket said.

The bird was hooded, but he could see from the sharp-edged beak that it was a raptor.

"It's a snake eagle."

"What do you use it for?"

"The Jarumi have trained eagles to intercept surveillance drones. We captured this one and we're waiting for the military to come pick it up. We think that if they tag it, the bird will fly back to their hideout. But no one from the Nigerian Armed Forces has come yet. And as I said, I don't think they'll be coming soon."

"What do you feed it?"

"It seems to like raw goat meat. Creates quite a mess."

He continued the tour, pointing out body armor in another cage.

"We keep the ammunition in a separate vault so that intruders will need separate access to use the guns—that is, if they don't already have ammunition. This presents problems for us, of course, if we need to mobilize our men quickly." He stopped at a cage filled with what looked like cans of Coca-Cola and a large kettle drum.

"These cans are all filled with explosives that we confiscated over the past weeks. That kettle drum is large enough to destroy this police station. Fortunately, we apprehended the assailant. We are now questioning him." In pronouncing the word *questioning*, the detective looked Bracket straight in the eye, a challenge of sorts to ask more. "Come, have a look."

"I don't think I can help with that."

"Come on, he's right over here." Idriss locked the armory behind him and slid aside a peephole on the door where Bracket had earlier heard the whimpering. "Don't worry, he won't be able to see you."

Inside he could make out two police officers, a man and a woman, sitting in front of a suspect. The boy couldn't have been more than seventeen. His mouth had been wedged open by a kind of brace, like headgear from an orthodontist. He had tribal scarification marks on his cheeks. On the table was what looked like an entire case of Coca-Cola. One of the interrogators used a straw to suck up some Coke, plugged it with her finger, and then dribbled the Coke over the man's teeth. He groaned and tried to gag it back up.

"You're force-feeding him."

"Not exactly. We're giving him what he deserves, the very weapon with which he tried to kill us. But instead of explosives hidden in the can, we use Coca-Cola itself. After a few days of this treatment his teeth begin to rot, exposing the root. Most farmers have good teeth because they don't eat sugar. He is evidently from the city—lots of cavities. It is quite painful for him."

On cue, the interrogator plugged another straw and sprinkled more soda over the boy's teeth again. He screeched.

"I've seen enough," Bracket declared.

"Do you want to talk to him? Ask him what his plans are? He seems to know quite a bit about the spaceport."

"No, I don't. You should stop this."

"Good choice. He is not very educated. He does not speak Kanuri very well or Hausa either. His Pidgin is not intelligible. He can barely read. But he seems to have been taught complex chemistry as a bomb maker, a contradiction we often find among the Jarumi." He slid the peephole shut again. "Don't worry. Boys like him will not come for the spaceport first. They'll come here where the guns are."

"You're going to let that boy live?" Bracket said.

"If we set him free, he'll be killed because the Jarumi will think he is a spy."

"What about a trial?"

"Anything is possible."

Max drove him back to Ibrahim Musa's compound to reunite with the movie production team. When he arrived, Musa was serving the entourage a sumptuous meal at the behest of his wives, and Baba was reclining with his belly shifted to the side after having stuffed himself with food. The producer too looked contented and mirthful, and was telling loud, ribald stories about other film shoots, to the delight of Musa's wives. Even Musa appeared to have loosened up, enjoying the moment.

Good, Bracket thought, *let them play. We need their fantasies, their make-believe personalities. Out there, monsters rile you in the night. Fifteen-year-old pregnant girls blow themselves up. Let them imagine a better future, let them tell bright stories where we sail among the stars and they are the passengers, and we are the pilots.*

CHAPTER 15

Never leave your Geckofone unattended. That was usually easy advice for Bracket to follow as its tactile, almost rubbery skin warmed to his fingerprints and eagerly lapped up his biometric data. But when he returned to Naijapool he became distracted by the delivery of the Chinese trader Xiao's water tankers, which were already reversing into the pool facility one by one to empty their cargo, some twenty of them in all.

His Geckofone had disappeared by the time he came back to his desk—it wasn't sitting on the power cells where he'd left it to charge and it wasn't perched on the ceiling near the overhead lighting. He called out to the device but it didn't respond. Under his desk he found the thin husk of the external battery, with the edges burned black. This was bad. *Someone had been in here.*

He opened the small freezer in the refrigerator and pulled out a frozen cup of *miya yakwa*, a mix of beef, onions, peanuts, and collard greens cooked in palm oil. He threw this in a microwave until it was steaming hot before chewing it down. Eventually, the particles from his breath salted the air and he spied a subtle movement near a pencil case near his hand. The Geckofone turned off its camouflage and slid before him. It was blinking with a red error message.

Attempted intrusion. Partition. 6% memory loss. Emergency code 465664.

A Digital Security guard arrived as Bracket was trying to make sense of the message, having been hailed automatically by the device.

"Malfunction, sir?" the officer said, picking up the Geckofone.

"Worse than that."

Her face had the soft symmetry of an attractive woman, with inviting dark brown eyes, and she had a slender, androgynous torso. She moved with a feminine air and was wearing a light perfume. First time he'd seen a transgender woman in Kano. She seemed to be about Sybil's age. The name on her badge read INI.

She examined the Geckofone for a minute. "This looks like a powerful attack," she concluded, handing it back to him. "Did you find the battery?"

Bracket fished the charred husk from under his desk. "I think it's an electrical shortage."

"Your G-fone ejected it. It must have overloaded the circuit intentionally. Smart."

At this the Geckofone began blaring out a warning signal and tried to scramble out of Bracket's pocket. He held it in place, calming it with his fingerprint signature.

"Hang on," the officer said, using her own Geckofone, a more powerful, rooted version of his own device with more controls. "I think the adversary is still here."

"Where?"

"Somewhere close by." She crouched down to look under the desk.

"What are we looking for?"

She held up the battery and pulled off a kind of furry hook from the surface. "This looks like a fang."

"Snake?"

"No, a spider."

Bracket felt his skin tingle. He had never liked spiders. Snakes he could marvel at in their streamlined, reductive elegance. Spiders were all spindly legs and neurotic movements. "You don't think it escaped?"

"Oh no, it's very close to us." The officer removed a wand from her hip belt. "I can neutralize it with this Taser."

"What should I do?"

"Keep looking. Just don't touch it—they're deadly."

They checked under his chair and the desk but didn't find anything, Bracket trying hard not to cower behind her. She courageously lifted up papers and moved aside a tiny coffee table. Nothing.

"The refrigerator," she whispered.

"I'll move it, and you take the damn thing out." He stepped close to it, feeling his heart pounding.

"Maybe I should call for backup—" the officer began, but Bracket was already wrenching the refrigerator from its socket. The spider was about twice the size of his hand, covered with furry bristles, and had a body the color of sand. It had eight optical cameras and one hardwired data transmission fang that poked out from its orifice. The electrical circuits had been woven into the carapace of the insect. Exposed in plain sight, it splayed out all eight of its legs. Then it shot out its bristles, which stung Bracket's skin.

"Damn! Shoot it!"

The spider scurried up the wall before the officer could fire, leaving a trail of bristles behind it. Bracket retreated to the door to close off its escape. It skittered across the ceiling, moving too quickly for a natural insect. Now it was over his head, its sensors scanning for an exit. It spied the G-fone in Bracket's pocket and reared up its forelegs. It leapt for Bracket's chest.

He saw a flash of light above his eyes as he ducked to the floor.

"Are you all right, Mr. Bracket?"

"You get it?"

"Yes, I've disabled it. You can open your eyes now."

"I was protecting the Geckofone."

"I'm sure you were, Mr. Bracket. I caught it in a Faraday cage. Sorry I had to shoot so close to your head. With all its sensors active, I wanted it to think I was firing a Taser. It wasn't prepared for the cage."

"You could have told me."

"No, it has microphones and full speech recognition. If someone is operating it remotely they would have known. The Faraday cage has neutralized it for the time being." She stooped down over the spider. "Now quite harmless with its circuits disabled. Looks like they removed the poison sac. Nothing to be afraid of."

Bracket watched the docile thing in the cage. It didn't try to escape. It just sat there.

"This is really quite fascinating, sir. It's very sophisticated. It was probably designed to infect the Geckofone with spyware. We'll take it back and analyze its code—you're lucky you bought that battery. The spider wasn't prepared for the Geckofone to lose its tail. Old defense against a new adversary."

"I'll have to thank my friend for that. Thanks for your help, Ini."

She smiled at him. "How did you know my name?"

"It's on your badge."

"Ah, of course. I've restored your basic communications functions, but I'm going to have to limit your access to the Loom in case it managed to slip in code we can't detect at the moment. You can keep your phone. Just give me permission to access it remotely." He pressed his thumb onto the screen of her device. "Thank you, sir."

Bracket watched her carry the revolting creature away, thinking, *Brave soul.*

He checked in with Josephine to give her an update on the pool and the film shoot, but she was preoccupied with mission testing. The spider caught her attention, though. "Did it get anything?" she asked.

"We don't know. DigiSec is going to check it out. We should be careful what we say."

"All right, let me know what else you learn. Don't say anything critical over these channels."

"Could have been the Jarumi, or someone trying to sabotage us."

"What did I just say, Kwesi? Don't say anything over these channels. Come see me if DigiSec learns something useful."

After signing off, his G-fone indicated that it had downloaded something. He thought Ini might already be poking around from her remote connection, but instead he found a message from his friend Onur, the geologist:

> **Kwesi,**
> **How's the cycling there, eh? Been too long, buddy. I looked at the photos. It could be a meteorite but I cannot tell. There is one expert I know who is specialized in meteorites and archaeology. His name is Dr. Wale Olufunmi. Last I hear, he is in South Africa and he is not in good health. A warning to you, my friend: he can be very crazy. Last time, he almost killed me.**
>
> **Wife and son are in good health. Too much soybeans. We stay on base at Ellington Field now and I ate a big piece of steak. Delicious! Transformers coming to Houston next year. Until then, we run emergency drills for the satellites when they begin to fall. We pray they will burn up—God help us! Can you send me one of those Geckofones? I hear they're cool. Be safe, my friend.**
>
> **Onur**

The fact that the transformers had not yet arrived did not bode well for Houston, because it meant the city would be dependent on solar arrays or wind farms. Even then, those power sources

were of limited utility without transformers, which were manu-
factured in Europe. And Europe had been knocked offline too.
Onur and his family would be safe on the military base—Elling-
ton Field—yet prisoners of sorts within its borders.

He took Onur's advice and sent Dr. Olufunmi a message with
photos of the artifact attached, which would sit in his outbox until
Ini over at Digital Security cleared his G-fone, so it might take
some time to reach him. Outside at the pool, Xiao's last tanker
dumped its load of water, and Bracket's crew switched back to the
local supply to fill the rest of it. The mock-ups of the space station
modules were now fully submerged, rippling below in the cloudy
water. The air on the pool deck too had changed, the humidity of
the water soothing Bracket's skin. He couldn't help but enjoy the
immensity of it, an aquifer of water rippling through the Sahel
like an oasis.

Then he saw a diver sitting on the far edge of the pool, his fins
dangling over the side.

"What the hell are you doing, Santander?"

Santander was a marine biologist from Mozambique who
had run a dive shop off its beautiful coastline before joining the
spaceport. He was busy smearing toothpaste inside his mask to
keep it from fogging up.

"Inspecting the pool, Kwesi. *Sixty freeze to death in Chicago.*"

"That water hasn't been cleaned yet. Besides, you should have
a dive buddy with you."

"I have dived in worse conditions, Kwesi. I saw something alive
in the water. *Hurricane-force winds pelting the island of St. Kitts.*"

"You're telling me you went down there already?"

"I did a quick swim around. *Won the Nairobi Grand Prix with
seven seconds to spare.*"

"We have no idea where the water was sourced from, Santander. There could be water-borne diseases, *E. coli*, anything. You
shouldn't have gone in there."

"Okay, no problem. *Tranquilo. An outbreak of rhesus disease.*"

The divers had been waiting for months to dive in the water, and in the meantime, Santander had become a newshound. Newshounding was an addiction that had devastated entire populations after the Flare, who had flocked to any Internet connectivity with obsession. You subscribed to a newsfeed and you were informed by multiple forms of breaking information based on your attention span. The feed was adjusted accordingly so that you could be jolted out of a daydream by a headline. Newshounds typically had jerky, unpredictable movements as they weaved through crowds. The worst services were illegal and combined haptic feedback with visualizations and heads-up displays . In areas cut off by the Flare, newshounds were sometimes worshipped as oracles. Santander had somehow devised his own newsfeed off the Loom, an impressive feat of engineering when information was so tightly controlled by the government. On a practical level, it made him annoying to talk to. He had the attention span of a gnat and interjected headlines into conversation without context.

"Take your suit back to the washing facility," Bracket ordered. "We need to disinfect it."

"I found a spotted stingray on the bottom, and I think it's blind," Santander said. "The fish are schooling. I've never seen anything like that—they have vestigial adipose fins—and their schooling patterns are phenomenal."

"We're not starting an aquarium," Bracket snarled. Watching the police torture that boy back at the police station in Kano had drawn out a hidden anger in him. "They'll all be dead by morning. We need everything decontaminated now. No more diving until I give the okay."

"We can't kill fish like that, Kwesi."

"We can kill them"—Bracket shook his head in disbelief—"and we will."

"I don't think you understand. These are special fish. Their schooling behavior is unusual—we need to research them. I mean, where is this water sourced from? That would be a start. *Cowries at four-point-one Naira at the close of trading in Johannesburg."*

It was a good question, Bracket realized. Where had Xiao gotten the water? From a lake? As powerful as the filters were, they would get clogged if they sucked a stingray through their pipes. But he wasn't about to negotiate over this. "We are not keeping them. We are not studying them. We are getting rid of them."

He tried to catch the fish with a skimming net, but the water was too cloudy to see properly. The fish schooled in tight bunches, as the diver had said, and when Bracket swept the net through the school they flitted away.

"I will go get some meat," Santander suggested. *"Chinese medical supply ship seized in Sea of Molucca."*

"You're going to throw meat in the pool?"

"No, you'll see."

He returned a short while later with strips of dried tilapia and two fishing rods. "I fish in the River Kano," he explained, "when I'm off duty. Catch and release into this bucket. Then I can study them properly."

Together they began fishing by the side of the pool, using the tilapia as bait. The stingray, surprisingly, was easy to catch once they found a line long enough to reach the bottom. It greedily ingested the bait and the hook, causing Santander some consternation as he tried to remove it without tearing a gill. The other fish only warily nibbled on the tilapia, zipping into the underwater modules of the space station every time Bracket jerked on the rod.

"I'm going to see if we can track them on camera," he decided. He climbed the stairs to the operations room and turned on the cameras, switching between viewing angles until he spotted the fish hovering nearly motionless in a school, their mouths sucking water in and out through their gills. Each little fish was dark brown with a singular bright green circle near its smallest fin, which looked like an eye. That's when he saw it: *the school rapidly shifted shape into a perfect half-circle.* Then the fish moved again to form a sort of zigzag shape. Just as quickly they returned to a normal circling vortex.

"Santander, get up here," he said over the intercom.

"I told you," Santander declared triumphantly when he saw the video screen. "Special fish."

"What in hell could be making them do that?"

Again the fish finned into a new position, this time an almost flawless square.

"Schooling fish use sensory cells called neuromasts to detect subtle changes in movement. That is how they school to evade predators. *Tech riots plague Guayaquil again.*"

"No predators are shaped like squares."

"You're right," the diver conceded. "It's a shape that's rarely found in nature."

A triangle this time, back to a half-circle, and then a sort of zigzag. It was hypnotizing to watch and also made Bracket's skin tingle. Their movements seemed unnatural, paranormal.

"You said something about movement," he said, to stamp some reality on the situation. "That they follow each other's movements."

"I meant vibrations," the diver admitted. "The neuromast cells enable the fish to detect subtle, infinitesimal vibrations so they can school. You'll see that their movements are too fast to allow for other forms of communication."

"So they're responding to vibrations in the pool?"

"Most likely. It could be a machine or some other signal. This is not their natural environment, so they may be disoriented. Fish are often harmed by electromagnetic signals—take the great white shark, for example, which has never been successfully domesticated in an aquarium—"

"I'm going to record this," Bracket concluded, as the fish schooled into a circle again. Seeta would want to see this for herself, but she had been so busy lately that he had hardly spoken to her. "Did you hear anything while you were underwater? Any sounds, like a whale?"

"Nothing out of the ordinary," Santander said. "I'll run an image search of the fish on the Loom. *More details emerge on Reims nuclear spill.*"

The diver slid his mask down over his face, where Bracket could view his newsfeed deluge on the built-in heads-up display. Santander muttered under his breath as he navigated through the various screens for several minutes. Soon he lifted the mask from his face.

"They're a variant of the Lake Rukwa minnow, from the Congo. Most likely Lake Kivu."

"You're telling me this water is from a thousand kilometers away?"

"I believe so. I can find no record of their schooling in such patterns in the scholarship. They're an endangered species that has been closely studied."

Endangered, Bracket thought. *No wonder Xiao sold me the water for so cheap.* The trader had somehow acquired illegal shipments of water and must have been willing to offload it at a cut-rate price to the first buyer. But Bracket would have to deal with him later.

"Let's keep this quiet for now."

"Of course. There's no sense in sharing our findings until we have more data."

"No, Santander," Bracket corrected. "There's no sense in sharing our findings because if anyone learns we've got endangered fish in this tank they'll shut us down. Don't get too attached to them either. The chlorine will kill them all by morning."

CHAPTER 16

Nurudeen Bello's face leapt onto the wall twenty meters across. He was wearing an emerald-green *fila* cap and sitting on a chair, with a round-edged granite monolith towering above him in the distance.

"Aso Rock," someone in the crowd whispered.

"Can't be. He's not the president."

"That's the view from the villa. I've been there. That's what it looks like."

"It must be doctored."

Aso Rock, someone was kind enough to explain to Bracket, was where the presidential villa in the capital of Abuja was located, and that Bello's appearance there was somewhat akin to a U.S. senator calling a press conference from the Oval Office.

The room was packed to the brim with scientists from Nigeria, India, and all across the African diaspora. On the other side of a scientist from Gujarat was a Trinidadian; next to her was a French-speaking Yoruba from Benin. Bracket didn't see Seeta anywhere and she hadn't responded to his message about the fish he'd found in Naijapool.

"My esteemed colleagues," Bello began, "as we approach our historic launch, we deserve a moment to pause and commemorate our achievements. I'm pleased to present to you a film featuring some of Nigeria's best actors about Nigeria's new frontiers. We believe their artistic expression will properly celebrate our grand forays into space." He explained that the film was being broadcasted on all networks throughout the country and then signed off.

Bracket eyed Josephine to see her reaction, and she edged closer to him.

"Where the hell is he?" she whispered.

"Someone said Aso Rock."

"He showed me that recording three weeks ago. That wasn't live."

"Well, I haven't seen Bello since he visited the tank."

"I'm concerned," she admitted. "He's not returning my messages."

"You think something happened to him?"

"I don't know. There was a brawl in the National Assembly. He's losing control of the legislature."

The film opened with an eagle soaring above a cliff, the bird's tail feathers pivoting in a majestic aerial display of strength and cunning. The clip made Bracket think of the Jarumi and the caged eagle he'd seen in Kano and the torture of that boy.

"Do you think the Jarumi sent the spider?" she continued.

"Could be, although I don't know why they'd be interested in our internal communications. Ini's looking into it."

"Ini?"

"Over at DigiSec. What I do know is that the Jarumi are on the move."

"How?"

"I have a source in town."

"I told Bello we need more protection," she complained. "We're vulnerable here. Our perimeter is set up to defend against organized soldiers, not terrorist attacks. Bello thinks the military will root them out. But where's the NAF? They haven't sent any troops."

"You think the mission is at risk?"

"I don't know. Maybe. He cares about the mission. But he behaved poorly the last time someone threatened the space program."

"What last time?" Bracket asked.

She shushed him when an engineer crowded too close to their conversation. They moved to the rear of the mess hall, Bracket feeling tempted now, encouraged by her rare show of trust, to tell her about the school of fish he'd seen and the strange recordings Seeta had made in the tank. But he'd learned after Abdul's disappearance that Josephine liked facts. And when the facts were bad, she wanted solutions—none of which he could provide at the moment.

"Bello never tells me where he's going," she complained. "He's so secretive that I don't know if we have anything left in our budget."

"What about his investors?"

"I've never met them. I don't know what he's promised them and I don't know who they are."

The film now showed footage of the solar flare rippling through the International Space Station. Interior shots depicted instrument panels shorting and the astronauts frantically rushing forward to seal off the module to stop a fizzling wire of electricity from striking oxygen and igniting the entire station. You could see the interior powered down with emergency lights and the now-famous image of Masha Kornokova flipping through a glossy binder as they prepared to leave her behind in the Soyuz capsule, a tear dripping from her eyelid into a tiny globule that drifted toward the camera and smeared the lens.

Josephine turned away from the film. "I shouldn't be here. I should be working." She paced quickly out of the mess hall.

On the big screen, the actors Baba George and Omotola Taiwo appeared together, causing excited cheers to ring out from the Nigerians when they recognized the actors. The next shot was so well edited that Bracket nearly missed the sleight of hand. Omotola Taiwo and Baba stood outside the neutral buoyancy pool, putting on their elaborately embroidered space suits. The shot seamlessly shifted to the two actors in their costumes at Ibrahim Musa's compound. The final scene depicted both of them thrusting their arms to their sides like superheroes, mingled with images of them making the same motion in Musa's swimming pool as they prepared to save Masha Kornokova. Once aboard the "space station," which was clearly filmed on a green screen and edited in later, the actors kicked off a heart-pounding, zero-gravity dance number, while residents of Mumbai—saved now from pieces of the station plummeting into the city—danced gleefully in the streets.

The room burst into applause as the film ended, and Bracket couldn't help but clap his hands too. They had shot and edited the film far faster than any Hollywood production could have. Josephine may have had her share of criticisms of Nurudeen Bello, but the man was a master of PR. And for all the difficulty of dealing with their entourage, Baba and Omotola Taiwo had both proved their on-screen talents. Bracket felt proud to have contributed to the blatantly propagandistic film. He liked the vision. The bombast.

And the timing was right—today would mark the first simulated space walk in Nigeria and all of Africa: a four-hour simulation that wouldn't end until evening. Naijapool, now smelling of chlorine, was like what you'd find at any swimming pool, if on the bottom of that ordinary pool was a mock-up of a space station. Cranes and hooks dangled into the water, and you could hear the skimming sound of the filtration system. The fish were gone now. The crew had run through the checks many times already, testing the hoses, the power, the cranes, and the communications systems. The divers waded slowly into the lukewarm water, checking their weight belts before strapping on their fins. Things could go badly quickly on a simulation. The astronauts were essentially locked into a 125-kilogram space suit, and if they sucked in water, they could drown within moments.

Bracket bit his lip as the crane lowered the Naijanauts into the water. Soon their helmets were fully submerged, their faces stretching behind their visors as mission control went through various safety checks over the comms channels. The Naijanauts began bounding smoothly through the bluish water with confidence, the divers closely circling them, keeping the supply lines untangled and double-checking their suits.

It works, Bracket thought, and smiled to himself. *Naijapool is operational.*

It was well after ten o'clock when the simulations finally ended for the day, and another hour before Bracket locked down the facility. The creature had not erupted from its walls, and the fish were nowhere to be seen. Nor had anyone reported any eerie sounds in the water. But he felt it was too early to celebrate—every time he had let his guard down in Kano, it seemed, some new problem arose to waylay his plans. "You should keep your eyes on where you're going," his crew liked to say to him, "not where you've stumbled." But in Nigeria, he feared that if he cast his gaze too far ahead he might not like what was planned for him.

Outside, he saw the hot yellow heat of a ground burn in a thruster test, fire and smoke and clouds burning amber beneath the stars. Scientists were peering over diagrams through their safety goggles as they performed their experiments—Seeta would no doubt be running acoustic scans as soon as the burn finished. Hoping to find Ini, he walked to Digital Security, which occupied a wing of the complex for Operational Security. A guard directed him to the rear corner of the building, and Bracket passed through a clear PVC strip door to get to her office. Inside, the walls were painted dark green and LEDs lit plants ensconced in the corners—ferns, ivies, epiphytes, and dieffenbachias. The air felt close on his skin and he could smell the moisture from the plant soil.

"Ini?" he called out. A large moth fluttered across his face. He swatted it away.

"Don't hurt it!" Ini said. She was huddled over a long white table, dressed in a full-length green jumper, the kind of tracksuit assigned to the Naijanauts. One of them must have given it to her.

"You let that thing fly around in here?" Bracket asked.

"Of course! It's a fascinating specimen. Its behavior is remarkably well adapted. Someone picked it up in Port Harcourt last year."

"I didn't know moths could live that long."

"They can't," Ini said. "At least not without being modified. Hold on, let me see if I can attract it."

She pulled a clear wand of plastic from a pencil case. She walked over to a sink, pouring some sugar and water into a little cup. Then she shut off the lights, giving the wand a shake until it emitted ultraviolet light and quickly dipping it in the cup. The moth soon appeared, circling the wand before landing on it and extending a proboscis to lap up the sugar. He now saw that its antenna looked thick, almost rigid.

"You're saying it's been modified."

"Yes, like the spider. It's a cybernetic organism developed by the Cameroonian military, I think. It has camouflage capability. Someone caught it outside her home, hovering around the lights. The antenna had been damaged, so it could only broadcast on a limited spectrum, and it lost contact with whoever was controlling it."

Bracket felt something tugging on his pants leg. He brushed at it and felt scales slip across his shin. "Shit!" he said, and kicked out.

Ini threw the lights back on just in time for Bracket to see a fluorescent green snake slithering out of view. "Stay where you are," Ini advised. She ran over to a desk and flicked on a screen. "That's great!"

"What's great?" Bracket said, looking about nervously. "What was that?"

"Body temperature thirty-seven degrees Celsius. Blood pressure at a hundred twenty-five over eighty-five. Then you can see the spike in your heartrate. I got it working again. It wasn't sending me back any data before."

"That was a snake?"

"It's a green racer. Poison's gone, of course."

"What else is in here?" Bracket winced.

"I've got about twenty specimens of varying sophistication and health," Ini said. "Almost all of them are designed to camouflage themselves, so you won't see them." She beckoned to Bracket with her finger and pulled him over to a white blooming orchid. "See this on the stem? It's a cicada—the height of biomimicry. It evolved in nature to imitate a leaf, and then was hacked with optrodes. Its motions are very basic but I love the audacity of it—a computer imitating a bug imitating a leaf. Genius."

Bracket could see two dark gray graphene wafers poking out of the insect's underbelly. Its green skin had healed around the wafers, but the wounds still had an oozing, disturbed quality. "Doesn't look very healthy," he said.

"Oh, it will live," Ini explained. "But you're right. All of these cyborgs are suffering in some way, because their immune systems reject the technology. I try to make it less painful for them. They're quite rare. We don't get to see too many cyborgs, not since the hacking of live creatures was banned under the Tallinn Agreement. That's why devices shifted to biomimicry—your G-fone, for example—and not to using real animals. Hacking animals was shoved underground to the black market and to the military. The fact is that evolution is still way ahead of us. People find these for me. I pay what I can, usually not a lot. Though I'll admit I paid a lot for the green racer. I love the efficiency of its movements. I can't always save them, though. Many of them die. Which reminds me—the spider—I was able to coax some information from it."

"Is it still alive?" Bracket asked, looking around the room. The last thing he wanted was for the thing to try to leap at his head again.

"Sadly, no." She sat down at a long countertop covered with metal tools and held up the curled-up light brown carcass with a pair of forceps. "I would have liked to have spent more time with this."

He found himself comforted by watching her. Something in her furrowed brow and her concern for the welfare of these creatures, maybe, reminded him of Sybil.

"I was able to salvage the electronics," Ini went on. "Most of the memory was still intact. The spider used a zero day attack against your G-fone, a vulnerability in the code that could give a remote adversary control of your device. You see, the G-fone code is patched almost instantaneously—it's self-repairing—so zero days are extremely difficult to find. I've never even seen a successful deployment before. In fact, we're lucky we caught this spider, because it appears to have infected a number of other G-fones around the base. Your device was warned of the attack by others. The remarkable thing is that it came up with the solution on its own of dropping its battery to escape."

"So you're saying the spider infected other devices."

"Eight other devices, to be exact, all in upper management. I believe they have been infected for about three months."

"Three months!"

"Yes, we have to assume that all their communications were compromised. We have sequestered the other devices. But the infiltration was limited to the identity each user selected to communicate on the phone. It appears you used the default identity, which in your case was Yankee."

"American."

"Yes, American. We're recommending that you use Kalibari from now on."

"I can't just be myself?"

"Not anymore, I'm afraid. Thankfully each identity is partitioned off from the next. You'll have to shed your Yankee roots, but you may find that changing your identity can work to your advantage. I know that I have. I never would have gotten my job if I'd signed up as a woman. The first question on the application was my gender."

"I would have liked to have seen that job interview," he said, laughing.

She smiled, and he realized it was the dimple on her left cheek that made her seem familiar. Just like Sybil. "When you shed your identity it can be liberating enough to discover who you really are. My favorite is Wodaabe."

"I haven't seen that as an option."

"It's not on the top-level Loom. Did you know that their men carry mirrors and are constantly touching up their makeup? Many of them use fake kohl made from battery acid to accentuate their eyes. It's terrible for them, but they take beauty to the extreme. One day I hope to catch a Geerewol ceremony. That's when they compete to be the most beautiful member of the clan. I can't attend a real one, of course, because I wouldn't be accepted, but there's a Geerewol happening on Naijaweb next month that I've signed up for. You should join, Mr. Bracket. I think you'd have a chance at winning with those lashes of yours. First you have to get used to wearing the Wodaabe tribal identity. It's not the same as the others."

Bracket told Ini to transfer him the tribal identity, thinking he might learn more about those women he had seen at the marketplace. It couldn't hurt.

"Either way," Ini went on, "we don't have much more information about the attacker, but we hope to find it soon. Zero days are worth a lot of money on the black market. Combined with a cyborg, you're talking about a hundred thousand cowries at least. I ran a search and this particular species of spider is not endemic to this region. The cyborg itself also appears to have been made in Nigeria. Whoever sent it must be extremely wealthy or connected to underground markets. You should be flattered—you're one of the most important people in the Nigerian space program."

"I don't really see it that way."

"Maybe your new identity will help you believe it. We'll send you more information as we receive it."

"Thank you, Ini."

"One more thing," Ini said, pointing at the data the snake had sent along. "Your blood pressure is a little high. You should try to relax."

As he walked away, frightened by the news, he started replaying his conversations over the Loom. Who had he talked to during the past three months? Sybil, mostly by convoclip. Seeta had sent him songs. He'd shared his blueprints of Naijapool with Josephine and had spoken with her daily. Whoever had been listening in would know about the progress of Naijapool and a little bit about Sybil. He'd sent a note about the artifact they had found too, but he doubted someone would be able to make any sense of that. Where had his Geckofone been when he'd slept with Seeta? In his pocket? On the ceiling? It angered him. They had no right to spy on him. He didn't think it was the Jarumi, either. They could send eagles to peck at drone cameras—and maybe even dig tunnels—but a biohack seemed beyond their means if it was as expensive as Ini reported.

He found himself meandering from his usual path home toward Seeta in her quarters, who slowly opened the door, wrapping him in her arms. Her tangled, thick black hair was unkempt, with clumps sticking out from the sides. She smelled as if she needed a bath but he liked the honesty of it, the grit. She was wearing pajamas. On the floor he could see a pair of muddy trousers and blouses scattered around.

"We're not crazy," she said.

"Did you see it again?"

"No, I didn't."

"Me either. And no one has reported another break-in. Makes me think that the creature is able to hide itself."

"Like a cloaking device?" she asked.

"Or stealth technology. It's strange that no one else saw it, not after it made so much noise in my quarters. And Op-Sec didn't find anything on the tapes. Also it had that glow to it. It doesn't make sense to me."

"I wish I had recorded the bloody thing," Seeta said. "I've never heard a sound like that before."

"I'm not sure if I want to hear it again."

He slumped down on the edge of her bed. Bracket was tired as hell from the double shifts and now thirsty for a drink. He told her about the zero day spider that had attacked his G-fone and what Ini had explained to him.

"You think there's a connection?"

"No. That nasty thing was designed and built by humans."

Since Seeta wasn't a director, her quarters were about half the size of Bracket's. There was a tiny bathroom, and she had crammed a desk into the space, leaving barely enough room for the single bed and her audio equipment. She had dangled an ivy plant from the ceiling, and a bright red succulent was perched in a window the size of a shoe box. He smelled sagebrush in the air, and sure enough, a dry smudge of sage dangled over the entryway.

"Did you learn anything more about the artifact from your friend Onur?" Seeta asked.

"No, he passed me along to a contact of his. Detective Idriss mentioned Bayero University in town. We can try one of the professors there."

"I won't be able to get off the spaceport until after the test launch." She sighed. "I'm completely spent as it is. Did you tell him about the creature?"

"I spoke to him about it, but he didn't believe me any more than Op-Sec did. He mentioned an albino—something about child abductions. Anyway, he said he can't conduct an investigation here without an official invitation."

"Maybe we should talk to Nurudeen Bello," she suggested. "He might listen to us since Josephine isn't taking us seriously."

"No one knows where he is." He explained how Josephine suspected he had disappeared, but Seeta was too exhausted to do more than sigh again. "One more thing. When we filled the pool, we saw some strange behavior from a school of fish."

"You put fish in Naijapool?" she laughed. "Why on *earth* would you do that?"

"They came through the water supply. I brought you a recording."

Together they watched the film as the school of fish quickly shifted between different shapes, Seeta's face growing more and more alarmed. "That's bizarre. It's almost as if they're following a set pattern. They might be genetically modified."

"One of my divers managed to trace them to Lake Kivu in the Congo."

"You sourced your water from the other side of Africa?"

"Trust me, it wasn't on purpose, Seeta. Josephine forced me to go to a local trader to fill the pool on schedule, and he offloaded it to us. Anyway, the diver – he's a biologist – said the fish have been closely studied, and no such behavior has been seen in the wild."

"I'd like to speak with him."

"All right, but I've got to warn you—he's been mainlining news off the Loom for months now."

"Oh no. I can't stand bloody newshounds."

Pypers and newshounds had a reputation for not getting along, she explained, because newshounds consumed DJ sets that Pypers spent weeks assembling in moments, compressing their playlists into audio files that the newshounds played back at ten, twenty, or even thirty times the usual speed. Pypers tried to help people center on the moment, while newshounds compressed moments into as little time as possible. "Did he find anything else? Any vocalizations like the ones I shared with you before?"

"I'm afraid not. Just these fish."

"If it's not a genetic modification, it's almost certainly related to signal interference," Seeta observed. "But it's not enough to draw any conclusions."

"It might mean the creature is still close by."

"We should be careful," she agreed.

They both stood there watching the video of the fish in the pool, hoping their schooling patterns would shed some secret. They were exhausted from their double shifts, and the mounting list of questions was only draining their energy further. She brushed a dark curl from her brow.

"Can you spin something?" Bracket suggested. "How about that 'Aesop's Fables' thing you did before?"

Seeta perked up. "Always in search of a happy ending, aren't you, Kwesi?"

"Never said that."

"You didn't have to. It's written all over your face." She swiped through some tracks on her stereo. "How about we listen to Add-ama instead? She's the musician I recorded at Lake Chad."

She dimmed the lights and played back the recording as they lay on the bed. The singer's voice sounded eerily close by, as if she were in the room with them. Bracket thought he could hear what Seeta heard, how the singer's subtle voice blended with all the sounds around her. Here a car horn; there a cricket; an *okada* motorcycle wheeling away into the night as the musician plucked at her lute. They listened for a while, intently, until they lost the will to make love and drifted off to sleep.

CHAPTER 17

Bracket awoke from a dream about his ex-wife, a recurring dream that he'd had since they'd gotten married. He was supposed to meet Lorraine at a movie theater at their local shopping mall but she didn't arrive when they had agreed, and when he finally found her in the food court, she was kissing another man. The dream had an almost laughable simplicity that didn't require any Freudian insight to understand. From their first date he'd felt as if she was slipping away, and all that was missing was the final time and place of the severance. The divorce hadn't cured him of the nightmare. It was as if a deep berm had been carved into his mind that his subconscious would flow through forever. It didn't matter either that he was sleeping in Seeta's quarters.

She was already dressed. "I've got to get to the platform," she said, pulling him in for a warm hug before leaving. That, at least, was different from his failed marriage. Lorraine had liked affection in the afternoon. Mornings were off-limits.

He pawed at his eyes to wake himself up, swiping through messages on his G-fone. Most were automated updates about various operations at the spaceport. But one read:

Mr. Kwesi Bracket. I am waiting to receive you at your office.

There was no signature, and the metadata had been stripped, so he couldn't guess who sent it. Only Nurudeen Bello called him by his full name. Thinking—hoping—that Bello might have returned from his trip, which would set Josephine and everyone else in a better mood, Bracket showered and dressed quickly, putting on a freshly pressed shirt. At Naijapool, two astronauts were preparing for their next EVA on the pool deck. A former fighter pilot from the Nigerian defense forces switched poses from a sturdy downward dog into warrior pose. A young neuroscientist from Port Harcourt had her nose buried in a large mug of coffee, trying to flush out her system, most likely, before she spent the next six hours confined in an EVA suit. On the second floor, he found a gigantic bear of a man standing outside the operations room wearing a black suit. He puffed out his chest as Bracket approached. He didn't look like Bello's security guard.

"You can't go in there."

The accent: *cont* instead of *can't*.

"That's my office. I'll go where I damn well please."

"Hold on," the man said, barring Bracket's way with a club of an arm.

He opened the door and whispered some words into the operations room, Bracket becoming more enraged with every passing moment.

"All right, you can go in."

"If you get in the way again, I'll have security throw you in the brig."

Seated at Bracket's desk, as if it were his own, was an older man in a double-breasted, pin-striped suit with tightly combed silver hair. He held a titanium cane topped with an ebony wood handle. All his suit buttons were cowrie shells, and gold rings adorned his fingers. There were cowries woven into the suit itself, such that he clattered with each movement, an extraordinary display of wealth. He did not appear to have a biomimicry device with him, and Bracket's G-fone confirmed this. Upon spotting Bracket, the man stood up and, with some effort, swapped the cane to his other hand.

"Mr. Bracket, I'm Dr. Olufunmi. Dr. Wale Olufunmi."

"How did you get in here?" Bracket demanded.

"I needed a place to rest. It's difficult for me to stand for too long."

He sat down again, somewhat heavily, using his free hand to unbutton the cowries on his jacket and remove a slip of paper. He handed it to Bracket. "You sent me a message about an artifact you found."

Bracket looked at the man again. He had just sent the message—at least that's what it felt like. He had expected a reply eventually, but not to meet the man in person. How had he gotten there so quickly?

"I don't recall sending you an invitation."

"We've had a problem with the uplink near Yaoundé for the past few days. So I hopped in my plane."

"Just like that."

"Well, yes."

"Didn't think to let me know you were coming?"

"There was no way to send you a message. Sadly, jet travel can move more quickly than a message these days."

Bracket was still reeling from the intrusion into his office. Bodyguard or not, Olufunmi should not have bypassed Op-Sec so easily.

"Forgive me for being forward," the man continued, "but do you have it?"

"Have what?"

He stabbed his finger into the printout. "The artifact you wrote me about."

"It's not here. First, I need you to explain yourself."

"I am at your disposal, as they say."

"Call off your man here. He's making me uncomfortable."

Olufunmi nodded at the bodyguard. "Wait by the plane, Clarence."

"By the plane? That's too far away for me to protect you—"

Olufunmi banged his cane on the ground: "By the *plane*!"

The bodyguard turned and left the facility, giving Bracket an angry look on the way out.

"Clarence is a former Springbok. Played sixteen games for his country before a fly-half knocked out his knee. He responds to the coaching mentality."

Bracket was relieved that the bodyguard had left the room, but he was still wary of Olufunmi. "We found two artifacts."

"Two? You only sent me a photo of one."

"That's because one of them was stolen from us. We found both of them while building the facility you're in right now."

Olufunmi looked about with appreciation. "Is that right? This must have been quite an undertaking. It's very impressive. Only I doubt a meteorite came from this area. There have been no known recordings of meteorites striking northern Nigeria. In all likelihood it came from somewhere else, transported across the Sahara perhaps."

"Could be. You know something about meteorites?"

Bracket was racking his brain to remember what his friend Onur in Houston had said about this man. He was obviously wealthy, but his friend hadn't said anything about that, certainly nothing about a private jet.

"I was a scientist at NASA's Lunar Geology Lab in Houston. I'd like to think that I made some modest discoveries during my time there."

"But you're not living there anymore."

"Oh no, I've relocated to South Africa. That's my home now."

"You weren't hit by the Flare?"

"Of course. But the old apartheid mentality remains. The country still thinks of itself as being cut off, a trauma, if you will. Certain transformers were shielded, and the solar grids survived. You could even say that I was in the right place at the right time."

Another thing: Bracket could see that one side of the man's face was slow to move, or not slow—paralyzed. His right arm appeared to be paralyzed too, but the other half seemed to be functioning all right. Bracket had a million things to do, and he wanted to know if the scientist could tell him anything about the artifact he had found, but he didn't like the fact that the man had so easily bypassed Op-Sec. He mistrusted pushy people as a matter of course.

"I can see that I've interrupted your schedule, Mr. Bracket. I have no desire to get in the way—we can wait until you've finished your work for the day before you show me the artifact." He smiled a half-smile that must have taken a lot of effort. "I'm eager to see your simulation tank."

"I don't have time to give you a tour."

"I'm happy to follow along. I promise not to get in the way."

Rich pushy people were even worse. The two scientists moved slowly down the corridor, Dr. Olufunmi leaning heavily on his cane to prevent his bad foot from dragging along the ground. Bracket pointed out the hyperbaric chamber, which would be used by the divers in the case of decompression sickness; the briefing room; and the diving equipment room.

"This is all excellent," Dr. Olufunmi kept on saying. "All excellent. It's like a modernized version of the NBL in Houston."

"You've been there?"

"Many times. I visited whenever I had a free chance to watch the simulations. It's where they practiced before launching the Hubble the first time. I saw many of those test runs."

"Then you probably saw me too."

"Oh no, that was too long ago. I left in 1993."

They reached the entrance to the changing rooms, where two astronauts were getting ready for their next simulation. Bracket held out a hand to block the scientist. "I can't let you in unless you tell me more about what you're doing here, and more importantly, how you got here. You can't just fly into Nigeria Spaceport without high-level clearance."

Dr. Olufunmi drew his breath in, suddenly annoyed. "I doubt you would understand."

"Try me."

"It's of a highly technical nature."

"I'm the director of this facility. I can handle technical issues pretty well."

"But you don't have a PhD."

"You'd better start talking or I'll put you back on that plane."

Something in the tone irked him, the implication being not only that he didn't have a PhD but he could never achieve one. The structural failures of his people imputed to him.

"I can see that you took offense," Olufunmi said. It did not feel like an apology. He curled over suddenly as if in pain, leaning on his cane. "Can we sit somewhere?"

Bracket grabbed two chairs from the briefing room—where the astronauts were now receiving their orders for the day before the EVA—and set them down in the hallway.

"You've got five minutes."

"All right. Five minutes. That should be enough time. I suppose I should start at the beginning. I should have been here twenty-five years ago, because I was one of the scientists recruited to lead Bello's program."

"What program? I'm a part of Bello's program." But he was remembering now something that Josephine had told him. *The last time,* she had said. Bello had done something wrong *the last time.*

"You're a part of his second program. What else do you know about Bello?"

"I know he was a whistleblower who was jailed, a man who exposed the human rights violations in this country. He's now one of the most powerful politicians in Nigeria."

"That's right, he unearthed the Ibeji counterterrorism organization. That's the official story. What you have failed to ask is why Bello was arrested in the first place."

There it was again: the professorial tone. The man was determined to make a student out of him.

"The official story does not include the part about how Bello himself was stealing money from the government. His dream was to create a space program in Nigeria, and he had planned to do so with funds he'd hidden from his own department, funds that were tied to oil revenues. He invited scientists like me to come run the program for him. I was to be stationed in Jos, but others were supposed to be stationed here."

"So you're claiming that he was a criminal. That's quite a story."

"That is the simplest explanation but not the correct one. You must still be new to Nigeria. The ministers in power were equally corrupt. They weren't worried about Bello stealing money so much as how he intended to use it—to build a space program. He planned to invest the money back in his people. It would have given him a real shot at joining the political elite." Olufunmi winced again in pain, but Bracket felt no need comfort him. "The timing could not have been worse. Abiola won the general election, and the government clamped down on all opposition. Canceled the elections. They placed Bello under house arrest. And the Ibeji operation killed everyone he had recruited."

"But not you?"

Olufunmi slowly unbuttoned his dress shirt with his good hand. He peeled back the seam and showed Bracket three scars that curled around his body, the skin thick and striated. "I survived."

"That does not explain what you're doing here. I sent you a message about an artifact I found. I didn't invite you here."

"I've known Nurudeen Bello for twenty-five years. He is all the security clearance I need. He knew about my expertise on meteorites and approved my flight."

Bracket caught the lie. He'd never told Bello about the meteorite. He took a long look at the doctor slumped before him, and for all the dignity he was striving to impart, Bracket sensed another, more desperate need lurking beneath. The man's wounds were more than physical. He seemed like someone who was still picking up the pieces after something had shattered him; whether it was the space program or the physical wounds, Bracket couldn't tell. Anyway, there was no way to verify the doctor's story because Bello had disappeared.

"All right, Doctor."

Olufunmi's eyes lit up. "You'll show me the artifact?"

"First I'm going to do my job."

"Of course! I won't tell anyone. I'll only watch."

Bracket went through his work plan for the day as the doctor shadowed him. Olufunmi asked numerous questions about the simulation and the qualifications of the astronauts in the water, pleased beyond measure.

"It happened," he kept muttering. "It truly happened. Bello did it."

Dr. Olufunmi avoided eye contact with the other staff in the operations room, wary of their attention, almost as if trying to stay out of view. This was the fifth time Bracket had watched the simulation and three more were scheduled that week, but Olufunmi celebrated each maneuver with joy. "Fantastic!"

Bracket normally didn't speak to the astronauts directly and instead monitored the various machines. The same people speaking to the astronauts in the water would remain in contact with them in space, only there wouldn't be divers hovering like pixies to protect them. And they would shift to the Nest—Josephine's mission control room—during the actual mission.

"You probably think I'm too old to have any interest in outer space," Olufunmi said quietly, "because I didn't grow up in the U.S. like you."

"Never said that."

"Nonsense. Americans think of others traveling into space as a concession. When I was ten years old, I volunteered for Operation Moonwatch in Agege, outside Lagos. It was run by Dr. Whipple at the Smithsonian, a way for amateurs to help track satellites in the night sky. My mother bought me some binoculars—for a king's

ransom at the time—and I would climb onto my neighbor's ve-
randa at night to spot satellites. That was when Agege was still
farmland. If I spotted a satellite, I'd wire in a message to Olifants-
fontein in South Africa." He smiled. "That was before the days of
radar, when scientists hadn't solved the acquisition problem and
thought that the best way to track a satellite was to spot it with
an optical telescope. There were five thousand of us volunteers all
around the world. That is when I knew I wanted to go into space."

"I thought you were a lunar geologist."

Olufunmi scowled and straightened his tie. "Everyone has the
right to imagine."

Aware that he'd somehow embarrassed him, Bracket volunteered: "I guess I caught the bug at a young age too."

"You're *still* young."

"I've got a daughter who's twenty-four years old. You should
tell her that." Bracket laughed. "Anyway, my mother used to
work for Raytheon up in Massachusetts. They hired her to weave
core rope for Apollo's memory guidance computers. She joked
that she was one of America's first space programmers."

He'd visited that Raytheon plant many times too and been
thrilled by the acres of advanced machinery and precision. That
was before his father's diagnosis, Bracket recalled, when his
parents had seemed immortal. But he suppressed that thought.
Nothing good could come of that memory. It was hard-woven
into him, tangled and knotted, with no programmer to delete it.
Instead Bracket told a few more tales about his mother and her
love for everything African. The dashikis, Kwanzaa holidays,
forced greetings in Swahili.

Olufunmi did not seem too impressed by these tales. It might
have been that he didn't want his dream to mingle with Bracket's—one African, one black American. The destination was the
same but the vision was a deeply personal and creative act. It was
like being deep asleep and having a total stranger walk into your
dream.

Bracket ran through some checks with the operations room staff, and when he looked back at the doctor, he was asleep, his head drooped to his side. That was when Josephine called Bracket on his Geckofone. He could see staff in the Nest scurrying about behind her. She was wearing thick black-rimmed glasses, having shed her contact lenses. "Where have you been, Kwesi?"

Bracket used a Kalibari identity, as Ini had advised him. "I've been in the operations room, right where I'm supposed to be."

"I'm sending you a new work plan for the day."

"Why? We're on schedule."

"Schedule's changed."

Bracket stepped into the hallway, motioning with his chin for one of the other staff to watch Dr. Olufunmi.

"I think Bello's in real trouble," Josephine said. "He appears to have stopped using his G-fone altogether. I've confirmed the Jarumi are returning—and soon. We don't know how much time we have, so we need to advance the test launch. It's happening in seventy-two hours."

"You're going to cause a revolt after the hours you've already been forcing people to work," Bracket warned.

"What do you want me to do?" she hissed. "Wait until a group of murderers attacks us?"

"No," he said, thinking it through. "Tell everyone Bello's going to be overseeing the launch personally. They need inspiration."

"But it's not true."

"We can deal with that after the launch. They just saw his film, and people will be more eager than ever to help out if they think he'll be here."

"What if someone finds out?"

"The end result is the same—they'll walk off the job. Bello is the reason these people are here, Josephine. You've worked them hard enough and you can't ask for more hours without a good reason."

"Fine," she agreed, seeing the logic in his plan. "You're the only one who knows the truth. I've got to call seven other people now." She signed off before Bracket could change his mind.

INTERLUDE

All of Masha Kornokova's dreams were of spinning: A chip of paint flexing like a butterfly. An errant screw gyrating like a worm. Whirls of motion filled her mind as she drifted off to sleep, fearing that one of these little objects would rip through the soft protective shells of the module and pull her into the vacuum of space. The satellites around her were no longer a constellation of man-made stars that corrected their own orbits, but free-floating missiles being sucked in by Earth's gravity. The ISS was falling too, and with each passing orbit she saw distinct features sharpen through the porthole: the equatorial band of Asia seemed to swoon with mysterious light, as if it had captured the moon itself, and Africa pulsed with a bright yellow eminence. It was easy to miss the United States now, when it slid by on the dark side, pale illumination trickling out of the military bases before a quick speckle in the Silicon Territories. Ukraine was the same: darkness flecked with searching tendrils of light. This was the world now.

Masha felt weak and hungry all the time, yet Josephine was constantly urging her to cut back on rations, turning her sustenance into a sort of game, varying her consumption targets: today mashed peas, and Wednesday a cup of rice, but tomorrow, a thick thigh of chicken. These surprises in her diet were designed to liven her up. Meanwhile, she was urged to exercise and spin like a top to prevent her spinal fluid from warping her vision permanently. So she spun and she spun, until she saw paint flecks and bolts turning beneath her eyelids.

Masha wanted to gaze upon Josephine's eyes again, not the polished, simulated image she was beaming up from Nigeria—blue eyes and white skin—but the frazzled, impassioned woman whom she had known on the surface. It would only be fair. Josephine could see Masha's real face, after all, and Masha knew that her own sunken cheeks, which had once looked fetching when they had first met during astronaut training, now appeared hollowed and made her eyes bulge.

Still, when she demanded the data, Josephine would give it to her. And the data told her that the Flare had unleashed thirty thousand pieces of debris, which were spinning, spinning now until they flamed out in the atmosphere, and on each orbit the chances increased that one would strike Masha first. Would it be a wingnut? A flake of silicon? Or her own hunger that tore her apart as she returned to whence she came?

CHAPTER 18

Bracket left Wale Olufunmi in the mess hall, where the scientist heaped a plate of Nigerian food so high that the cassava spilled off the sides. As the doctor dug in, Bracket went to the rocket platform to look for Seeta, who was conducting final acoustic tests on the rocket platform. She had pulled her hair back in a ponytail and was wearing a white lab coat and baggy cargo pants. A dark lock fell over her cheek as he leaned in for a kiss.

"Josephine has been riding me," she said, looking down at a clipboard, "and it's driving me bloody crazy."

"It's not only you. She's moved up all our schedules."

"You're defending her?"

"I happen to agree with her this time."

"I don't give a fig if Bello is coming here. We had politicians come through Sriharikota all the time. They only care about themselves. They try to snap photos with you, tell you about some bullshit physics fact they read about on the Internet. Then they squeeze your ass."

"She doesn't think he's coming."

"She doesn't?" Seeta asked. Then, thinking it through: "Smart move. All the bootlickers are climbing over themselves to impress him."

Bracket nodded. "That lunar geologist I wrote to just flew in from South Africa."

"I heard that he was here. At lunch everyone was talking about it. They were excited to meet a founder of Moonstream."

"He didn't say anything to me about that."

"You've heard of the Moonlight Sect?"

"Rumors of it. Something people cooked up to distract themselves from the Flare."

"It's not a rumor. I forget how little information reaches the U.S. sometimes. There are millions of lighting systems using Moonstream technology right now. They were originally designed in South Africa to provide lighting during electricity blackouts. When the Flare hit, Moonstream was in the right place at the right time. We have entire cities running on Moonstream in India. In Bhutan, Moonstream is even believed to be divine; the president said it brought people closer to the gods, and that raised the gross national happiness index by ten percent. It was invented by a man named Dayo Olufunmi. Wale Olufunmi is his father."

"Wale told me he was a scientist, not a businessman. Bragged about his PhD."

"Find me a PhD who hasn't. Maybe he was a scientist before. Now he lives off his son's fortune. They're one of the great Nigerian success stories."

"You think I can trust him?"

"Can you trust any rich people who don't need you?"

She said she would finish up what she was doing and meet him over at Naijapool with the artifact. Everywhere scientists were scurrying in a frenzy of motion, encouraged by Bello's impending arrival. Bracket found Dr. Olufunmi seated alone in the cafeteria polishing off his plate, his bodyguard standing silently above him. Not far away, though, tables of young scientists were eyeing his every movement.

"I've found the artifact, Dr. Olufunmi."

"Call me Wale," Olufunmi said.

"Sure."

"You're mispronouncing my name anyway."

"I say it the way you say it."

"It's a tonal language." He cracked a turkey bone with his molars and slurped out the marrow. Then he wiped his hands with a handkerchief and grabbed his cane. "All right, let's go."

As they exited the cafeteria, Wale limping along, one of the young women asked the scientist for his autograph.

"My son's still not married," he said, as he scrawled on a photo of himself sporting a colorful business suit. He gave her a business card. "Call my assistant and we can arrange a conversation. He likes smart women."

She curtsied in the Yoruba custom before scurrying away, Bracket thinking that Wale had said that his son likes smart women, which implied that Wale did not. He wondered what he'd think of Seeta.

"We need a safe space," Wale said quietly.

"My crew needs to use the operations room," Bracket explained. "Naijapool is too busy right now for any privacy."

"How about your quarters?"

Bracket did not intend to let the man into his own home.

"Fine," Wale said, leaning heavily on his cane. "Let's go to my plane. No one will bother us in there. Clarence, put in a call to Nanjala."

"You want to leave?" Clarence asked.

"Have her fetch us."

Fifteen minutes later, a friendly Kenyan woman, about forty, with close-cropped hair arrived in a golf cart. She offered Wale a glass of cold water, which he declined as they motored out to the private jet, a sleek two-engine plane of Brazilian design with about eight portholes on each side. The tail fin was painted with two intertwining yellow crescent moons against a midnight-blue background. They climbed the small staircase into the passenger section of the plane, and Nanjala left again in the golf cart to pick up Seeta from the rocket platform. Inside, a leather couch lined one wall of the cabin, and walnut coffee tables were perched between four leather chairs that could recline. Clarence posted himself at the entrance, scanning for any threats.

"No one's coming, Clarence," Wale said, sitting heavily in one of the armchairs. His paralyzed leg must have made standing uncomfortable for him, but he was too proud to ask for help. "Drinks."

"Coming right up, Doctor."

Clarence shut the cabin door and disappeared behind a cloth partition, where Bracket saw what he guessed was a shower and bathroom, ringed by handrails for Wale to hold. A painting hung at the front of the cabin, a portrait of a handsome young black man wearing a stylish T-shirt that read CRESCENT.

"My son," Wale explained. "He's in Manila right now for a business opportunity. Can never get him to wear a collared shirt." He pointed at the lights on the ceiling. "Here's how we make our money." He pressed a button on a control panel built into one of the armchairs, and the windows of the plane darkened as liquid crystal coursed through the glass. Soon it was pitch-dark. The next thing Bracket knew, the interior had been flooded by moonlight, exceptionally pure light that turned the cabin into a haunting parallel image of what he had seen a moment before. The armchairs, tables, and couch were all there. But they were different, magical. He waved his hand through the light, which made his skin look at once natural and exotic. He felt nostalgia for the cold, moonlit nights he'd once experienced in Massachusetts as a child, as if they were right there. With that memory: his mother, and then regret.

The moonlight slowly faded and became regular white light again, sourced from an LED bulb. "We normally ease people into it," Wale said, "but I thought you might enjoy the total effect. Those are our latest Moonstream bulbs. They're not on the market yet."

"Strange things," Bracket grunted, trying to hide his amazement. He felt disoriented and very much alone in the plane, even with the scientist sitting there beside him. He was relieved when the hatch opened again and Seeta stepped in.

"I've got until seventeen hundred hours," she announced. If she was impressed by the opulence of the jet, she didn't show it. Clarence returned from the rear, carrying a tray with Guinness beer and chilled mugs, which he set down on one of the coffee tables.

"Beer?" he asked.

"Bloody hate Guinness," Seeta said, "but yes."

"It's an acquired taste," Wale said. He was being more than polite, though, and seemed to be assessing Seeta as he passed her a bottle. "Seventeen hundred hours, you say? About four hours from now?"

"Yes, until I have to test the platform again."

"Should be enough time. Nanjala?"

The Kenyan woman emerged from the front of the plane and he whispered in her ear, and then she left again. Wale struck up a conversation with Seeta, and far from being intimidated by her intelligence, he appeared to warm to her.

"And where did you attend school?" Wale continued.

"I got my doctorate from Trinity College, Oxford, and I had a postdoc at LIGO."

"The gravitational-wave observatory? That's quite impressive. LIGO Hanford or LIGO Livingston?"

"Both. My research focused on eliminating noise, so I calibrated the mirrors at both sites," Seeta said, flattered.

"Seeta Chandrasekhan," Wale went on. "You wouldn't by any chance be connected to the prominent textile family from Gujarat? They're investors in Moonstream."

Again, she was taken aback. "I'm connected to my uncle by blood. But he would deny that he's connected to me."

"I see."

"I doubt you do."

Bracket heard something clunk below him in the cabin and the sound of the turbines powering on. Probably for the electricity, he guessed.

Seeta set the cloth-wrapped artifact down on one of the walnut coffee tables, causing a smile to spread across Wale's face from ear to ear.

"Fantastic!" he said. "You haven't touched it, have you? It should be in a glove box."

"We don't have one," Bracket said.

"Then latex gloves. A clean surface to work on. This is standard protocol."

They waited as Clarence searched around in the hold and returned with some latex gloves and a dusting brush. Once he had the proper equipment, Wale marveled at the little pottery as he unwrapped it from the handkerchief with a pair of tweezers.

"Look at the markings!" he said. "Extraordinary! I've seen these symbols on other specimens, but rarely as clear as these."

"Has anyone deciphered them?" Bracket asked.

"No, there aren't enough to begin unraveling the text. It's one of the great mysteries of African archaeology. But this is a fine specimen that will surely make a contribution."

Outside, the engines were growing louder, and Bracket felt the plane begin to move. "What are you doing, Wale? We didn't come here to get on a flight."

"I can spend these four hours explaining everything on paper, or I can show you directly."

"I don't have time for this," Seeta said, getting up from her seat. "Turn off the engines. Let us out of here."

"You want to know about this artifact? I can take you there to see who made it right now."

Bracket looked at Seeta, trying to gauge her reaction. He didn't like Wale's assumption that they would go along with him, but he couldn't help but be intrigued. "Where?"

"Lake Chad," Wale said.

"You can't just fly into Lake Chad," Seeta said. "It's a full day's drive along terrible roads."

"Not where we're going. We'll be southwest. I can give you my word that we'll be back on time for your schedule. But please— we're wasting time as we speak. What do you want to do?"

"All right," Seeta said.

Bracket nodded his agreement, and Wale whispered something into his cane. The engines increased their power, and the jet began to turn on the runway, then they were rushing forward and lifting off, the nose banking upward at a sharp angle. Seeta grabbed on to the artifact as they all leaned backward during the long climb into the sky. Bracket hadn't flown since he'd first arrived in Nigeria, and he had forgotten the power and speed of an airplane. And unlike a commercial flight, no warning lights came on and the pilot didn't make any grating announcements. They were simply flying. He peered out the window at the rocket towers and the Nest.

As the jet leveled out at cruising altitude, Wale explained that he couldn't confirm the artifact contained a meteorite without taking a sample and analyzing it in his geology lab in Cape Town.

"Perhaps you yourself could run a deep acoustic scan?" Wale suggested. "You evidently have the expertise."

"It might help," Seeta acknowledged, enjoying the compliment. "But my equipment is designed to analyze much larger structures. To do it properly, I'll need a controlled environment and a full day to conduct the test. A full day that I don't have."

"Then that will have to wait," Wale decided, suddenly reasonable.

"You said you know who made it," Bracket said.

"I have a theory," Wale admitted. "But it is rather complex." He took another slug of the Guinness, his eyes fixed on the orange recessed lighting of the cabin.

Trying to figure out how to explain it to us, Bracket thought.

"Are you familiar with celestial navigation?" Wale asked.

"It was standard training at NASA," Bracket said.

"Manual or on a computer?"

"On a computer."

"What I am about to tell you is not taught in your standard trainings. In fact, it is rarely taught at all."

Bracket looked out the window as they pulled free of Kano, nothing but dry Sahel and fields of Guinea corn interspersed with dust-laden roads. He thought he saw a lone cattle munching away at some bramble.

"Man has been looking up at the sky from the moment he slept on his back. No country can claim the right to own this experience, you see. It's a universal desire to understand what we're looking at. My research in lunar geology was always a metaphor for me to ask that question, mediated through the lens of science. But I'm a dreamer just like anyone else. So I began learning more about the explorers and astronomers who came before us, when the notion of space meant something, when it bridged the spiritual and the physical, when it was not just another equation for an engineer to calculate."

"Come on, you're talking like you were born a hundred years ago," Seeta argued. "You didn't use a slide rule, Dr. Olufunmi. You're not that old."

Wale held up a finger excitedly. "That's exactly my point, young lady. The slide rule! The slide rule can be traced back literally thousands of years. It was introduced in the sixteen hundreds to make calculations based on a logarithmic scale, but the slide rule wasn't invented out of thin air. It has a direct line to celestial navigation. Want another?"

Grabbing a bottle from the tray, Wale opened it ritualistically, giving it one shake and then tapping on the bottle top twice with his middle finger. "It tastes better here than South Africa, it truly does. Nigerians brew the best Guinness in the world. See the curve in this bottle? There was a time when counterfeiters in Lagos had copied the old bottle exactly, and you never knew what the beer would taste like. They sorted that problem out, fortunately, by making the bottle almost impossible to manufacture, stretching their injection molds to the very limit. Delicious.

"As I was saying, while I was in exile I studied a time when lunar geology mattered, when meteorites mattered. That's when I found out about the ancient city of Harran, a tremendous culture that sat at the nexus of Mesopotamian civilizations. In Harran, they worshipped the moon. As a scientist I wanted to know how the Harranians had measured the stars. They used astrolabes, which are almost like analog computers—the progenitors of the slide rule—that operate from the vantage point of man on Earth. By identifying key stars with the instrument, they could predict sunrises, sunsets, the passing of comets, and even solar eclipses. With a little trigonometry, they could also measure distances and angles with precision. Astrolabes were invented by the Greeks, passed along to the Arabs, then to the Jews, and eventually to European culture. They enabled navigation by the stars. And the city of Harran sat in the middle of these cultures, inheriting a rich tradition. Most Harranian astrolabes were lost, of course, because they were made of wood. Metal astrolabes were only available to the very rich or to powerful religious leaders, and crafted by renowned builders such as Bastulus and Ali ibn Surad."

Out the window, Bracket saw what may have been an old bus abandoned by the side of the road, then a cluster of huts nearby, but no people.

"I was able to find an astrolabe by al-Ijliya, the first known woman astrolabe maker. I convinced the Kunstmuseum to allow me to examine it, which they did after a generous donation. The briefcase, Clarence."

The bodyguard picked up their empty bottles and disappeared toward the rear of the plane, returning with a silver attaché briefcase, which he handed to Wale. Wale used his thumbprint to open it and removed a metal object from a velvet bag.

"You bought the astrolabe?" Seeta asked.

"It's not the original. I took high-resolution photos and had it modeled with a 3-D printer. I hired a metallurgist to re-create it. It cost a small fortune to make, nearly as much as the real astrolabe. Would have been easier to buy it, frankly." Something in his look told Bracket that he regretted not having done that. Bracket found himself reaching for it. Maybe it was the curves on its face, or the way the polished brass caught the light, but he wanted the astrolabe in his hands.

It looked like a giant pocket watch, a circular metal plate with looping lines and miniature heads of dragons, ornamented around the edges with topiary motifs. Wale explained the various pieces, such as the alidade and the rete or ankabut, which pointed to the bright stars of major constellations. The arcing lines marked off the tropics, the equator, the horizon, azimuths, and times for prayer.

Wale let them each hold the astrolabe for a moment. Heavier than Bracket expected. It could endure. This object was made with the long view, not years but generations. Centuries. He felt a sort of reverence, a connection to the seekers of before. He could only imagine what impression the original would have had upon the ancients. The precision of each arc was extraordinary, as if diamond-cut.

"This astrolabe was forged in the tenth century," Wale explained. "Look at these symbols along the edge. Most astrolabes were designed to work locally, so that you could navigate in the general region where they had been designed. But al-Ijliya crafted hers as a universal astrolabe with interlocking plates called tympans." He removed three metal disks from the cloth. "These tympans were interchangeable—if you moved several hundred kilometers to the west, for example, you could swap in this tympan and still navigate perfectly; to the east, this one." Wale was growing animated now. "But this tympan intrigued me the most." The tympan fit snugly within the astrolabe and was circled by a chain of engraved insects around its edge.

Bracket felt a subtle thump as the pilot nosed the plane down, and they began their descent. They seemed to be following a river, which was dotted with canoes, and the land around it was lush with vegetation.

Seeta was still focused on the astrolabe. "Are those ants?"

"That is what I thought at first glance. Except I could identify no culture in the region that worshipped ants or gave them any particular importance. You can use this magnifying glass."

"There *is* something connecting them," Bracket chimed in. "Their antennae—or a string, maybe. And they have four legs instead of six."

"That's correct. Look here."

"Waves," Seeta guessed. "They're by the sea."

Wale slapped the desk with glee. "Not waves: sand. They're camels."

"It was a desert?"

"You have it precisely, young lady! This tympan was used to cross the desert, and not just any desert, but the Sahara itself. We had always known that the Arabs penetrated into North Africa, but this tympan means that the trade routes had been established much earlier than suspected. The image is a caravanserai. The only question that I needed to solve was *where* in the Sahara the tympan was meant to be used. My natural guess, of course, was Timbuktu, which is an ancient trade route and city. But when I traveled to Mali, the astrolabe did not work. This was to be expected, because of the precession of the equinoxes and the wobbling motion of the Earth that occurs over the centuries, but I had made adjustments for that. I tried it again in Alexandria in Egypt and Tamanrasset in Algeria. Still nothing. And then I decided to head further south to the Lake Chad region—and that is where it worked again."

"That's where you're taking us," Bracket said.

"Precisely," Wale said triumphantly. "But there is a deeper question, isn't there?"

"Yes," Seeta agreed. "Why would the tympan work there? What was there that deserved it?"

"Exactly, young lady. Up until that point, the great Arab centers of civilization fell within the Maghreb region, spreading from Aleppo to Córdoba, Spain. Yet there was clearly a city in Nigeria important enough for travelers from Harran to cross the desert."

The landing gear opened, and the plane began drifting in for the landing. Bracket couldn't see a runway or anything approaching a road, and he braced himself for an impact. He looked for a seat belt, but he couldn't find one in the lounge chair. And then suddenly there was a spit of concrete and the plane landed smoothly on the runway. They coasted for a quarter of a kilometer before the pilot stepped on the brakes, causing them all to pitch forward in their seats.

"Short runway," Wale explained, still focused on the astrolabe. "Look here, below the caravanserai: it's a figure, a head. See the features? It looks like a black African."

"It's hard to tell," Bracket said, trying to catch a view of the landscape outside.

"I've blown up the image a dozen times. It most resembles carvings from the Nok civilization. The Nok people lived all over northern Nigeria and are known for their intricate terra-cotta sculptures, which show realistic portraits of their people—even their hairstyles. They traded gold, slaves, and ivory for salt, cowries, and metals."

Clarence peered out the porthole and opened up the hatch. "Let me check it out, boss." He drew his pistol, but there was little to see besides dusty scrubland. Not even a road or a village. They must have long since left behind the rivers they had been following in the air. It was a low-flung plain, and the heat poured into the cabin, somehow even hotter than at the spaceport, and on the horizon Bracket could see thunderclouds so far away they appeared like foamy waves cresting over a beach.

Clarence seemed on edge as he scanned the area. "Hold on, boss. Let me get the rifle." He unlocked a compartment and emerged carrying a large rifle that was so big it even looked heavy for him. He stepped out onto the runway and signaled that they could join him.

"Where's the airport?" Seeta asked, making her way down the steps.

"There isn't one," Wale explained. "I built this to facilitate our research. The lake is still another ten kilometers north of here. You're making them nervous, Clarence."

"This is for your safety," the bodyguard explained. He was now in his element and wasn't going to let Wale order him around. "Nanjala," he said, speaking into a small walkie-talkie, "turn the plane around while we're out there, hey?"

"You got it," the pilot replied.

"All right," Clarence explained to them. "Most predator attacks come from the front. So I want you in a line behind me."

"Oh, come on, Clarence," Wale said. "You see one lion out here and you think we'll get eaten alive."

"I think we should listen to him," Bracket said.

"Yeah," Seeta agreed, glancing around.

Wale set a quick pace with his cane, forcing the bodyguard to keep ahead of him with his elephant gun. Now they were walking through scrubland that rose above head height, and Bracket could barely see a few meters on each side, the vegetation drawing in close. Seeta crowded near him. Clarence spotted a cobra slithering away into the bush, but otherwise they saw little.

"Our excavations here," Wale said over his shoulder, "point to an advanced Iron Age culture that suddenly collapsed. But oral traditions in the region suggest the Nok culture continued as isolates. These descendants were sometimes called the Sao. The Nok—or the Sao—are the only trading culture that was powerful enough to have merited their own astrolabe. You'll see soon enough—we're not far away."

They were climbing a small embankment and Bracket felt his anticipation rising, eager to learn more about the people who had made the artifact that had caused him so much trouble.

Clarence motioned for them to stop walking, peering down at the ground and running his fingers through the dust.

"Lion?" Bracket whispered, surprised at how casual the word sounded on his lips.

"No." Clarence shook his head. "Someone's been here."

He crawled forward on his arms as the scientists waited nervously behind him. He looked into the scope of his rifle, before standing up and shouldering the weapon.

"They're gone. But we shouldn't stay long."

Finally they came to the rise of the hill. Before him Bracket saw three shipping containers, probably airlifted in, spread out in a U shape over about an acre of land cleared of brush. Between the containers was a long pit, which appeared to have been excavated about four meters at its deepest end, with different gradations in other places. Indeed, nearby was a backhoe, but its tires had been slashed through, and the machine seemed to be melting into the earth itself.

"No!" Wale shouted. "They couldn't have!"

He practically hopped down the hill to the edge of the pit. Here, there were numerous cavities in the earth, with the soil clumsily turned over. They continued walking along the dig until they found the remains of an old brick wall. This too had been chipped away, and the center of it was gone, hacked with a pickax.

Wale turned accusingly toward Clarence. "How could they have gotten through the perimeter security? You told me it was a state-of-the-art system."

Clarence scanned the area with his rifle scope, shaking his head. "The tripods are still there, but they don't look online. I don't know. I'll check it out."

Wale was beside himself with anger. "This was one of the world's best-preserved sites of Nok archaeology," he said, pointing to the old brick wall. "This tunnel was one of only three that have been recorded around Nigeria. I suspect it goes back several hundred yards, and it's hewn directly from the rock with incredible precision. The Nok are the only known culture to have built such tunnels. Thankfully the thieves only took the keystone of the arch, so we could in theory resume our work. It was heavily carved and quite beautiful, but mostly ornamental. We've been excavating here for months, carefully documenting and preserving the find. Everything points to successive settlements over the centuries."

"What do you think happened?" Seeta asked.

"Looted," Bracket said. He recalled what Detective Idriss had told him, that artifacts held value on the black market.

Clarence busied himself by inspecting the perimeter, holding the rifle at the ready in both hands.

"But who would do this?" Seeta asked.

"Vagabonds," Wale sneered, "trying to make a little money, destroying their own heritage in the process." Then, suddenly remembering himself: "Where's Ahmat? He should be here. Clarence, do you see Ahmat anywhere?"

Ahmat looked after the site and was the lead researcher, Wale explained, stooping down to pick up different artifacts, shaking his head as he did so.

"This is the largest Nok site to date. We've found beads made from quartz, glass, and carnelian in the alluvial soil—Lake Chad once extended this far south. This indicates a cross-Sahara trade. See these shards here, the comblike marks carved into the terra-cotta? These were once giant storage pots. Ahmat has been analyzing the patterns, and our best guess—it's still inconclusive—is that the Nok used a special accounting system. And an accounting system suggests that—"

"There was someone to account to," Seeta said. "You're saying that they had to keep track of their trades because someone else was in charge. This was an outpost."

"Yes," Wale said, growing increasingly impressed with Seeta. "This site was not the center of the Nok empire. We suspect that location is farther to the south based on our analysis of the trade routes. Of course, now the site has been spoiled. Not totally ruined, but the looters have likely stolen specimens that contained more of the script. Hopefully, if they're like typical thieves, they only stole things that looked valuable and left behind the most important archaeological evidence."

Clarence called the group over to one of the shipping containers, which was closed shut. There was a ventilation chimney spinning slowly on top, and the roof was lined with solar cells.

"Stay back," Clarence warned, loading his rifle. "Someone's in there."

Bracket could hear it too: nervous scampering movements inside.

"Ahmat!" Wale shouted. "Don't be afraid. We're coming inside. It's Dr. Olufunmi. I'm here with Clarence and some fellow researchers."

But they heard only a muffled whimper.

Crying? Seeta mouthed at Bracket.

Clarence motioned for them to stand back. He tried the door, but it had been wedged shut by a drift of sand. He plowed some away with his boot and then yanked the door open.

He was met with a rush of fur.

"Yissus!" he shouted. The beast knocked him to the ground with its full force. He shot his rifle into the air, blowing a hole through the side of the cargo container. The hyena lunged for him as he scrambled to his feet, but seeing the giant man rear up to his full height, it crouched from fear and then turned and sprinted away into the bush.

Bracket ran over to him. "You all right, man?"

"Tore me up," Clarence said, chest heaving. "But he couldn't bite through my armor." Beneath the torn shirt, Bracket could see a thick layer of Kevlar protecting the bodyguard's chest. Once

Clarence dusted himself off, he picked up the rifle, reloaded it, and stepped inside the container. Bracket smelled a terrible stench.

"He's here, boss," Clarence shouted from inside.

"Dr. Chandresekhan, you may want to wait here," Wale advised.

"Don't bloody coddle me," she said.

Inside, splayed out on the ground, they found Ahmat, a squat, balding man with a thin goatee. He had been shot through the back of the head, and blood and grime covered the desk above him. Half his chest had been stripped away in mangled shreds.

"Hyena had a go at him," Clarence concluded, gritting his teeth. "Must have gotten trapped in here by the sand."

Ahmat's hand had been severed and it was dangling from the lightbulb on the ceiling of the container, buzzing with flies. Red string had been tied around one of the fingers.

"Jarumi," Clarence concluded. "The string."

"The computer?" Wale asked.

"Stolen."

Wale's eyes teared over. "He was one of the best archaeologists in Nigeria, a brilliant mind. Let's get him out of here. We can put him in one of the pits. He would have wanted that, to be close to his ancestors."

"I'll tell Nanjala to put out a call on the emergency band," Clarence said. He pulled out a walkie-talkie and walked off to warn the pilot. "I'm going to inspect the other containers. Stay close together and within sight."

"He lived out here all by himself?" Seeta asked.

Wale shook his head. "He often had a team of graduate students with him, but he was closing down the site before the Harmattan comes. This was all meant to be covered in tarpaulin and locked up by now."

Together, Seeta and Bracket dragged the putrescent body over to one of the pits, trying to avoid touching the stump of an arm as they did so, Wale circling about giving unhelpful instructions.

Now that the corpse was in the open, hooded vultures began wheeling in the sky at the scent. Bracket and Seeta shoveled dirt over the dead researcher as best they could, and then piled stones on top to prevent the animals from returning to defile him even more.

Dusty, thirsty, and exhausted, the group sat down at the edge of the dig to rest. Seeta hadn't said a word since first touching the body. Bracket could smell the stench on his fingertips.

"You okay?" he asked.

"I'm thinking about Addama," she said. "The singer I recorded. What will happen to her if the Jarumi come to her village? She lives close to here."

Bracket put his arm around her shoulders, unsure of what to say. The heat and the smell had stained his nostrils. After finishing his inspections of the site, Clarence returned with more bad news. "They managed to break into the food storage container," he said. "But they couldn't break the lock on the equipment container."

"So our equipment is still there?" Wale asked.

"For the time being," Clarence said. "My guess is that they'll be back again soon for it, boss. We should get going. I checked out the tripods, and someone disrupted the perimeter lasers with mirrors and took out the guns with a drone. It was a carefully coordinated attack."

"That system cost me a million cowries," Wale said. "And you're telling me a bunch of illiterate bandits disabled it?"

Bracket recalled the trader Musa's words about the Jarumi: *These men are ignorant but not stupid. Their struggle has made them inventive.*

"Ahmat wouldn't have had a chance," Clarence added, "once they disabled it."

"No, he was a gentle soul," Wale lamented. "We were so close to finding the southern capital of the Nok. This will set us back months. Perhaps years."

"What about the artifact we found?" Bracket asked.

"It could help," Wale admitted. "The artifact has certainly narrowed down the possible range of their trade routes, but without the accounting records, we'll be guessing blindly. It could be near the spaceport or Kano—which would fit, given how old the city is—but an area of twenty square kilometers can take a decade to properly explore. Even then it might only be another trade outpost."

They went to inspect the shipping container, where Wale fished around among the shovels, PVC boxes, sample bags, and brooms until he found a three-wheeled wheelbarrow with an electronic box in the middle and a handle for the operator to push the thing forward.

"Metal detector?" Bracket asked.

"No," Seeta said, perking up. "Much better than that. A GPR. Ground-penetrating radar. That's exactly what we need. It can give us a better acoustic image than my instruments at the spaceport."

"Quiet!" Clarence hissed. The bodyguard cupped his hand to his ear, and Bracket too could hear an engine in the distance.

"Nanjala's spinning up the plane," Wale guessed.

"No, boss, that's a truck." He rushed up a nearby embankment and raised the scope again. "Two trucks," he said. "Moving fast."

"Coming this way?" Bracket asked.

"No, they're heading to the plane."

"Police?" Seeta asked hopefully.

"No, must have seen us land." Clarence shook his head. He fingered the trigger of the rifle. "Out of range too. Come on. Time to go. I can carry you, boss."

"I won't be carried like some invalid," Wale declared. He raised his cane over the site, waving it about like a staff, for what purpose, Bracket couldn't tell. Then they all ran back through the bush, moving as quickly as they could in the stifling heat, Seeta pushing the GPR before her.

"I'll distract them," Clarence said, peeling off into the bushes. "Keep moving!"

They kept running through the bushes, twisting this way and that as the path meandered, until, finally, the runway opened up before them, the plane already powered on, with the stepladder ready to accept them. But the two trucks were headed that way too and would reach the plane sooner. Bracket could make out the militants more clearly now, about ten on each vehicle, and see their bright red armbands.

Then a man in one of the trucks suddenly exploded out of his seat, flying into the dirt. The second truck kept barreling forward until the windshield spiderwebbed and the truck drifted to the side as the driver slumped over, dead. Clarence had fired only two shots.

"Go, Wale! Go!" Bracket shouted.

The Jarumi leapt out of their trucks as the scientists barreled up the stairs into the cabin, Bracket helping Seeta lift the GPR into the cargo hold. Nanjala released the brakes and the plane inched forward, moving slowly, Clarence running alongside until he could climb onto the stairs, and he pulled the hatch closed with the militants firing wildly in their direction. Now the jet was rocketing ahead on the runway and took off at what felt like an impossible angle. Seeta lifted open the arm of the lounge chair to remove her seat belt, and Bracket desperately copied her as the plane banked sharply once, then twice.

They all looked out the windows as the militants' trucks shrunk in the distance, and soon the men were specks and hardly seemed a threat at all. Nanjala banked again over Lake Chad, and Bracket could see the silver water scintillating in the late-afternoon sun, a flock of spoonbills white on the surface as the birds rose up and descended again to the water.

They flew in silence for a while as they recovered themselves, and the plane climbed to its cruising altitude. When they leveled out, Bracket moved to the bathroom to clean off the stench of Ahmat's body, rubbing his hands compulsively under the warm water.

When he came out, he accepted Clarence's offer of a Guinness, slurping it down as much for the cold as the alcohol. But instead of the drink calming him, Bracket grew angry. Clarence had known that they were in danger the moment they had landed. So had Wale. And the scientist hadn't warned them.

"Wale," Bracket growled, "you knew full well that the Jarumi were in the area when you invited us out here. Your own researcher was murdered in cold blood, and you risked all our lives without so much as an afterthought. How do we know this isn't some crazy vanity project?"

He hadn't meant for it come out as an accusation, but the stench on his hands—still there after washing them—had removed any pretense at being polite.

"Vanity project?" Wale asked in disbelief. "This isn't a vanity project. What about you, Dr. Chandrasekhan, do you think it's a vanity project?"

"I'm with Kwesi on this, Wale," Seeta admitted. "I'll grant you that it's interesting scholarly research. But it doesn't seem worth the risk, if you ask me. And certainly not worth *our* risk. It's a lot of speculation."

Wale threw his cane to the floor in frustration. "Vanity project!"

Bracket moved to pick it up for him. He felt an intense electric shock when he touched it. "Damn!"

"You shouldn't touch that," Wale explained.

"What is that thing?" Seeta asked.

He lifted the cane above his head, ignoring her. "I'll show you why this isn't a vanity project."

The cane emitted a thin beam of light that slowly expanded into three interlocking beams that swirled around, meeting in the middle in a 3-D image near the cabin ceiling. Wale twisted the cane in his hands, causing the lights in the cabin to dim.

The image crystallized into an ancient Chinese manuscript with stylized renditions of mountains and a fisherman in a turgid sea.

"This was recorded in a court during the Song dynasty," Wale said, "around the year eleven hundred. See that red streak in the top left-hand corner? What do you suppose that is?"

"Could be a stain," Seeta said, "or a rainbow."

"Have a look at this one from Al-Andalus in Spain." With a subtle shift of the cane that Bracket couldn't perceive, the image swapped. This one was a landscape of rolling hills. Again, there was a streak across the sky, this time blue. "That is from Xàtiva, a town near Valencia. And this is a carving from ancient Harran." He flipped through several more images, noting the peculiar streaks or arcs in each of them.

"You're saying these marks were all recorded around the same time," Bracket guessed.

"Not around the same time!" Wale hissed. "On the exact same date. It was likely an aurora from a coronal mass injection. Charged particles colliding with the atmosphere."

"A solar flare?" Seeta asked.

"The most powerful solar flare in recorded history, much larger than the Carrington event in the eighteen hundreds."

Bracket was beginning to sense it now, Wale's wild speculations coalescing into a sort of deranged logic. He felt the plane descending again, headed now back to the spaceport.

"I believe that this flare may have given rise to a new civilization," Wale said. "Within a few decades, an advanced Iron Age culture appeared in northern Nigeria that merited being recorded on astrolabes thousands of kilometers away. The Nok weren't simple traders. They were much more than that! They were extraordinarily tall and powerful warriors who could easily defeat their enemies. They could leap enormous distances! They had the power to melt stone. That is what I am looking for. I'm talking about a civilization that once possessed technologies as great as our own. A civilization forged right here in Nigeria that captured the imagination of kings and queens living on the other side of the world."

Bracket felt his skin tingle. *Extraordinarily tall. The ability to leap enormous distances.* He peered over at Seeta and could see that she was thinking the same thing. Together, they'd seen that.

"I think the first flare ignited the civilization of the Nok," Wale continued. "And the second flare—the very one that brought you here to Nigeria—may have unearthed it once again. I don't know why, or how, but something must have changed. These artifacts have been buried for a millennium and now you found them again."

"They're here," Seeta said.

"Well, possibly," Wale said, misunderstanding her. "I'm confident in my findings. But you're right that it's still only a theory that requires more archaeological evidence. If we could correlate this specimen to the accounting methods I described—"

"You don't understand, Dr. Olufunmi," Seeta explained. "We've already found your evidence. The Nok are still alive."

CHAPTER 19

The cryogenically cooled fuel shrunk the titanium walls of the rocket like a candy wrapper as the *Masquerade* pointed skyward. It was the real ship, finally rolled out into the fresh air, a Nigerian spaceship powered by Indian rockets. It wasn't a pathetic little capsule perched atop a rocket like the red nose of a clown. The *Masquerade* was a starcraft.

Bracket heard the countdown, then the ignition, and saw the white flame burn blue and the torrent of cool water rush down to protect the rocket against its own flames. The bolts blew off the trusses and the *Masquerade* lifted into the air in a hurricane of fire.

The antenna array swiveled to track the launch, downlinking huge quantities of data for the rescue mission. The *Masquerade* would be traveling fifteen thousand kilometers per hour when it separated from the rockets, which would return to Earth to land again. The starship, meanwhile, would orbit the planet two times before touching down on the airstrip. There was no one on board.

"Show a little humility," Josephine had warned Bello, when he complained that the test launch would be unmanned. "We're not going to send a crew into space on an untested machine. We'll follow the Soviets. They launched the *Buran* shuttle without a crew and with no press watching. The Americans launched the *Columbia* without a single test mission and three thousand journalists observing—and it could have killed them all. They lost half a dozen heat tiles on liftoff alone."

Watching the launch from two kilometers away, Bracket's skin tingled as the *Masquerade* sailed clear of the cloud layer. All around him the scientists were cheering openly, some hugging, while others, like him, said nothing. Beside him, Wale shook his head with tears in his eyes.

"We did it," he whispered. "We finally did it."

But Bracket remained quiet—the mission wasn't over yet. He had watched the *Challenger* space shuttle explode on television, when African American astronaut Ronald McNair had been incinerated before his eyes. He remembered the white burst, the tiniest error multiplied into a fireball of doom, and how his mother had locked herself in her room for two days. The Indians too had lost one of their own in the *Columbia* disaster, when Kalpana Chawla had died.

Seeta was positioned much nearer to the rocket, and when she had clearance from Josephine, she rushed in to examine the platform with her acoustic instruments to find any evidence of damage. Here and there, long streaks of soot snaked up the angled exhaust basin, curling over the lip and singing the grass. Six thousand degrees of exhaust had emblazoned the basin in flame and then been deluged with three million liters of water.

Inside the Nest, he found Josephine surrounded by half a dozen directors, who were all celebrating. He could see the ends of her orange-tipped dreadlocks beginning to fray.

"Bello?" Bracket whispered to her.

She shook her head and stepped inside her privacy cone, which folded around her before he could say anything more.

He returned to the pool deck just as the two rockets returned to their platforms, executing a perfect landing to more cheers.

It's happening, Bracket thought. *The dream became real.*

But as he passed by the hyperbaric chamber, he saw that it had been sealed shut. Santander, the biologist, was lying on a plank along the wall. He lurched up when Bracket knocked on the glass.

"What are you doing in there, Santander?" he asked through the intercom.

Santander's eyes were red and swollen. For once, Bracket seemed to have his full attention, when the diver was normally enveloped in a newscloud.

"I've got decompression sickness, Kwesi," Santander responded thro-ugh the comm. "I surfaced too quickly after I heard a noise in the pool."

"What did you hear?"

The diver looked too scared to continue, lowering his voice for fear someone might overhear him. "It was as if someone was *calling* for me."

So he had heard it too, Bracket realized with terror. "You could understand it?"

"Not the words, but the meaning. It was a longing—a lamentation, as if someone had lost something."

"Could you communicate with it?"

"No, it couldn't hear me. I haven't been back in the water. Doctor said I can't dive for a month."

Bracket could see how despondent the diver had become, because he would almost certainly miss all the simulations for the rescue mission. He'd be stuck in the hyberbaric chamber with nothing to keep him occupied as everyone else focused on the launch.

"Tell you what, Santander," he said, trying to appear calm. "I could use some help. I need some information."

"The doctor told me I had to stop downloading the news. It's not good for me."

"I'm sure she's right – but make an exception for me, will you? Can you drop in and scrape whatever you can about Nurudeen Bello over the past few days? I want you to look at the Loom, Naijaweb, and any local mesh networks. Whatever you can find."

"I can do that!" Santander replied excitedly, relieved to have a purpose again. "Whatever you need! You want me to scrape for Bello, or something else too?"

"Bello. Anything about him. This information is top priority."

It felt almost cruel to be asking for it. Telling a newshound that information was top priority was like dangling fine wine in front of an alcoholic.

"I'll drop in right away."

"Thanks, buddy. Hang in there."

CHAPTER 20

"It was too risky for you to use the Songstones outside," Durel said. "You could put us all in danger."

"They didn't follow me here," Balewa argued.

"The police didn't follow you, but you've been seen and now you've raised their suspicions. They'll be watching for us. We told you to leave the stones alone."

"Now the Jarumi might know," Abir added.

"They don't know," Balewa said. "No one knows where the Jarumi are anymore. Not since the bombing."

Durel stoked the glowing coals at the base of her teakettle. She had bought a new one after Balewa had crushed the last tea set with her Songstone. "Now you've done the exact opposite, Balewa. It was foolhardy for you to use the Songstone in the first place."

"I don't think you should have taken such a risk either," Abir said. Balewa turned to look at Abir, wondering why she hadn't spoken out sooner. Had she lost her trust too?

Durel poured out the tea among the women, dropping in flecks of sugar. They sipped slowly as it steamed from their small silver cups. Balewa's pregnancy was making it more difficult to sit for long stretches, but she had been blessed with a strong back, and at least the morning sickness had subsided. Not long ago she would have had trouble drinking tea at all. The Songstones had given her inner strength, a fortitude she had not felt since before they fled to Kano—although her newfound confidence also meant she found herself arguing more often with the other women, who preferred to keep the hierarchies of the clan, especially since some of them weren't as adept at bringing the stones to life.

"This is excellent tea, Durel," one of the women said, politely trying to change the topic of conversation.

"We sold plenty of medicine this week. I thought we deserved better tea for once."

"Even if the Jarumi found a Songstone," Balewa said, pressing her point, "they wouldn't know what to do with it."

"Can you please drop this for once, young lady?" Durel snapped. "Your stones are what ruined the tea set that I received from my mother-in-law. I scrimped and saved to buy a new one, using money that we could have spent on finding our children."

"Yes, we've spoken about the stones enough," another agreed. "You're too reckless with them. They're dangerous."

"You're about to have a baby," Durel insisted. "You should concern yourself with that, not with these stones all the time. You could hurt yourself."

That's exactly what I want, Balewa thought. She still had no desire to raise the child of her rapist, who might be born with similar eyes or nose, or some other feature that would always remind her of what had happened. How could she love such a creature?

"I'm merely saying that if the police saw me we shouldn't be too concerned."

"Then why are they still looking for you?" Abir pointed out.

Balewa was trying to understand why Abir had turned against her. Normally they vouched for each other and stood strong against the critical snipes of the other women. She felt as if she was losing her closest friend.

Feeling even more alone, she retreated to one of the remote chambers to sing softly to herself. By now she had grown familiar with the figures painted on the wall and strung the various pictures into a kind of story in her mind in order to calm her nerves. One of the figures in the drawing had big breasts and long tresses and was surrounded by a group of people.

That one was the musician, Balewa decided. Beautiful melodies would have poured from her mouth. People would have adored her and sought out her companionship.

Farther down the wall, the same figure appeared again, holding something in her hand. This time, lines zigzagged from her head like lightning, and the other people seemed to be running away from her.

It's because she found a stone like me, Balewa thought. Before, her people had thought that woman had only a pretty voice, and now they knew the power of her Songstone. Balewa wanted to be like the woman, to unleash a strength that the others would be forced to respect.

Soon they will respect me instead of mocking me for my suffering. They're no better than I am. Just because they gang up on me doesn't make them right.

Consoling herself, she hummed some soft notes, trying out a new melody in her throat, a dark one that meandered through a somber minor scale.

Suddenly, the picture on the wall started vibrating. Then it was still again. Had it responded to the notes? She kept silent for a moment, until the entire rock wall seemed to shift.

She ran back to where the others were gathered. "Did you feel that?" she asked.

"Yes!"

"We felt it!"

"Did you do that?"

"No," Balewa said. "I didn't."

"Where is it coming from?"

"Quiet!"

The rumbling started again, the tea sloshing over the rims of the silver teacups. Durel had the presence of mind to throw sand on the coals. They felt a stronger shake now. The walls of the chamber seemed to shift and chips of rock began falling from the ceiling. The very ground beneath their feet was swaying. Abir tripped and fell on her side. One of the other women banged her head on a wall painfully.

"They've found us!" Durel hissed. "I told you that they would find us!"

"Use your voices to protect yourselves!" Balewa shouted. "Nothing can get through the Songstones."

But the violent shaking of the chamber made it too difficult for them to concentrate, and Durel had never found much success with the stones anyway. Two of the women tried to sing and became frightened by the quaking ground. Balewa focused her mind as the walls were bending around her.

The sounds are right here in our throats, she thought. *The music will keep us safe. Can't they understand that?*

A chunk of stone cracked from the ceiling right over Durel, who threw her arms above her head to protect herself.

"Watch out!" Abir shouted.

Balewa shifted her voice outward to move the aura around Durel. The rock slid harmlessly off the aura onto the ground beside them. After another violent shake, the rumbling subsided.

"I don't think anyone is coming inside," Abir observed.

"Then what is happening?"

"I don't know. We should go outside to see."

"That's exactly what they would want us to do. Expose ourselves."

"We don't know that."

"I'm going to look," Balewa announced. "I don't want to wait for them to find us first. This is our home now, and they have no right to enter it without our permission."

She emerged cautiously into the night with her Songstone held aloft to fight off any intruders. But she didn't see anyone nearby. Above her, the stars traced a band of light along the Milky Way, and the air felt cooler than within the cave. She traced a long stream of smoke across the sky to a distant flame. They weren't digging here at all, as Durel had feared. They had sent some kind of airplane framed with spearpoints into the dome of the sky, a new destructive force that had belched fire and smoke.

These people are much more powerful than we believed, Balewa thought. *They would be able to do more than dig into our home if they ever found us. They could destroy us completely.*

Soon the giant vessel shrank to a small circle of light in the night.

Balewa realized she would have to prepare the women much better to protect them against such forces. If the Jarumi arrived with that much strength, there wouldn't be a moment to spare. Every note, every rhythm, every melody, would have to blend perfectly together in a harmonious defense. They needed much more practice. A rigorous training regimen. *We've been too casual about our use of the Songstones,* she thought, *wasting our time bickering among ourselves every night and longing for our children. It's time for us to sing without fear, to truly share our voices.* She descended back into the chamber to tell them what she'd discovered.

CHAPTER 21

The *Masquerade* fired its ram's-horn thrusters after its second orbit around Earth, sending the craft flaming through the atmosphere. On its descent the ship began a series of slow turns, using friction to lower its velocity for the landing. The blazing heat assaulted its underbelly, but the grooves in its crocodile-like bio-skin deflected the energy outward. The ship spread its hundred-meter-wide white egret wings to glide through the clouds toward the airstrip. As it neared the runway, the spacecraft ejected folds upon folds of parachutes adorned with brilliant green and white polymer beads like an enormous *egungun* dancer. The *Masquerade* touched down on the runway as the fire suppression trucks raced out to meet it. Both the *Masquerade* and the Indian rockets had returned to the base exactly as they had been designed and would now be refurbished and refueled for the crewed mission.

Amid the celebrations, Bracket observed the successful landing from the operations room, feeling triumphant but distracted. He dialed Wale through the Wodaabe identity that Ini had installed on his G-fone. In the image, his eyes widened and they were highlighted with eye shadow. His jaw stretched longer, with his teeth shining brilliant white as he spoke. It was as if he had become a more slender, effeminate version of himself, except that the identity also made his voice deeper.

"Why are you dressed like a woman?" Wale asked, frowning.

"I'm not a woman—it's my secure identity."

"You're wearing makeup." He avoided looking at the camera directly whenever Bracket spoke, as if he might be contaminated by his androgyny. "You told me on the plane that you've seen the Nok at two different locations," Wale summarized. "Can you take me to where your worker disappeared?"

"Yes. But if the creature—"

"The Nok."

"If the Nok are still there, we'll need security. It's not safe to go at night."

"Clarence is all the security we need," Wale insisted confidently.

"You're right," Bracket agreed. "But I doubt he's ever seen anything like this. Let's go at six. I'll see you in the morning."

"What about Dr. Chandresekhan?"

"She's working a double shift right now."

They picked Bracket up in the golf cart at Naijapool just after dawn. In the back of the cart, the scientist had brought a shovel, a broom, and his usual box of latex gloves. He was wearing a khaki-colored pith helmet like a British explorer. The open-air cart felt dangerously exposed to attack as they drove along in the soft morning light, people watching the motley trio curiously on their way to the mess hall for breakfast.

"Stop here," Bracket said, when they drew near the tracking station. Together, they dismounted, and he pointed at the area where Abdul Haruna had disappeared.

"You believe that he was taken into the ground at this spot."

"Yes. He left behind a lot of blood."

"Curious," Wale said, furrowing his brow. He poked at the ground with the butt of his cane.

Clarence scrutinized the area. "You didn't see anyone take him, Mr. Bracket?"

"No one saw anything. He disappeared out of sight."

"I can see several old tracks here, but the prints have been obscured by the sand."

"Those could be from my crew," Bracket guessed. "They helped me chase him down after he grabbed the artifact."

Wale rubbed his chin. "Strange that you found the artifact out by the pool too. You would think that it would have been deposited closer to this area, if we're in the right place. Is that the tracking station over there?"

"Yes."

Wale hobbled over to the door to peer inside. "So this is it! Fifty years of space history right here in Kano! How appropriate that the Nok might have been sitting underneath it all along. Let's have a look."

He moved to open the door with his good hand, but Clarence stopped him.

"Get out of my way, Clarence! We're talking about decades of history. This station once tracked John Glenn around the Earth. This was Africa's chance to join the space age—wasted, of course."

"Let me check it out first, boss."

"There's nothing in there," Bracket objected. "I went inside when we found the first artifact."

"People who aren't trained in archaeology often overlook things of value," Wale insisted.

Clarence drew a pistol from a shoulder holster strapped under his suit and cautiously stepped inside. He came back about two minutes later. "You can go in. There is no evidence of tampering. There is an old blanket from when a cowherd may have lived here. The person did not stay long and moved away."

"How long ago would you say that was?"

"A year ago at least."

Dust had silted the countertops. The shelving and drawers had already been stripped clean, save for some old folding chairs and rusted file cabinets. Bracket could see from a dirty line that ringed the walls that there must have been a flood at some point. Indeed, in the corner of the room silt had piled up. Wale walked over to the Bendix machine.

"This is marvelous," he said. "Kano was on the old minitrack network, which used Yagi antennae, not the parabolic dishes that are standard today."

The machine had a label that read ANTENNA SUBSYSTEM MONITOR. There were red plastic indicator lights for the reflector, elevation, alidade, and pedestal. There were also a number of buttons for brakes, lubrication, and hydrostatic bearing. At the top of the panel was a button that said SYSTEM POWER. Wale pressed it before Bracket could stop him. The indicator lights powered on.

"Oh." Wale took a step back.

The machine sputtered for a moment before powering off again.

"Still works after all this time?" Bracket said.

Wale switched it off again. "I didn't expect that. A station like this would have had generators to keep it operational, either two hundred fifty or five hundred thousand watts. One would run the core electronics and the other would keep the station cool. I'm sure Bendix would have removed them when they pulled out. Unless . . ."

"Unless what?"

"Unless they didn't have time for some reason."

"Someone else would have taken them," Bracket observed. "People don't waste things like that around here."

"The tanks may have been buried."

"Why would they do that?"

"Every tracking station was different, depending on the local needs and environment. This land was filled with nomadic herders before NASA arrived, simple people. It could have been too much of a shock to have all of the equipment jutting everywhere."

"Do you have any idea why they shut this station down?" Bracket asked.

"No one knows. The Zanzibar tracking station was taken offline after a coup d'état, but nothing like that ever happened here. There were rumors that the Kano tracking equipment showed some anomalies, strange data that didn't make sense.

I've never been able to confirm that. It's been classified for fifty years."

"I've had computers short-circuit on me," Bracket said. "My colleagues have also been reporting inaccurate readings on their instruments."

"Might be a connection," Wale said neutrally.

Bracket didn't know what he'd been expecting—a staircase, maybe? a hatch leading down into the abyss?—but they didn't find any entrance. They couldn't find any proof of the Nok. If the civilization was as ancient as Wale implied, there was no reason for them to remain undiscovered for so long. Still, he found it alarming that NASA had left quickly without warning or explanation. Had they discovered something too?

"How do you know all this, Wale?"

Wale frowned as if troubled by the question. "When I was a boy, I had hoped to work here one day. Every boy in Nigeria did."

They found nothing else of value in the station and stepped outside again, where the sun was already blaring down on the dry ground. Wale set off behind the station and scampered up a small hillock, Clarence running along to keep up with him.

"These mounds," Wale said. "Were they part of your construction site?"

"No, we're far away from the dig," Bracket said, making his way toward them.

"How about the antenna array?"

"No."

"These could be earthworks. Look—they stretch for hundreds of meters. Go fetch the shovel, Clarence. Let's conduct an exploratory excavation."

Turning around, Bracket saw that Wale was right, the mounds went on for a long distance. But there was nothing particularly remarkable about them. They weren't unusually large and did not have any special features, looking like embankments you might find near the side of any road. He felt an unpleasant dissonance in his blood, a dry pucker in his gums, as if some dark vortex coalesced at the very spot he was standing on.

The thought crept up on him slowly as Clarence returned carrying the shovel.

In the United States, Mexican drug smugglers had ferried in cocaine through tunnels until the Flare, when it became more profitable for Americans to use the same tunnels to escape to Mexico and then press on to Central America.

"What if it's a tunnel built by the Jarumi? Abdul could have used one to escape."

"The vegetation is quite thick here, Mr. Bracket," Clarence observed, thinking through Bracket's suggestion. "Plants don't grow quickly in the Sahel—that means the Jarumi would have needed to build any tunnels before the spaceport was constructed. They don't plan so strategically. They specialize in skirmishes and targeted strikes."

"There's no sense in speculating," Wale said. "Let's dig."

The bodyguard stripped off his suit coat and began shoveling out piles from the mound, but he unearthed only dirt and stones. Bracket relaxed as he realized that the mounds weren't hollow after all.

"Clarence is right," Wale insisted. "You can forget your theory about the Jarumi. If these mounds are older, we most likely wouldn't find anything inside. There could still be something below them—over the centuries the earth would have been pushed up. We'll have to come back with the ground-penetrating radar machine."

"Alright, let's get going."

Bracket called Seeta on the ride back to Naijapool, where she was at the rocket platform examining the stability of a concrete escarpment. "Kwesi, are you wearing eyeliner?"

"Digital Security wants me to use this identity," he said, and sighed.

"Looks like a silly woman," Wale huffed.

"You look very fetching," Seeta replied, laughing. She aimed her camera at the ground. "See that? It's a microfissure. I've found six of them now. We'll have to seal them. I told Josephine that we were short by a hundred thousand liters of water, but she didn't listen. Thankfully, I deflected most of the energy down the shoot. Burned the bloody hell out of the brush on the other side."

"We didn't find anything at the tracking station," Bracket said.

"These things take patience," Wale chimed in. "You can't unearth an ancient civilization in a day. I need you to help me use the GPR, young lady, so we can be more methodical next time."

"Time," Seeta said, "I don't have. My job right now is to keep the astronauts from being fried like a sausage."

Wale looked disappointed.

"Then our best lead for now continues to be the meteorite," Bracket concluded.

"Maybe we can gather more information once we understand its structure," Wale admitted. "Can you initiate a deeper acoustic scan, Doctor?"

"I just told you I don't have the time."

"Let me carry it forward once you begin. You both can attend to your duties, and I'll monitor the experiment."

Seeta thought over the proposition. "All right, I'll come down to the pool. Meet me there in a half hour."

When Seeta arrived, they searched for a quiet area and ended up settling on the dive equipment room, which was empty. Inside they were surrounded by racks of dive fins, masks, and wetsuits on hangers that had a sour smell. On the other wall, hidden behind a locked grate, were air tanks and oxygen lines.

"I need you to keep your people out of here," Seeta ordered. "I have to calibrate my instruments."

They stepped outside as Seeta began setting up her equipment.

"Quite a feisty young woman," Wale said casually.

"Please don't say that to her face."

"Of course not. She's quite well educated."

"What is it with you and your PhDs?"

"Education is a mark of achievement. Pedigree and upbringing are as important as your current status because a wise man looks at things differently from an imbecile."

"How about an imbecile with a PhD?"

"There are sadly too many."

There was a high-pitched whinnying sound that grated at Bracket's ears. Then the glass from the door of the equipment room splintered, the shards exploding outward. He fell to the ground, and Wale tripped over backward, his cane rattling on the concrete.

Bracket kicked the door open and found Seeta slumped over the artifact on the floor. "Seeta! Are you all right?"

"Ugh."

He gently tried to raise her head. "Let me look at you."

She slowly, painfully, allowed herself to be stretched out. He searched her torso for any kind of injury and then checked out her limbs. She hadn't been harmed except for a nick on the back of her hand, which she must have picked up from the blast.

"Talk to me. Let me know you're okay."

"I'm okay," she said.

Now Bracket became aware of the sound of air hissing around him. One of the air lines had ruptured. He quickly twisted the valve shut, grateful that nothing worse had happened.

Wale poked his head in, saw that she was okay, and huffed: "The artifact?"

"Now is not the time, Wale."

"Well, what happened to it?"

"It broke! Okay, it broke!" Seeta snapped.

"Christ," Bracket said. Although he knew it could have been a lot worse—there were more than a dozen oxygen tanks in the room.

"And where were you, Clarence? I pay you to look after me, not to flee at any sign of danger."

"I was pushed back by the explosion."

"That was some distance."

Seeta leaned against the wall of the hyperbaric chamber. "The tones, Kwesi. What I heard in there."

"What tones?"

"I calibrated the instrument across several frequencies. The pottery was responding somehow, as if it was listening. I felt subtle vibrations as I played back the same tones. The rock inside was growing warm...the next thing I know the pottery exploded. It responded to sound in a way I've never encountered before. I wasn't playing a strong amplitude, certainly not strong enough to break it."

"We need gloves," Wale declared, holding up his hands. "Don't touch anything."

Clarence brought them each a pair of latex gloves, and they carefully collected the broken pieces of the artifact. Wale picked up the inky black rock, which was pocked with crystalline structures. They carried the fragments upstairs to Bracket's desk in the operations room.

"Careful," Wale said, "careful. We'll have to number these shards." Once they placed everything on Bracket's desk, he bent over the objects. "It's true then. This is almost certainly a meteorite. It looks like a monomict brecciated eucrite. The outer layer has annealed as you would expect, and it's glassy in appearance, but these etchings are unusual. They appear to have been carved in a geometric pattern by a human hand. Only diamond could have cut this. You didn't touch it, did you?"

"We used the gloves as you said. But the tones the rock responded to. They reminded me of something..." She trailed off, looking past all of them.

"What you recorded in the pool?" Bracket volunteered.

"No, but close. Of. . . Addama. They reminded me of a song that Addama played on her lute. The very same notes. Not in the same order, but they were there."

"Who are you talking about?" Wale asked.

"I recorded a musician near Lake Chad who played a lute and sang the most lovely melodies, an ethereal voice. And it all fit the soundscape, Wale, in a way that only the best musicians can. While I listened to her, the timbre of her voice made me feel as if I were there and somewhere else at the same time. This meteorite responded to the same frequencies as her own notes. There is a connection. I don't know how or why, but there is a connection to her."

"Out by Lake Chad, you say?" Wale asked.

"Yes, about fifty kilometers from your dig."

"That would fit if the oral traditions had been passed down. The Nok mixed with peoples from all over the region—there is evidence of their settlements over an enormous area."

"Maybe their civilization didn't totally disappear," Seeta agreed. "Maybe they passed along their music."

"We're not going back to Lake Chad," Bracket declared, anticipating where this was going.

"I agree, boss," Clarence chimed in. "It's not safe with the Jarumi in the area."

"I suppose that's reasonable," Wale conceded, disappointed. "It could be the way the meteorite is carved. A eucrite like this shouldn't have any unusual response to air pressure."

"What does air pressure have to do with it?" Bracket asked.

"Sound is caused by the vibration of air molecules," Seeta explained. "The frequency tells you how much air is displaced. The lower the frequency, the more air that is displaced. That's why you feel deep bass in your chest and high notes in your ears."

Bracket felt he was onto something. He remembered the strange patterns he'd seen on the artifact, the script that Wale said no one had yet deciphered. "You said the sounds made that thing shatter, right, Seeta? The music?"

"Yes."

"If it is music, maybe the markings on the artifact weren't an accounting system as you suspected. It could have something to do with the music instead."

"You mean like musical notation?" Seeta said, growing animated. "It could be. Wale, pull up images of the artifact."

Wale obediently displayed the images from his cane on the wall of the operations room, and they closely inspected the markings. "It's not like any musical notation I've seen before," she said. "I'll need more time with them. Do you have any more samples from your dig, Wale?"

"I have thousands of images."

"We could run them through a pattern recognition program on the Loom," Seeta said. "That could be the key that we've been waiting for! It may take a skillful musician to play the right melody. The astrolabe didn't contain the coordinates to find the Nok. The coordinates must come from the music."

They arranged for Wale to access the artificial intelligence systems embedded in the Loom—a difficult task because of the proximity to the launch, when departments would be running final calculations. But they managed to find a half-hour window when the AI had not been booked—at 3:30 in the morning. Together, Wale and Seeta would build on the work of Ahmat, the researcher who had been overseeing the archaeological dig at Lake Chad. Santander hailed Bracket on his Geckofone as the scientists were discussing how to design the algorithm to feed into the Loom.

"What is it, Santander?"

Wale leaned over to see Santander's image. "What's wrong with that man? What is that all over his face?"

It was true, the diver's face appeared to be covered in insects. "They're malflies," Santander explained.

Bracket shuddered. The most hard-core newshounds willingly accepted malflies into their feeds, knowing that even though the microdrones carried malicious code, they also contained information about trends: who was sending viruses or launching botnet attacks; what product was being peddled; giving insight into the black market. It was dangerous work, but expert newshounds could isolate the malflies in digital honeypots so that they were unable to infect anything else.

"Disgusting habit," Wale frowned.

"What did you find, Santander?"

"I tapped into my feed again like you said."

"See, an addict!"

"Ignore him, Santander. What did you find out?"

"Nurudeen Bello lost a motion in the Senate. He was formally requesting a budgetary allocation to fund the space program beyond the interim period of the rescue mission, but the Senate delayed the vote."

So Bello lost, Bracket thought. *Josephine would not be pleased at the news.* "Anything else?"

"I only report the news. Mr. Bello was last spotted," he added, "in a silver Mercedes in Abuja, which was driving at high speed out of the city."

"What about military support to stop the Jarumi?" Bracket asked. "Did your newsfeed say anything about that?"

"I don't know about that. You asked me to scan for news about Bello, not the Jarumi."

"That's right," Bracket said, trying to encourage the man.

"Would you like other news, Mr. Bracket? Perhaps something more local?"

"What else you got?"

"I don't have any news about the Jarumi."

"That's fine. Tell us what you have."

"Some citizens captured an albino magician in Kano."

"What does that even mean?" Seeta asked.

"An albino has been accused of child abductions," Bracked explained. "The locals sometimes sell off their body parts for medicine, thinking they have magical properties."

Seeta looked confused. "You mean—"

"It was recorded on personal devices," Santander chimed in.

"Go ahead, show us."

Santander patched his newsfeed into Bracket's G-fone, which projected the image on the wall. At first, random streams of characters moved across the screen in various directions. The most recent news items scrolled quickly in the foreground in bold colors, while the older items hovered slowly behind, gradually fading as they left the news cycle. Every newshound organized his feed differently. Some color-coded them by mesh, others by type of news, such as sports or entertainment, and still others by their emotional content. It was maddening to watch, like looking into the subconscious of a deranged man.

"Can you isolate the video?" Seeta said.

"I do not like so many distractions," Wale agreed.

"Here it is," Santander said. "Unedited."

On the screen, the first video showed a group of people standing by the side of the road, mostly merchants and pedestrians. An *okada* scooter weaved through the traffic. It appeared to be dusk. You could hear a shout go up and the camera suddenly shifted its angle to the side. Now people were running toward something in the bramble along the road. Then, far in the distance, a bluish glow emerged in the corner of the picture, like a spark igniting a fire, and it shot impossibly fast out of view.

"What was that?" Wale asked.

"It moved too quickly," Bracket agreed.

The second video was shot from farther away with a higher resolution. The person also had a steadier hand. You could see that several men were running off into the distance between some bushes. Then, as they faded out of view, the bluish field appeared and rushed across the distance as rapidly as before.

"Slow it down," Bracket said. "Half speed."

This time they saw the blue field rise up and begin to dance about, and the thing bounded at impossible speed into the distance. It looked fast even in slow motion, skipping across the video frames.

"That's it," Seeta said. "That's the creature."

"What creature?" Wale asked.

"It's the same thing that Kwesi and I saw."

"But you said you thought it was the Nok. That's supposed to be an albino."

"Good point," Bracket agreed. "Santander, how do you know it's an albino?"

"There is a malfly feed of the albino being captured," Santander explained. "I've stripped the bad code from the video."

So it was true—an albino had conducted magic. Had Detective Idriss been right all along? The creature in his quarters had been an albino?

"Albinos don't have magical powers," Seeta argued, folding her arms. "They lack melanin in their skin. It doesn't matter what country you're in—the biology is the same. Right, Wale?"

But a change had come over Wale's face, and he looked frightened. "I don't know," he said.

"You all right, boss?" Clarence asked.

"Get me a glass of water."

The bodyguard quickly left the room.

Seeta put her hand on his arm as he stared absently ahead. "Wale, have you seen something like this before? Like the flash on the video?"

"No," the scientist said, leaning on his cane. He drew his finger along his chest. "These wounds. An albino woman gave them to me. She attacked me in my laboratory in Cape Town. She had skin that glowed in the moonlight."

"What happened to her?" Bracket asked.

"She disappeared," he mumbled. "She was last seen in Nigeria."

"You don't think this albino is the same woman, do you?" Seeta asked.

"I'm not sure," Wale said, shaking his head. "But it's not likely. That was a long time ago."

Clarence came back carrying the water. Wale mopped his brow and then said to Bracket, "Play the video."

Bracket watched the video closely as the cleaned image appeared on the screen. The feed started with an albino man urging a motorcycle rider to drive ahead. The albino had the features of a Nigerian man but his skin was white, lighter even than Bracket's, and his eyes were faded blue. It was as if a makeup artist had swept in and powdered a black man with talcum. A mob of people clouded the screen and it was too late—some angry men wrested the driver to the ground and kicked the motorcycle to pieces. The albino started shrieking for mercy. As the video rolled, the mob began battering him until someone arrived with a machete and the crowd cleared a way to let him through. The albino held his hands together, imploring them to spare him. But he was quickly slashed through the throat. The rest of the mob descended on him until all you could see was the blood beginning to flow.

The room grew quiet.

"Should I play it again?" Santander asked.

"I've seen enough," Wale said. "It wasn't her."

"Then who was it?" Seeta asked. "And why didn't he use any magic?"

"Maybe he was too frightened," Bracket volunteered.

He kept seeing the machete go up into the air and slash down again as the man screamed. It reminded him of watching Abdul Haruna's blood oozing near the tracking station—only this time the evidence was obvious for anyone to see. Wale looked crest-fallen, but it wasn't clear whether he was saddened by the killing, or because the video meant the Nok still being alive might be a product of their collective imaginations.

CHAPTER 22

The model for the *Masquerade*'s mission to the International Space Station was the rescue of the Salyut 7, the 1980s-era station operated by the Soviet Union that preceded the Mir. On that mission, two cosmonauts revived the offline Salyut as it spun dangerously out of orbit, without power, meaning that they had to work largely in the dark in subzero temperatures. Technology had improved a millionfold since the Salyut, and the current mission benefited from the fact that Masha Kornokova could communicate with ground control.

Josephine Gauthier had done everything in her power to rescue Kornokova and had found the engineers the materials they needed. She had secured for the astronauts the best training, equipment, food, tech, and resources to achieve their objectives. But she had offered nothing about albino magicians.

"We found out about the intruder that broke into my quarters," Bracket told her on the deck of Naijapool. She was wearing a turquoise head wrap, looking nervous, a hint of self-doubt that he'd rarely seen in her. "He was an albino man who was caught outside Kano."

"Op-Sec didn't report anything to me."

"They wouldn't have. They didn't know about it."

"Where is he?"

"Dead," Bracket said.

She shook her head, taking another glance at Bracket, surprised that he knew more than she did. "I've ordered Op-Sec to increase their patrols."

"Good. We'll be all right," he reassured her, touching her arm.

She flinched: "Shit!"

"I'm sorry! I shouldn't have done that."

But he could see blood seeping through her shirtsleeve.

"You're injured, Josephine! Let me see that."

She turned away from him. "It's nothing."

"You're bleeding."

Finally, she sighed and peeled back her sleeve. He saw a thick, macerated scar on her forearm. It had scabbed over and bled out many times in clumsy lettering: MASHA.

"I need to see her again," she said softly.

He didn't know what to say.

"Oh, don't act like a fool, Kwesi! You knew that Masha was my lover. I never should have told Ini about my identity. I'm sure she told everyone."

Her lover, Bracket thought. Ini had never mentioned that.

"I didn't know that you were connected, Josephine. What identity are you talking about?"

"Caucasian, all right? I use it to talk to her."

She rolled her sleeve back into place, obviously in pain. *How many times has she cut her arm? Picked at it like a flagellant?* Bracket knew Josephine was feeling enough pain, but he couldn't help but wonder: *Caucasian? Why? Why would she communicate through a Caucasian identity? Especially if they had known each other in the flesh?*

She stared down at the ISS on the bottom of the empty pool. The simulations had stopped so the Naijanauts could prepare their bodies for the launch.

"Masha is the daughter of a logger," Josephine added. "She comes from a poor family. Grew up with nothing. No hope. Made it into the Russian air force through her hard work and brains. Bello talks about black empowerment and Indian achievement, or whatever you Americans call it. But I don't believe in such propaganda. She's trying to accomplish the same thing we are."

"That's what Bello wants," Bracket said. "Except he wants to include Africans. I don't see anything wrong with that."

She plugged a cigarette into her mouth. Bracket didn't remember her smoking, but he let her puff on the pool deck even though it was strictly off-limits, seeing that she needed whatever it represented to her.

"*Merde putain*. Bello. I warned him about the Jarumi."

"He had to leave Abuja."

"Where did you hear that?"

"He lost a vote in the Senate and it looks like he fled."

She narrowed her eyes, and he could feel her calculating who might have told him. Then she relented, snubbed out her cigarette on the floor, and hoofed away.

Bracket returned to Digital Security, where he found Ini huddled over the carcasses of various machines. This time he ducked his head as he entered the room, checking to see if any of her biocomputers were going to pester him. He had already seen a green racer, a cicada, and a moth, and he had a feeling there were more sinister creatures waiting to spring out from the murky corners of her lab.

Her face lit up when she saw him. "Mr. Bracket! A pleasure to see you again." She was wearing a tight-fitting velvet tracksuit that showed off her butt, causing Bracket to frown with disapproval. He never would have let Sybil wear a tracksuit like that. She also wore new press-on fingernails that clicked against the screen as she typed.

"I've been able to dissect the spider," she explained, getting up from her desk. "The cyborg is so complex that I knew it would hold some more clues. You see, the engineers were forced to make certain design decisions that would be unique, leaving a sort of fingerprint. And I found this." She displayed an article on one of her monitors.

Port Harcourt—*The Rivers State Zoo reported the theft of a number of animals yesterday. No suspects have been apprehended. The thieves appear to have climbed over a low wall in the gorilla pit after sedating the animals with tranquilizers. They proceeded to break into the reptile pit, bird aviary, and insect hut. The thieves made off with a green spitting cobra and a large bird-eating spider.*

"We don't know why they took these things," zookeeper Roderick Kachikwu said. "They are not popular animals."

While rare, the stolen specimens do not carry a special value on the black market because they are extremely venomous. Police are continuing their inquiries.

"I am guessing," Ini said, "this is the bird-eating spider, poor thing. But it made me think that I should search through the code to find out how it was communicating. I found multiple logs with the same address buried in temporary memory. It normally communicates through an onion router, which would have disguised the destination, but I forced it to default to an unencrypted connection. The address leads directly to a particular house in Abuja owned by Senator Willie Kidibe of Cross Rivers State."

"Never heard of him."

"I just sent you more information about him."

Bracket scanned through the articles on his G-fone as Ini continued examining the spider—or the code that had been embedded in the spider's electronics. Willie Kidibe, he learned, was a former militant from the Niger delta who used to sabotage pipelines and kidnap oil executives for ransom. During peace settlements in the region, he and his bandits agreed to lay down their weapons for a hefty settlement from the government. He then used the money and his popularity as a rebel to run for public office, which he had held ever since, first in the House of Representatives and now in the Senate. According to one article, the politician had gained a reputation for being just as corrupt in office as he was as a rebel fighter.

"Why would a senator be spying on the space program?" Bracket asked.

"I don't know. We should assume that he knows a significant amount of information about all of our activities here."

He ambled over to a small fish tank, where he saw a lizard with green skin flecked with orange spots resting on a bed of pebbles. The water was cloudy with algae. "Salamander?"

"Yes," Ini said, not looking up. "They insulated the electronics against the moisture. It can record an image but it has no wireless capability. You need to physically download it from the salamander through its anus."

"Amphibious," Bracket found himself saying. "That's impressive." He was learning to see things from Ini's point of view, where everything was curious.

"That's exactly right," she agreed. "I think this salamander may have been built by Roland Ibe himself, the inventor of the Geckofone. He won't return my messages, though. Wait. Here, the spider's transmitting again. Some figures: 334-TY339."

"That's not a hexadecimal code," Bracket said. "I know that much."

"You're right. I'll run a search on it."

"Thanks, Ini," he said, turning to leave. "Let me know if you find anything."

"Hold on—I've got a hit at the Federal Road Safety Commission. It's a license plate number. Belongs to...no, it can't be."

"Who?" Bracket said, suddenly interested.

"Omotola Taiwo."

"The actress?"

"I'm certain of it. It's her personal car, a Mercedes Benz 500 SL. There's more. The spider's transmitting a message. 'Northeast.' Does that mean anything to you?"

"Yeah," Bracket said. "Omotola Taiwo is Bello's fiancée. Someone on my crew told me he was spotted leaving the city, and this must mean he's heading northeast from Abuja. The senator knows exactly where they're going. We should warn Bello."

"His Geckofone has been turned off for some time," Ini confirmed. "I'll see if I can reach him another way."

"Think we should scramble the spider's messages, just in case? Send some false information?"

"No," Ini said. "We have to let the traffic continue or he'll know we're listening and switch to another channel. I'll let you know if I learn anything more."

"Thanks, Ini. I'd better go tell Josephine." He gave her a polite smile and left.

Josephine was in the Nest analyzing telemetry data from the test launch when Bracket called. She answered, maybe on purpose, with her Caucasian identity, which narrowed her nose a bit, turned her eyes hazel, and squeezed in her lips. Her voice sounded slightly higher. So this would be their shared secret. It was fine. He knew it must have been difficult for her to admit her love for Kornokova.

"What do you think we should do, Kwesi?"

It was the first time she had ever asked him for advice.

"We need to take the threat seriously. There's a chance the senator might be preparing to kidnap Bello. Or do him harm. I've read his files—it's in his history. He used to be a thug. I don't know why he chose Bello, but there's a real risk."

"I'm not trained to deal with someone like that, Kwesi."

"Neither am I," he admitted. "I don't trust Op-Sec with this either. We've got to bring this to the Kano police."

"No way. They're imbeciles."

"Detective Idriss might be corrupt, but he's no imbecile. I've double-checked everything at Naijapool, Josephine, and my crew is ready for any situation. The tank is operational and the filters are functioning properly."

"I've seen your reports," she said impatiently.

"What I'm saying is that Bello isn't the only problem—I think there's something else that might be threatening the mission, something that could ruin all the work we've done here. Whether it's the Jarumi or someone else, I don't know. I need to look into it. Let me go talk to the police. I know them—if anyone can help us, they can."

He could see Josephine thinking it over, which her Caucasian identity interpreted by making her cheeks blush. He felt he had finally caught her attention. Maybe she was listening to him now because she had bared her scars for him to see. "All right," she decided, "you've got until the rescue launch. That's forty-eight hours."

"Don't worry," he said, "I'll make sure we complete the mission."

"We'll complete the mission."

And like a newshound, he couldn't tell if she had heard him or was merely repeating what he had said.

CHAPTER 23

The wind was gusting across the road as Max drove Bracket into downtown Kano, giving a taste of the Harmattan that would sweep across the Sahel in the coming weeks. The roadsides were eerily empty of market sellers and the normally crowded intersections were bare. The residents had closed their shutters, maybe against the wind, but more likely because the Jarumi were coming. Even the cowherds appeared to have moved their cattle away from the city. Bracket found himself peering down every alleyway expecting to see a gun-toting militant storming toward them. Max too was tense and hurtled through intersections without stopping for the signals. They passed through the industrial markets and found all the storefronts barred.

Detective Idriss had asked Bracket to meet him in a poorer residential area, where the buildings were crammed closely together and the windows striped by iron security grates. An enormous, solitary kapok tree towered over the neighborhood. They stopped at a building where three Mitsubishi police trucks were parked out front with their lights flashing and a crowd had gathered nearby to see what was happening. The officers recognized Bracket this time and waved him into the home past the onlookers, who were craning their necks to peer into the building.

Bracket stepped into a vestibule a few paces wide to find an officer beaming a flashlight beneath a couch. The cushions had been thrown to the floor.

"Step straight through, Mr. Bracket!" Idriss shouted from the next room. "We don't know if it's booby-trapped." A corridor branched into two adjoining rooms and a simple kitchen with a sink, gas stove, and breakfast nook. Detective Idriss was directing other officers inside the room on the left. One of them held a sledgehammer, and he brought it down on a machine gun, hitting it until the barrel crumpled.

Idriss looked up calmly. "Give me a moment." The detective pointed to another twenty guns lined up along one wall—"These too"—and the officer dutifully began crushing them with his sledgehammer.

"Mr. Bracket, I appreciate you coming to see us here."

"We're in trouble at the spaceport," Bracket said. "I need your help."

"And I shall provide it. But first I need *your* assistance." He picked up a framed photo that was sealed in a clear Ziploc bag. "Do you recognize this man?"

The photo showed a white man with a blond ponytail, with his arms around two children—a boy and a girl, maybe about ten and fourteen years old—and a smiling wife. Eero Saarinen's Gateway Arch towered over them in the background. It looked like one of those stock photos that you take on a green screen at tourist sites, where they digitally add the monument later.

"I've never seen him before," Bracket said.

"He's American and here illegally, as you might have surmised. Do you recognize anything in the photo that could be useful to us?"

"That was probably taken in St. Louis," Bracket guessed, "before the Flare. The elevator to the top of the arch wouldn't have been working afterward. Unlikely he's from St. Louis or he wouldn't have kept the photo, because people tend to take tourist sites for granted when they live near them. The ponytail means he didn't hold a typical job. Either worked for a small business or held a backroom role of some kind. Maybe a coder."

"I'm impressed at your powers of observation. That might help us in our investigation, if we have time for it," Idriss said. "Let me show you something else, Mr. Bracket." He beckoned for Bracket to follow him into the adjacent room, which smelled of ozone. There, partitioned behind some mosquito netting, the floor was covered with thousands of writhing bugs. He reflexively itched at his neck, thinking of the zero day spider. In the middle of the room was a large computer server, and next to that was a glass-and-metal box about one meter square.

"Malfly hatchery," Idriss explained. "We were tipped off by a neighbor who saw him transporting in reels of polymer. We were very fortunate to find it."

Now Bracket peered closer at the ground to see that they weren't insects at all, but the typical microdrones that hounded electronics, and their tiny wing-blades and servo motors had been fried. Malfly drones preyed on devices that didn't connect regularly to the Internet, where it was more efficient to transmit malware through wireless spectrum. These would likely be shipped overseas and released to pester Americans desperate for basic goods. He felt his Geckofone rustling in his pocket, alert to the threat.

"You killed them all," he observed.

"Local EMP. They won't fly again. It's a minor hatchery that releases at most a thousand malflies a day through that extruder. They're shoddily made."

"You think this was run by the guy in the photo?"

"Not all of you are lucky enough to work at the spaceport, Mr. Bracket. Anyway he's not very good at it, judging from the quality of these malflies. He appears to have been warned that we were coming and fled some time ago."

Bracket bent closer to pick up a malfly, which hummed lightly at his fingertips as the propeller tried to spin up. He fed it to his Geckofone.

"It seems like overkill," Bracket said, thinking it through, "for him to have all those weapons for a small hatchery like this."

"I couldn't agree more, Mr. Bracket. This hatchery can't be worth more than a thousand cowries a month. Those weapons are meant for the Jarumi."

The Jarumi? He had known that Americans—and Europeans too, for that matter—ran illicit businesses in Nigeria. But helping Islamic militants seemed like too much. "You actually think that guy's a member of Boko Haram?"

Idriss chuckled. "I doubt he is a member of the Jarumi. This house is full of illicit material: pornography, stimulants, steroids, opioids, and so forth. I suspect he was merely dealing weapons to make money."

Bracket tried not to think about what the man might be doing with that money as they made their way back to the room where Idriss's officers were busy destroying the guns. Sending money to his family? If so, where were they living? Or was the man blowing it all on sex, which he had seen plenty of expatriates do? Bracket had rarely encountered undocumented Americans in Kano, and when he did he usually regretted it. They'd offer him some shady deal or desperately ask him for a job he couldn't provide, their eyes burning with resentment.

"Nurudeen Bello has disappeared," Bracket announced to Idriss.

The detective lifted an eyebrow as Bracket explained to him what had happened, and how Digital Security had figured out the spider belonged to Senator Kidibe. "So you think he's been kidnapped, do you?"

"I don't know. It's a possibility."

"I wouldn't be surprised. Mr. Bello makes a show of his money. In Kano, people think your rockets are made of gold."

"By weight, they're not far off. Nitrogen tetroxide is hard to find in Kano."

"And you believe he was traveling this way, do you? That would seem to be a foolhardy thing to do."

"He was warned against it."

"The pigeon that feeds among the hawks doesn't fear death. That was poor judgment on his part."

"What do you suggest we do, Detective?"

Idriss leaned over to examine the twisted barrel of a shotgun, pushing his spectacles back up his nose as they slipped. "He could still be a victim of an ordinary car theft. The security systems in Mercedes cars are robust enough that they are difficult to hijack remotely, increasing the chance of a carjacking when the driver is still inside. That way the thieves can force the owner to bypass the security systems so they can repurpose the car and sell it. I can put out an all-points bulletin on the vehicle, but the thieves will have taken it off the road. On the other hand, if Bello has been kidnapped, as you suspect, they'll be in touch soon enough."

"How do you know that?"

"They would never expect you to send any money without proving to you that Bello was alive. No fool would do that. They'll contact you if what you say is true. But I wouldn't speak to Senator Kidibe, not until you have concrete evidence that he's behind it."

Idriss was merely talking through these various strategies as if they were a thought exercise.

"Can't you do anything else?" Bracket insisted. "No one's doing anything at the spaceport. This is what you wanted. It's in your jurisdiction."

"Right now the Jarumi are headed toward Kano. They are well armed and have a certain degree of discipline. We will almost certainly be outgunned. We're fortunate to have found their weapons first."

"They're coming tonight? They're already this close?"

"You still have time, Mr. Bracket. They won't be here for another three hours at least. I'll make sure that my officers escort you to the edge of the city. If Bello was driving northeast from Abuja, as you say, he would not have met them that far to the south. But perhaps they're better organized than we know."

Bracket looked at the detective, trying to fathom how he could resign himself to defeat so easily.

"My job is to serve this city, Mr. Bracket. We will not abandon it. We've requested a Super Tucano plane from the air force. There is the chance that some of the younger fighters will be intimidated by it. Even if the Jarumi do come, maybe they'll learn what it means to help people instead of enslave women, murder their neighbors, and make their own children ignorant. They'll see there is another way."

Bracket recalled the young man whom the detective had been torturing when he had visited the police station, the screams of pain and anguish they had inflicted on the boy with the Coca-Cola.

That way? That way won't teach the Jarumi anything.

"The other day I came by," Bracket said, "you told me that you'd heard of albino sightings. Did you see the video of the killing on Naijaweb?"

"We examined it, Mr. Bracket, and it's a hoax."

"You think the video was doctored?"

"It wasn't doctored. That albino was actually killed. But it happened over two months ago in the city of Yola. Two of the vigilantes already confessed to the killing."

"But what about the other videos?" Bracket said. "The ones of the blue light shooting into the distance."

"No one can explain those films," Idriss acknowledged. "I suspect they've been faked too, but we haven't been able to properly analyze them. They should never have been grouped together with the albino video. It shows you can never trust what you find on Naijaweb. Now, if you please, Mr. Bracket, we've got work to do."

Bracket was trying to make sense of what the detective had said. If the albino video wasn't connected, then what was the blue light in those videos? The albino was supposed to be a magician, which went against Bracket's own beliefs, but he had forced himself to consider it as a real possibility. Now that the albino video was a hoax, then what was that blue light? Was it the creature of the Nok, as he and Seeta had suspected? If so, he realized with a shudder, *the creature might still be alive.*

Bracket exited the building into a darkening sky heavy with dust. Far up in the air, he could see a small reconnaissance drone hovering. It rose and fell in the tufts of wind as it soared.

"Let's get out of here, Max."

"What's wrong, *oyibo?*"

"Jarumi."

He felt a loud explosion in his chest. Glass shattered as he ducked beneath the dashboard and hopped into the pickup truck. The crowd scattered away, shrieking.

"It came from above!" Max shouted.

Bracket looked up to find that the corner of the home he'd just left had been torn off and the shingles had caught fire. Now he saw the drone was carrying something by small hooks as it rose again above the building. It dropped it down onto the roof. Shards of shingles exploded outward.

Down the street, Bracket saw two children who hadn't fled. They couldn't have been more than ten years old.

"Hey!" he shouted. "Get out of here!"

The two children began walking toward the truck as if they hadn't heard him.

"Hey!" Max joined in, switching to Pidgin. "Get out of here! It's not safe!"

But they continued walking along, ignoring him.

"What's wrong with them?" Bracket asked.

Bracket recognized the red armbands just as the boys turned to face them. *The boys were holding pistols.*

"Drive, Max! Drive!"

Max reversed when the first shots sprayed around them. The bullets cracked the front windshield. He hit the brakes and swung the car around. Now the kids were firing into the back window.

Max plunged down an alley. But the way was blocked by a cow-herd, who had coaxed his animals inside to protect them for the night. Max honked madly, but the cows just stared back at them.

He reversed out of the alley as the cowherd berated them. When the car came out into the main street again, Bracket could see that the two children were locked in a gunfight with the police officers. Max accelerated down the main strip, then turned onto the highway leading out of town.

When they arrived at the spaceport, guards were already positioned in the towers, manning the machine guns, as Max slowed the car to a stop outside the gate.

"Aren't you coming with me, Max? It's safe in here."

"I have to go to my family."

Bracket knew not to argue with him anymore about family. "Go get them, then. Go get them and bring them back here. I'll make sure they let you in."

Max shook his head. "It's okay, *oyibo*. Pay me for the ride. I'll see you again."

"You sure?"

"I'll see you again. I'll fix things for you."

Bracket transferred the cowries, adding in extra for the damage to the pickup truck, and Max drove away into the night. He finally caught his breath now that he was inside the base. He hadn't expected children to dress and behave like soldiers. The Jarumi were waging a war against a defenseless population, and the attack had happened so fast that he hadn't had the time to contemplate what it really meant. Nothing had touched him. There were no bruises on his body, only a fragmenting in the recesses of his mind that he would have to reckon with later.

He dialed Seeta as soon as he returned to his quarters. When she picked up, he could hear the wind howling around her, wherever it was.

"Hey, Kwesi."

"Wale with you?"

"Yeah. Can you turn off that stupid identity? I want to see your face."

He tried to switch it off, but Ini had apparently locked it in place. "The Jarumi are attacking Kano," he said.

"For fuck's sake."

In the background he heard: "Language, young lady!"

"Where are you, Seeta? Are you safe?"

"We're out by the tracking station."

"You've got to get out of there! I talked to Detective Idriss about that albino video. He said that it was faked."

"It doesn't matter, Kwesi. We're so close to finding the Nok. The pattern recognition program came back with a range of frequencies, and we think we've found a positive correlation with the musical notation. We're testing them now. We found another shard, so we think the entrance must be around here."

"No, you don't understand, Seeta. The other videos were real—"

"Look!" he heard Wale shout. "I found another one!"

"I've got to go, Kwesi." She disconnected.

A bloody moon was perched in the evening sky as Bracket pedaled on his bike out to the tracking station. The color was rich and fulsome—there was no hint of orange in it. Dust seeded the atmosphere, scattering the light. Even as a scientist he felt the moon's power and what it portended: a reckoning—someone would die tonight. There was death in the sky.

Seeta and Wale weren't at the station when he arrived, and he couldn't see more than a hundred paces in the dust. In the distance, towering thunderheads of clouds touched the top of the sky. He started circling around the tracking station, keeping it always on his left, and calling out for the two scientists. He made one rotation, didn't find them, and widened it. The wind was rising steadily.

He heard them before he could see them: a high-pitched tone, followed by another lower tone, and another. The sound pierced through the wind and the noise. He moved toward the source, squinting his eyes against the rush of sand. There, he could make out Seeta crouching behind one of the mounds of earth. Wale was hunched over the ground, and his bodyguard stood anxiously between them.

"Hey!" Bracket yelled.

As he got closer, he could see Clarence pushing forward the ground-penetrating radar machine, and Seeta was scribbling something in a notebook. She had wrapped a shawl around her head so that you could barely see her brown-green eyes. Wale, by contrast, stood totally erect, leaning on his cane as if impervious to the storm raging around them.

"Two meters forward," Seeta was saying. "I'll try two-twenty-one."

"We just tried that!" Wale said.

"Two meters forward!"

"Dr. Olufunmi, we should get going," Clarence said.

"We're not going anywhere. We're too close."

"It's a dust storm, boss. We should get you safe and under cover."

"Nothing's stopping you from going back to the building, Clarence."

"There's more slag here," Seeta said.

"As I said there would be," Wale boasted.

"There must be tons of it. Let's fire the GPR again."

"It may be magnetite," Wale guessed. "I can't be sure. It's not unusual for it to be mixed in with iron deposits, but not at such a high concentration."

"If that's true," Seeta agreed, "that would explain why the instruments haven't been working properly. All this iron and magnetite would have skewed the readings. NASA must not have realized they were right on top of a thousand tons of iron slag. That may be why they had to close the tracking station."

Wale turned excitedly to Bracket, who was growing increasingly frustrated that they seemed to be deliberately ignoring him. "You're looking at the remains of a major Iron Age civilization here. There's enough slag to suggest dozens of smelting furnaces. The slag wasn't inside the mounds but buried deep beneath the surface. Fire the GPR, Clarence."

Seeta's headphones were draped around her neck, and Bracket saw they had rigged up a sort of cage for the meteorite, so that Seeta could dangle it from a string.

"Hold on a moment," Bracket said, holding up his hands. "This can wait. I'm as curious as you are about all this, but now is not the time."

"If we're going to be killed by bandits," Wale said, "then I want to gaze upon the cradle of the Nok civilization before I die. I've waited years for this. Now if you would please step back, Mr. Bracket, I would like to do some proper scientific work."

"No, I need you to listen to me. That albino video was faked."

"You told us already," Seeta said.

"But the other videos were *real*. There's still no explanation for them. That creature may still be out here! It's dangerous. I want to find out about this as much as you do, but we should come back with more security. And wait for the storm to pass."

"Clarence is our security," Wale insisted.

"Boss, I agree with Mr. Bracket that you should leave the spaceport before the Jarumi attack."

"In this storm?" Wale asked.

"We need to get you safe, Doctor."

"How is flying into a dust storm considered safe in any way, shape, or form, Clarence?"

"Please," Seeta chimed in. "This is happening. This may be the biggest breakthrough in vibroacoustics in a hundred years."

Wale bent forward to look at her instruments. "I told you, it's thirty-four. You made a mistake, young lady."

"Quit calling me that."

"You must be more methodical."

"And you need to get off my back, Wale! All right, I'll try thirty-four. Move the GPR two meters forward."

Bracket could see a black cloud surging toward them, the lightning flaring within it. Soon they would be buried in dust. He realized he had a fear of being buried alive that he hadn't quite articulated until this very moment.

"Let's wait it out at the tracking station," he tried to compromise.

"I agree, boss."

"These storms are all bluster," Wale said. "It'll be over in a minute."

"I don't know, boss. It looks quite bad."

"Ready!" Wale shouted.

"Thirty-four. Go!"

The sound started first as a low pitch. Then the meteorite began vibrating, and Bracket could see color in the inky black: gray peeking through the void, becoming blue. The sound—repeating quickly like the trills of some bird in estrus, the flitting tongue trapped in sedge, now the high screech of a grackle, the machine pushing it through the frequencies, and Bracket could feel weight on his chest, the old ghost come to claim him.

"It's hot!" Seeta said.

"Don't drop it!"

"Turn it off!" Bracket found himself shouting. "Turn it off!"

The bodyguard was pulling at the scientist, who was in turn hitting him with his cane. And Seeta had closed her eyes, her arms spread out like a yogi, embracing the sound.

The pressure on his chest. The noise in his ears. Then slipping, sliding into the earth around him, toward the center, his hair wispy in the static of the dust storm. He was falling, and there was no bottom, and it all seemed wrong. Now the sky was closed. Now the red moon was smoking as the ground pulled him in. The sand, it was filling his nostrils: *Turn it off! Turn it off! Turn it off!*

CHAPTER 24

The window, Bracket thought. *Open it. There's no air in this place.*
He was slowly suffocating and there was a wetness on his skin.
He couldn't see anything; he could feel only the coldness of some
dank, interstitial space. His arm touched flesh.

"Seeta?"

"Mmm."

"You all right?" He felt around in the dark for her, followed her
arm up to the soft folds under her neck. He raised her head gently
in his arms.

"What happened?" she whispered.

"I don't know. I can't see anything."

"What's that noise?"

Only now did he discern the sound, an endless repeating of
voices, an incessant play of pressure in his eardrums.

"I don't know."

"Someone's singing. Is Wale here?"

"I don't see him. Wait here. I'll see if I can find him."

He got up painfully from the ground. He thought he could
make out something in the distance, a soft blue flame glowing
like a pilot light. He took a step forward.

"Shit!"

"What? What happened, Kwesi?"

"It stung me!"

"What stung you?"

"The light. I touched it and it . . . damn!"

"I don't see anything." He could hear her trying to get up from the ground, her clothes scratching against the earth.

"Careful, Seeta, or—"

"Ow! Bloody hell!"

"I told you. Did you see it?"

"Yeah, it's like a sheet of plastic. It's an electric fence or something."

"Let me try my Geckofone."

He saw her face illuminated by the LED light as he turned the device on, how dust had coated her disheveled locks. Behind her he could see piles of rocks that sloped toward them, reaching to the top of the narrow space. The ceiling was rock too, and there was no natural light. The walls were lined with crude stone shelves, and on each shelf was a little mound. He scratched away some of the dirt and saw a bleached-white bone. It looked like a finger. On the next shelf he found two dark leather slippers half hidden in the dirt, leaning in closer to discover they weren't slippers at all.

They were dried human skin.

He found a flat rock to begin scooping away the dirt. As he dug, more of the grotesque thing began to take form. It was a body. Or the shell of a body, nothing but flattened skin and hair. He felt a stench rear up as he uncovered it, but the flesh had been squeezed of any blood. The person's face had been flattened to maybe four centimeters wide and the nose was matted into the cheeks. The eye sockets too were gone. A strip of cotton cloth was matted to the flesh, the same dark green color the workers wore around the site. Every feature was stretched and elongated like a fun-house mirror, the remaining splintered teeth mashed into where the neck should be. He reached over to touch the flesh. It felt like tanned leather, like a chrysalis abandoned for some new phase of life. Skin should never feel like that. No one should ever look like that.

"It's Abdul Haruna," he said.

Seeta took one look at the shelf and turned away. "How horrible."

"He didn't arrive here like this. Someone moved him here."

He began scooping some soil back over the mangled corpse to try to mask the stench, which was making the space feel even more nauseating.

"They're here," Seeta whispered, looking down the tunnel.

"Who?"

"Can't you see them?"

"I don't see anything. It's like the air stops."

"No, in between, I can see their faces, beyond it."

"Beyond what?"

Bracket saw what looked like an aura, a mottled shifting presence. It reminded him of when he'd once had migraine headaches in his youth, a black-and-blue orb that seemed to move in and out of his sight. The image was not so much before him spatially as inside his eyelids.

"I'm going to try something, Kwesi."

"You think you can find a way out?"

"Maybe. Don't say anything."

"Why not?"

"Keep your mouth shut. I'm going to try to talk to them."

"Who are you talking about?"

"Quiet."

Seeta was fiddling with her measurement instrument. "Dammit, I can't see enough. I'll have to eyeball it."

"You need help?"

"What did I tell you? Keep your bloody mouth shut. I think they can hear us." She began muttering to herself. "The sound is coming in at forty-six cycles. I'm going to roll a sine wave on top." She pressed a button on her machine. The blue aura closed in on them like a shroud.

"No, Seeta! Turn it off! What did you do?"

"Hold on! That was the wrong one!"

"I can't breathe!"

He felt the weight of it, crushing in on him, that awful pressure on his chest, the strength of a constrictor compressing his lungs. "Quick, Seeta . . . please."

"One second, almost . . . there!"

He heard four discordant notes and immediately felt a loosening in his chest. The air rushed in around them, and he sucked it into his lungs gratefully. It was still damp, but there was oxygen in it this time.

"Oh my god," Seeta said.

He turned around. Before them he could see several enormous beings. Each stood about seven feet tall. But like the aura he'd seen earlier, they seemed to shift and stutter in place, their outlines becoming hazy as they moved. There were three of the creatures. Two of them had a silken blue shape to them, while the other one seemed to be made from the earth itself, a looming entity with electric skin.

"That's the one who attacked us," he whispered. That's the one he had touched, and he remembered the strange longing from its quarters, the static feel of the body on his fingertips.

"We mean you no harm," Seeta announced.

The creatures turned toward one another. He could see no means for them to speak, since their mouths were merely placeholders for orifices, their entire faces like ceremonial masks, when he could perceive faces at all. They stared back without a hint of emotion.

"What did you do with our friend?" Bracket tried. As soon as he said this, he saw one of the creatures shift, and the undulating field wrapped around him like a net. The air was pressed out of his chest again.

"No, wait!" Seeta said.

This time it was constricting much harder, pulling at his ribs. He thought they would crack, that his heart would explode out of his chest. He heard a voice too, a strident chant that rang through his ears that was at once familiar and terrifying. And with each cycle of the chant more breath was drained from his body.

Now it stopped again, almost as swiftly as it had started.

"Don't do that to him again," Seeta warned, holding up her recording instrument.

"What did you do?" he gasped.

"They're using music."

Now another one of the creatures lurched for Seeta, and the field that had entrapped him flew out in her direction. Seeta was quicker. She sent out a blast of notes that seemed to weaken the field, until the creature retracted it back to surround itself.

"I saw someone," Bracket said, crawling back behind Seeta. "While it was coming toward you. There was someone there. A woman, I think. A girl."

"Human?"

"Yes."

"You mean controlling these things?"

"I don't know. I couldn't be sure...watch out!"

Seeta fingered her instrument but it was too late. Two of the other creatures crossed the distance between them in long strides. Seeta and Bracket tried to run but were trapped by the rubble behind them.

"Get back!" Bracket threw himself over Seeta, preparing to take the blow. They would hack him next, he thought. Or crush his skull. He cowered over her, protecting her from the attack even if he knew there was nothing he could do to stop it.

He could hear them hovering nearby, the eerie sounds of their soft music moving among them. It was like a hundred melodies clashing against one another in a cacophony. But the blow never came.

"What are they doing?" Seeta said.

"I don't know. Don't move."

"Don't touch that!" she said. "You can't have it! No, don't!"

The creatures dragged her measurement instruments away.

"He touch you?" a voice said.

"Who said that?"

The aura re-formed around the group, preventing Bracket from seeing anything.

"He touch you?"

"Did who touch who?"

One of the aurae moved over in Bracket's direction, prodding him with what felt like a cattle rod. "Ow!"

"Him? You mean Kwesi? No, no, he didn't touch me. We're friends."

Bracket thinking: *That all we are?*

"Come!" the voice said to Seeta.

"No, if I go, he comes too! We're together. We go together."

Again, he heard a flurry of notes pass among the creatures, which he now knew responded to the people somehow, whoever they were.

"Come," they said.

"Where are we going?"

"Come. Come."

Now the creatures started moving away from them, their soft light following them as they walked. Bracket could make out their surroundings better. They were in some sort of tunnel. They walked for a long time, twisting and turning in the seemingly endless branching tunnels, before he started to feel the air becoming fresher, and soon the tunnel opened into a room with a high, cavernous ceiling. The walls were covered with strange inscriptions. The creatures retreated to the edge of this space, positioning themselves defensively in what looked like another tunnel, and Bracket could dimly make out two figures lying on the ground.

"Wale!"

The scientist was crumpled up on his side.

"My cane," he muttered. "Help me find my cane."

"Are you all right?"

"They took it from me. Those monsters took my cane."

"I don't see it anywhere. Here, let me give you a hand."

"No, I need my cane. I won't depend on someone to get around like an invalid!"

"Let him bloody well help you up, Wale!" Seeta snapped. "We can find it later."

All this time, the creatures watched from a distance, observing their interactions.

Bracket went over to Wale's bodyguard. "Can you get up, Clarence?" He tried to turn the giant man over and felt warm fluid on his hand. "He's injured."

"He's dead," Wale said softly.

"What are you talking about? They killed him?"

"I told him to drop the weapon when they came, but they were attacking me. So he fired at them. And, I don't know, they stopped it. Then they swallowed him in one of their fields and when he came out again he was dead. The poor man. Clarence was only doing his job. Why won't they give me my cane back? I need it to walk."

"We'll get your cane back, Wale. It'll be okay."

"It's not dignified, to walk without a cane, to depend on other people to get around."

Seeta began humming to herself.

"What are you doing?" Bracket said.

"Join me."

"They'll kill us, young lady. Don't do that. They took my cane."

Bracket realized he'd never heard Seeta sing before, and was surprised at the raspiness of her voice, how she was slightly out of tune. He always assumed she could sing like a lark because she could describe music with precision and poetry. He followed her lead, trying to mimic the notes as best he could. He didn't see any shift in the creatures this time, no change in their aurae.

Soon their wavering voices roused Wale out of his stupor. He joined their motley chorus, but sang the notes truer and more forcefully until he began leading the song. One by one Bracket watched as the creatures wavered before his very eyes, and the blue aurae disappeared. The dirt skin flaked away from their terra-cotta forms and dropped to the earth in small clouds of dust. Before them stood five tall, elegant women holding dark stones in front of their chests like offerings. They stopped singing.

Bracket recognized them immediately: the long, lithe bodies; the garb harkening back to another era.

"You're both tone deaf," Wale observed. "That's what happens when you don't speak a tonal language."

"They're from Kano," Bracket said.

"You've seen them before?"

"They're Wodaabe traders. They sell medicines at the market in town, and that one"—he pointed at the youngest of them, causing the others to crowd around her, protectively—"was at the suicide bombing."

"Her?"

"I'm sure of it. She was singing a song like that at the bombing. She was singing it again just now, but it was different, more complex than before. She must have survived. I don't know how or why. But they're the ones."

Wale was leaning heavily on Bracket's shoulder. "These aren't the Nok," he said, disappointed. "I thought we would find the Nok."

"It has to be them," Seeta argued. "You saw what they did back there. This place is ancient. It's surely the home of the Nok. Look at the inscriptions. That room where we arrived—those bones were hundreds of years old. These women must be related to them, carrying on their traditions."

"You're right that this space is old," Wale said, looking now around the chamber. "But the Wodaabe would rarely have come this far south. It doesn't fit the evidence."

"Then how do they know how to use the meteorites?" Bracket asked.

Finally, the eldest among the tall women stepped forward. The others transformed themselves again, building up their aurae as they walked, so that it was clear they would protect her if the scientists tried to harm her. Bracket had learned his lesson and stayed put.

Like the others, the woman had a long, thin nose and braided hair that fell to her shoulders. She wore three rows of looped rings on each ear and had a leather necklace festooned with blue beads and cowrie shells. She had a brightly colored orange wrapper and shrewd light brown eyes that observed them closely. She might have been forty or even fifty, but her smooth bronze skin made it difficult to tell.

"*As-salaam alaikum,*" Wale said.

The woman paused, and then said: "*Alaikum salaam.*"

She began speaking rapidly in a language Bracket didn't understand.

"What is she saying?" Bracket whispered.

"I don't speak Fulfulde," Wale said. He responded with a few words in Pidgin, and soon they were talking back and forth.

"What's she saying?" Seeta asked.

"My Pidgin is a little out of date. I haven't spoken it for twenty years."

"Well?"

"Don't be so impatient, young lady. These things take time. I can try to translate."

The woman was watching them closely and repeated whatever phrase she'd said before. "My name is Durel. How did you find us?"

Wale explained to her, with a lot of gesturing, how they'd found the location through the use of the meteorite they had found.

"You found a Songstone," Durel said. "It belongs to us."

Wale clutched at the pocket of his suit and said something.

Durel recoiled at Wale's words, and the other women moved in closer, their aurae building around them.

"What did you say, Wale?" Bracket asked.

"I told them we found a monomict brecciated eucrite. It belongs to the Nok, to learned people who can read and write, not to ignorant murderers."

"Give it to them, Wale," Seeta ordered.

"Why should I? It's not theirs!"

"Don't be absurd. Who else does it belong to?"

Bracket grabbed the stone from Wale's pocket as the scientist leaned against him.

"Don't you touch that!" Wale protested.

Bracket held out the stone in his hand for Durel, but before she could grab it, Wale stepped in front of her.

"What the hell, Wale, do you want to get us all killed?"

"They're traders," he said. "You don't just give things away, even if you think that it belongs to them, which it doesn't." He spoke to Durel again directly, who watched him and nodded.

One of the women left the group and retreated down one of the tunnels. She came back carrying Wale's cane. Durel handed it to him, and he reluctantly gave her the meteorite. Wale continued translating in his broken Pidgin.

"Have you awakened it?" Durel asked.

"What does she mean by awakened?" Seeta asked.

"She wants to know if you were able to provoke a response," Bracket suggested, "to get the meteorite to react in some way."

"We were able to get a reaction between two thousand and twenty-two hundred hertz," Seeta said. "If you'll give me back my recording instruments, I can show you."

"You mean the electronics we found with you," Durel said. "We can't allow you to use them again."

"Why not?"

"Because you can tell people where we are."

"Ask them how many of these Songstones they have," Bracket said.

"They're not Songstones," Wale said, "they're meteorites." Clarence's death seemed to have brought out the curmudgeon in the old scientist.

"Ask her, Wale. Get off your high horse."

"Fine, but it's inaccurate. Durel, how many Songstones do you have?"

"We have eleven stones. With this one, we now have twelve."

The idea crept up on Bracket slowly, and then became a burning question. "Did you find one of the stones in a cracked vase?"

Durel seemed startled, her eyes narrowing. "Yes, we did. What do you know about it?"

"We found it at Naijapool—I mean where I work. One of my workers stole it and disappeared in the same area where we were searching for you. When we got close enough to stop him, we only found blood."

"Yes," Durel said evenly. "We found a stone in one of the tunnels."

"You didn't find anyone with it?"

"We found a thief."

So it was true. The flattened, compressed skin, squeezed of any life—they had killed him, a man whom Bracket had worked beside for months. If they could kill Abdul Haruna so dispassionately, they could easily kill them too.

"We were protecting ourselves from him," she continued. "We can use the stones to find other stones. They respond to each other. That is how we knew there was a stone at the spaceport."

"The spaceport?" Bracket said.

"That's why we went there. We did not intend to hurt anyone. We didn't know that you would learn how to use it."

The other women began speaking to Durel now in their language and she suddenly retreated.

"Wait!" Seeta said. "Please tell us more. You've been here for hundreds of years. Where are the rest of your people? Where are the men? Where are the children?"

Durel finished conferring with the others, who began singing in low voices. Soon they were surrounded by their aurae again, and their faces were not friendly. They enrobed the three scientists in one of their songs, ushering them through the tunnel for several minutes until they arrived at a large chamber lined with stone humanoid statues that towered over them. Here, the walls were also covered in inscriptions that Bracket couldn't make any sense of. The heads of the statues looked partly like birds, with beaks that wrapped around them like a phallus or a snake. All the sculptures were hewn from the rock, and he could see depressions where there might once have been inlaid stones or jewels. Wale marveled over the stretched, wiry limbs and stylized, elongated necks.

"Magnificent." He scurried about reading the text, which looped and circled and seemed to follow no logical pattern. "There should be enough script in here to decipher their language entirely. This structure must have been carved from sound: either by the meteorites themselves, or some means of amplifying their energy. If you look closely, you can see no evidence of scraping or chiseling." He began waving his cane over the inscriptions, presumably snapping images. "I'm going to record this moment. This is a major discovery. Possibly the greatest discovery in African archaeology."

Bracket carefully removed his Geckofone from his pocket, checking for a signal. But nothing was getting through the tons of magnetite above them. "I don't think we're under the spaceport anymore. It says we've walked two kilometers since we've been underground."

"But why would they build this underground in the first place?" Seeta asked. "It's like a hidden cave. If the civilization was as powerful as Wale suggested, it wouldn't need to hide."

"The seat of power of many Nigerian cultures remained hidden from view in order to imbue their leaders with spiritual strength," Wale observed. "Even in Europe, ordinary people rarely saw or spoke with royalty. Of course, it may not have been hidden. You saw the dust storm outside. Over a thousand years of Harmattan winds, it's possible the structure was buried. It may also have served as a defense of some kind—you can tell from the moisture in the air that there is a natural spring here, a source of moisture, which would have been valuable. It's difficult to be sure without exploring the structure. I think the inscriptions might tell us more."

"This isn't the time for that," Bracket said. "We need to get out of here."

"You got us into this trouble, Wale," Seeta added. "They could tell what you thought of them, and now we're stuck here."

Wale turned from the wall, suddenly angry. "They killed Clarence. I don't owe them an apology. He has a family back in Cape Town, now a family without a father. They should apologize. And they should give those meteorites back before they do any more harm, not just to us, but to themselves too. This is no place for amateurs."

"How are you so sure that they're not the Nok?"

"I know Fulfulde when I hear it. They carve calabashes and wood, not stone."

"But they know how to use the Songstones—"

"Meteorites."

"—someone must have taught it to them."

Wale grunted, conceding this point. He scraped at his teeth with a toothpick he'd produced from somewhere. As they sat there thinking through their predicament, one of the women returned with two calabashes of millet porridge and a tin cup full of water. It was the same girl Bracket had seen in the market, and she'd stuck a large silver hairpin into her braided hair. She wore a necklace of talismans, little leather pouches and twisted amulets with crisscrossing stiches. Bracket realized he hadn't eaten since breakfast and reached for one of the bowls, slurping it down. Wale waved away the bowl but sipped at the water.

"Wait!" Seeta said. She pointed at the girl's belly. "Baby. You're having a baby. Tell her, Wale."

"I'm sure she knows that already."

"Translate it!"

Wale reluctantly translated. The girl stepped back, pulling out a Songstone and dangling it before herself on a chain. She sang quick notes, sharply and perfectly on pitch, and the dirt clung to her aura and shrouded her from view.

"Where are the men of your group?" Seeta insisted. "Where are the rest of you?"

The girl, almost hovering, swiveled and left the room too quickly for a human to walk, leaving the three of them behind.

"We need to find something to trade them," Wale declared.

"Oh, quit it with your Nigerian prejudices."

"We have been dealing with other tribes for thousands of years. What we say about the Wodaabe, we learned by dealing with the Wodaabe."

"Everything you learned about them is negative."

"No, the Wodaabe are excellent herdsmen and bush doctors. They make the loveliest calabashes." He pointed to one of the calabashes of millet, which was intricately carved with starlike patterns. "They're experts in awl-carving. Also their camels are top-notch."

"When did you ever buy a camel?"

"You're missing the point."

"Missing something," Bracket muttered. He spent the time searching the capacious chamber for another exit, but the room seemed to have only the one entrance. It was easy for him to imagine that it had once been a place where rituals were performed, owing to the fire pit, and the smell of woodsmoke, and the cold, secret damp, and the reverent feeling the statues instilled in him. Wale continued examining the inscriptions and rooted through the shards that had fallen from the base of the statues, grumbling to himself. Seeta seemed to be trying to figure out where she went wrong with the girl and softly tried to imitate the song she had been singing.

After some time, Wale grew tired of snapping images of the room, bundled up his blazer as a pillow, and took a nap, laying his cane over his chest. Bracket poked around in the fire pit to see if he could find anything of interest, watching tiny clouds of ash rise up and spill back to the ground. Time passed slowly. The girl returned to fetch their calabashes. She lingered about, watching them.

"Where do you come from?" the girl said in English.

Wale jerked awake and repeated what he had explained before, telling her about the meteorite and how they came from the spaceport.

"But this white man isn't from Kano. The woman isn't from Nigeria. Where do you come from?"

"I'm a Yankee," Bracket corrected. "I'm from the United States."

The girl watched him closely as he spoke, out of curiosity or revulsion, he couldn't tell. He couldn't read anything in her dark brown eyes.

"I'm from India," Seeta said. She pointed at the brown patterns covering the girl's hands. "We have henna like that in India."

The girl nodded but kept her eyes on Bracket. "I'm Balewa," she said, and left.

"Well, that was bloody obvious," Seeta said.

"What was obvious?"

"Did you see the way she looked at you?"

"No."

"God, you're thick. She was all over you."

"Nigerians don't go for my type."

"The Wodaabe love a long, thin nose and white teeth," Wale said from his pillow, half asleep. "Also light skin."

"But I wasn't using my Wodaabe identity," he said.

"Keep your pants on," Seeta said. "We're still prisoners here."

"It's just—well, huh."

"Stay away from Wodaabe," Wale advised. "They're not worth the trouble."

"Next time they come back, Wale, let Kwesi ask her what they're doing here."

"Why me?"

"Because she'll listen to you."

"I think you're blowing this out of proportion. She didn't make a pass at me. She's pregnant."

"Try it."

Bracket dug around in the fire pit some more and found what looked like a fossilized chicken bone. He felt like he was wallowing in a nightmare and out of it might erupt a vision of a lady in a lake or a monster from the deep. He twirled the chicken bone until he started thinking it looked more like a finger than a drumstick. And it bothered him that the bone was warm to the touch in this cold purgatory. He peered down into the fire pit, thinking that it wasn't meant for fires at all, scratching until he found more small bones flayed out like a wing. Steam rose up the deeper he dug.

Sure enough, Balewa returned, this time with a small calabash of groundnuts, which she placed at Bracket's feet without looking him in the eye. He waited for her to retreat before picking up the bowl. He passed the bowl around to Seeta and Wale as the girl waited. Then he said, Wale translating: "Balewa, I'd like to speak with you for a moment."

She retreated a step. "Yes?"

"We're sorry that we offended you. We're scientists. Asking questions is part of our profession."

She nodded, again without looking him in the eye.

"Can you tell us what you're doing here? Maybe we can help you, if you need it."

Making some show of it by pounding his cane into the floor and clearing his throat, Wale asked Balewa to tell her story. She looked back and forth among the three scientists, assessing how much she should say, Bracket guessed. She got up and went down the tunnel, and he could overhear her speaking softly with one of the other women. She came back with a woven mat and sat down upon it in one smooth motion, her belly swelling to the side.

"I'm allowed to tell you some things, but not all of them."

"That's fine," Bracket said. She nodded, making it clear that she wasn't actually looking for his approval.

"We're called the Wodaabe," she began, "and we have roamed this area for many generations. We raise cattle, goats, sheep, and camels, and we live like birds in the wild, moving from place to place. Our men and boys raise our cattle and plot our migrations, and we women manage the house, the *suudu*. Every year we follow the rains to nurture our herds, and every year we celebrate the end of the year with our cousins at the Geerewol, our most important ceremony."

She didn't look anyone directly in the eye as she spoke and glanced over her shoulder from time to time. Every once in a while, the eldest woman, Durel, would lean into the room with a suspicious look.

"We lived this way for as long as we can remember," Balewa added, "following the migration routes. Not long ago, we began to hear that some bad men were coming into our lands, men who slaughtered cattle and stole children. So we planned our routes to avoid them."

"The Jarumi," Seeta said.

Balewa sucked in her teeth. "That's what we call them. Our men are excellent scouts and they made sure that we never encountered these people. This meant that sometimes our pastures weren't as green as we needed for the cattle, but they still grazed enough to fill their udders with milk, and we had secret watering holes that we used during drought, as we always have. One day, a man came to our village whom we hadn't seen in some time. His name was Latif, and he had once been part of our lineage before he fell on hard times when his cattle died from plague. He had left for the city to make a new life there as a trader, and we had learned that he'd married a girl he met in the marketplace. Many of us had known Latif as a young man. So we were all quite surprised when he arrived at our encampment after we hadn't seen him for several years. He looked very bad. Before he left for the city, he had bright, flashing eyes and strong arms, and he had always paid close attention to his manner of dress, being one of the most popular dancers at the Geerewol. Now his clothes were in poor condition and his teeth had grown yellow from smoking tobacco. He had a red armband around his forearm. But we don't abandon anyone who leaves us, especially if they wish to return, so our men welcomed him back, saying, *'On jabbaama, on jabbaama'*—even killing a small goat for him to eat, since he was clearly hungry. We should have suspected that something was wrong when he ate all of the food, because it's not polite for a guest to finish all of the food offered to him."

Shouldn't have finished that porridge, Bracket thought.

"Our men spoke with Latif for some time, and they found his answers very strange. He wouldn't tell them where he was living or what had happened to his wife in the city. He also acted differently. Latif was always loved for his *togu*, his charm and good manners, but he had become quiet and bitter. After finishing his tea, he excused himself and called someone on a mobile phone. When the men asked him about it, he only said he was talking to some friends. We didn't think too much of it since we use phones to call ahead to watering holes if we can find a signal.

"We were preparing tea the next morning—it was chilly—when our dog began barking. The men had just gotten onto their camels to take out the herds." She paused, swallowing. She seemed to be steeling herself, deciding whether to go on, and looked over at Durel, who moved away down the hallway. "We saw trucks arriving in the distance, with the dust clouds rising behind them like a sandstorm. The first thing they did was shoot my husband. I saw him slump in the saddle of his camel, and then they shot his camel too, as if for sport, like children playing at a game. There were ten large trucks. Our men formed up in their camels to try to stop them, but we only carried swords because we're not a fighting people. They were gunned down right before our eyes. We gathered together in the *suudu* of Durel, who was the strongest woman among us—she has the most *munyal*, as we call it, of all of us. But the men soon came to the *suudu* and Latif joined them. We knew then that Latif had betrayed us, that he had told them our location because he knew our routes, and because the bandits were friendly with him when they arrived.

"These were terrible men. They all wore red armbands. Latif came after me and raped me."

"Oh no," Seeta said.

But Balewa kept speaking as if she were talking about someone else. "We were all attacked. After he raped me, I was beaten many times and lost consciousness. When I awoke, the men were loading our children onto the trucks along with all the young girls, many of whom were much too young to marry. We managed to run away into the bush while they were distracted and hid behind some bramble. They shot the remaining cattle as they drove in the direction of our next watering hole."

Seeta moved over to comfort Balewa, but she shrugged her away. She did not want sympathy.

"Aren't you Muslim?" Bracket asked. "Why would they attack you?"

"They called us infidels. Latif said we were heathens who knew nothing of the Koran and told us we believed only what we wished to believe. We said that it's written that you can fight those who stand in the way of God, but that you aren't permitted to be the aggressor. But Latif only replied that we were the aggressors for not following the way of God. He could interpret everything we said to make us out to be infidels—his mind had been twisted by his time in the city.

"Five of us escaped. We waited until we were sure they were far away, then we began walking to the south toward Lake Chad. Some generous people were kind enough to give us food and water, but they were poor and couldn't share much, and they warned us that the Jarumi had attacked them too, so we continued walking south through the bush, staying out of sight. We knew how to find other lineages on the migration routes, but with Latif among them, he would know every watering hole and pasture. So we continued south until we came to Kano. We managed to sell some of our medicines for food in the city, but we were afraid to stay in town because we saw that Wodaabe women were treated very badly, forced to sell their own bodies to survive. We traded our medicines in the marketplace during the day and retreated to the safety of the bush at night, where we would sleep in the open air.

"One night, we built a fire to keep warm, and we began singing songs to try to pick up our mood. And as we sang, it was as if the ground itself were pulling on our chests. The next thing we knew, one of the tunnels opened to us. That is how we found this place."

"Is that how you found the meteorites?" Wale asked.

"They were here when we arrived, waiting for us, a gift, I believe, from our ancestors. We learned how to use them. This place is made from music—everything about it. We practice for the day when we'll see Latif again so we can bring him to justice."

"Are you carrying his child?" Seeta interjected.

Balewa rose from her mat, rolling it up neatly. "I'm sorry that I can't tell you more." She began collecting the bowl of groundnuts.

"I know where the Songstones came from," Wale said.

"You do?" Balewa asked.

"If you tell the others to come, I can show you."

Bracket glanced over at Seeta, wondering if Wale had hidden some secret from them.

"What proof do you have?" Balewa asked.

"My proof is that I found you here. I've been trying to find this place for years. I know how it works and how it was created. If you bring the others, I will tell you."

She quickly got to her feet and left. The swiftness of her exit left the room feeling cold, the damp air closing in on them; a decision had been made they didn't yet understand.

"She'll be back," Wale said assuredly.

"I thought you said we had nothing to offer them," Seeta whispered.

"I just thought of something."

"Be careful, Wale," Bracket said. "What are you going to tell them?"

"You'll see."

Bracket's eyes turned back to the fire pit. He bent over it and began clawing out the dirt in fistfuls. The chicken bones he'd seen. They looked far too old to have been eaten by the women recently, but he sensed the power of the place, the hidden, torrential energy waiting to be sprung at any moment. More of the bones of the animal came up, some of them charred. This was a goat maybe. Every time his fingers plunged deeper, he felt the sharp prick of another bone.

"They didn't make fires here," he said.

"Of course they didn't," Wale said. "There isn't any ventilation."

"Then what is this pit for?" Seeta asked.

"Sacrifices," Bracket said.

Saying it aloud startled them all out of their stupor. Wale hobbled over and poked around in the pit with his cane. "You're right. The carbon traces you'd normally find around a real fire are missing. But these animals weren't killed by these women. The bones are too old." He pointed to the wall behind one of the statues. "There are lines that run to the ceiling, grooves in the wall. They're flecked with breccia rock from the meteorites, annealed to the wall by heat."

Bracket saw the grooves now, which vaulted the chamber in obsidian-black.

"Balewa said this entire place was made for music," Seeta said. "The grooves may be designed to amplify the stones. It's an old technique found in temples around the world, to design the room to strengthen the acoustics to create sounds that would reach the gods. The acoustic architecture can create a B tone of two close frequencies to induce a meditative state. With the Songstones, the effect would be much more powerful."

"Powerful enough to kill a goat," Bracket said. "Or maybe us."

"They wouldn't do that to us," Seeta objected.

"They have no reason to trust us."

"They're not killers. They're afraid."

"Then why did they kill Clarence?" Wale asked.

That's what bothered Bracket, the fear of these women, and what might have happened to that fear as they seethed without their children or their families or their way of life. No one opening their arms to them in the cold night except to take advantage. Fear like that could grow into something else.

"It's a shame," Wale said, following the same train of thought. "This would have been one of the greatest archaeological discoveries of our time. An African discovery by Africans, not some gentleman explorer. These women are slowly destroying the place by inhabiting it, damaging the scientific record. Instead it's an African discovery ruined by Africans. We have no respect for our own past."

Bracket couldn't blame the women for being traumatized by what happened, nor for the horror they had faced. It would twist your mind, upturn your sense of right and wrong, especially when they could no longer follow their migration routes. They used to find spiritual guidance in the lowing of the cattle, the comfort of their friends and family as they drank from the well. All of these lodestars were gone for them. They were probably frightened, alone, and angry.

Balewa returned with the other women, who retreated behind her in what seemed like defensive positions, each of them carrying a Songstone.

"Do not be alarmed," Wale warned, picking up his cane. "My cane will create an image on this rock wall here. It is not dangerous." With a quick shift of his fingers, he projected the same images he had shown Bracket earlier of the ancient artwork with the solar flare from a thousand years ago. He also showed them pictures and descriptions of the Nok in colonial and Arabic texts, as well as the astrolabe, narrating along as he did so. The women watched all this impassively, but Bracket could see that at least Balewa was interested.

"So you see," Wale concluded, "your Songstones were activated by a solar flare. Or I should say reactivated. Those are charged particles emanating from the sun itself. The meteorites are possessed of a powerful energy, and the solar flare that struck the world last year must have ignited them again. All of these so-called magical properties can be explained by modern science."

He slid his hand down his cane as if cleaning it of some dirt. The tip of it let out a spark, and two bolts of electricity shot toward Durel, who collapsed on the ground. Her legs began convulsing.

"Wale! What are you doing?" Bracket shouted.

"Getting us out of here!"

He fired the Taser from his cane one more time but missed, and the women were already protecting themselves with the aurae of their Songstones. They were entirely coated in the crackling shields of their own voices. They forced Wale to move first, transporting him onto the fire pit. He dropped his cane and began hurling insults at them. Strips of their aurae leapt to the wall like charges of electricity and shot along the meteorite ribs to disappear somewhere in the statues. They pinned back Bracket and Seeta to the far wall as Wale writhed in the middle. Wale put up a tremendous fight, screaming in anger as he banged against the nebulous prison surrounding him. They amplified their music to an awful intensity and clapped so that the polyrhythms played off each other in the chamber. Now their fields created a blue-green channel to the grooves on the walls. The eyes of the statues began to flicker.

"Wait!" Bracket cried. "I can find them!" It was as if his throat were caked in ash. He felt the pressure on his lungs, but forced his voice to open up. "Your children! I can find your children! I know where they are!"

The crackling aurae quieted down. Balewa began pleading with the others, until they too stopped their singing. Wale fell to the middle of the pit, and Seeta rushed over to help him up. The scientist's face was exhausted from the effort, ashen and drained of blood. He wouldn't be able to survive another attack. The side of his body that wasn't paralyzed winced in pain.

"Tell them, Wale," Bracket said. "Tell them I can find their children."

The scientist half whispered the translation.

"How do you know where they are?" Durel asked.

"I saw some children in the city. Two children about ten years old, wearing the same red armband you describe."

"Did they tell you their names?"

"I didn't ask," Bracket said. How could he tell them that their loved ones had become child soldiers? "But Latif must be with them. He's as dangerous to us as he is to you. He may destroy our rockets and everything we've fought to build here. They're coming this way right now."

"We trusted this old man, and he hurt us."

"Please—go see for yourselves. We'll come with you if you like. No lies. No trickery."

The women discussed it among themselves, and he could see no change in their mien. It had been a gamble, but he had nothing to lose, given that they were slated for execution or whatever euphemism the women had called it in their language. Bracket looked at Balewa hopefully, but he knew that she wouldn't make the final decision. It was the eldest one, Durel, whom Wale had just shot with hundreds of volts of electricity into her skin.

Finally, Durel said: "You'll accompany us until we find the Jarumi. But the old man will remain here."

"He's in no condition to stay here after what you did to him."

"No further harm will come to him if you keep your word."

Bracket looked at Wale, who seemed too tired to stand up by himself. "I need a good working flashlight," Wale said in a quiet voice, "and food and water if I'm going to get any proper work done down here."

Seeta gave the old man a hug. "We'll come back for you, Wale."

"Come back with some latex gloves, a duster, and an archival program. All archaeology is destruction. The least we can do is properly catalog what we've found. We're ruining history with every breath we take."

CHAPTER 25

They followed the Wodaabe women through the tunnels for a long while before Balewa lifted her Songstone and sang a short melody that parted the very rock before them. Sand fell into the passageway as the entrance split, and Bracket and Seeta found themselves far outside the spaceport amid the scrubland. He realized they had passed the entire night underground. The mid morning sun blazed in their eyes, causing them to squint, and they could smell smoke in the air—the scent of burning plastic. The Harmattan had coated the landscape in a fine layer of silt, but the winds had died down, leaving an eerie calm.

One of the Wodaabe women hissed something, and everyone instantly squatted to their knees, causing the scientists to crouch too.

"What is it?" Bracket whispered, forgetting that the women couldn't understand him.

But they didn't need to. "Jarumi," Durel mouthed.

Keeping his head low, Bracket stole a look in the direction she was pointing and saw a caravan of Jeeps and cargo trucks spread out before them in the distance. There were perhaps fifty different vehicles, all in different states of repair: some were riddled with bullet holes, while others were burned-out shells from mortar fire. There were another ten or fifteen *okada* motorcycles zipping up and down the length of the caravan, the riders shouldering machine guns. The trucks themselves weren't moving, though. The entire caravan appeared to have stopped. Indeed, he could see smoke billowing up near the vehicles, where women were cooking a meal, the soldiers hovering nearby.

He hadn't expected them to be so close. If anything, he had hoped the Jarumi would still be in Kano, held back by Detective Idriss and his men.

Not far from the caravan, Bracket spied the scarred wreckage of a large aircraft. It was still smoking, and the charred body of the pilot—it might have been a woman, maybe a man—had its hands fixed to the gear stick, as if preparing to fly itself into the afterlife. Bloodied bodies were scattered beside it, either victims of the crash or all indiscriminately murdered, and covered in a layer of thick sand from the dust storm, looking like the petrified dead after a volcanic eruption.

The Jarumi must have taken the aircraft down, he realized. Maybe shot it, or perhaps—yes, there, in the sky far above him, he saw three eagles wheeling in the wind, scanning for hostile drones. The birds might have done something to the plane, although he couldn't say how. He anxiously looked back toward the spaceport, where the *Masquerade* was affixed to the two Indian rockets, its nose pointed toward the sky.

"Josephine wouldn't have fueled the rockets yet," Seeta whispered. "Not with the Jarumi so close by."

The perimeter fence was intact, and the guns in the guard towers also seemed to be operational, as far as he could tell, but the guards weren't firing. The Jarumi must have been out of their range. And looking more closely, he spotted some crumpled bodies not far from the perimeter. The Jarumi had probably launched an attack and then been repulsed, and were now reconsidering their strategy. Meanwhile, no one would be getting in or out of the spaceport.

That's when Bracket remembered his Geckofone and discreetly turned it on again by rubbing its back with his four fingertips in his pocket.

"Can you get a signal?" Seeta asked.

"No. Nothing. We should be in range."

"They could be jamming our communications."

"Then they're cutting us all off."

Looking more closely at the road where the caravan was situated, he began to understand—it seemed to be a dirt path that snaked deep into the Sahel. The Jarumi would have been expected to move along the main highway from Kano and to attack the spaceport from the entrance road. Instead they must have flanked the city on backroads to attain the much larger prize of the spaceport; if they could gain control of that, the rockets, the *Masquerade*, and even the mission itself could fund an entire army of rebels for years, outfitted with the most advanced weapons. For the time being, the Jarumi had laid siege to the spaceport and were locked in a stalemate.

Next to him, the Wodaabe women were also carefully studying the caravan, their silver hairpins and loop earrings glinting in the sun.

Bracket pointed at his arm, encircling it with his fingers. "Armband—see? They have the same armband. The children are there."

Close to where the women were cooking a meal, a group of children were sitting sullenly together smoking cigarettes. He tried to explain to her that there were more of them, and they were now soldiers, but she didn't understand him.

"You may not like what you find has happened to them," he said aloud.

The women consulted among themselves and pointed up at the sun, tracing an arc across the sky.

"They want to wait," Seeta guessed.

"For what?" Bracket asked.

But Durel seemed uncomprehending.

"They'll try to get back their children," Seeta said.

"Let us help you," Bracket insisted. "We can get support. Weapons." Him gesturing through all of this like a mime. "We can get more people." But even as he was saying it, he knew the women wouldn't trust him anyway, not after Wale had attacked Durel with his cane. Balewa reopened the entrance to the tunnel, surpris-

ing him by using the Songstone outside the cave, as if the ability to
activate it in daylight made it more real somehow. They all climbed
back down, where they waited in silence as she closed the portal
behind them.

Twice Balewa reopened the entrance to the tunnel, only to have
the other women decide that something wasn't right. One of them
left down a tunnel and returned with porridge for all of them.
Bracket fell into a dreamless sleep as the women ate peacefully in
silence. He awoke when Balewa opened the passageway again, and
the sky was turning a deep cobalt blue. The women started walking into the crepuscule, with Bracket and Seeta following behind.

"We should send everyone we can to help," Bracket hissed. "The
Jarumi have guns. Powerful weapons."

"Kwesi—"

"They want to let themselves get butchered?" He pointed at
Balewa's bulging stomach. "She's pregnant, Seeta. She's in no condition to fight!"

"They want to do it their way."

The women removed their sandals as they moved through the
scratchy bushes of the flat Sahel, padding along quietly, and soon
he could barely find their silhouettes in the dusk. He crouched back
down with Seeta.

"Can you get this entrance back open?" Seeta asked him.

"No. I couldn't catch the tune."

"They're two distinct melodies, I think: one on the way in and
one on the way out. But it was too subtle for me."

"Then we'll have to wait for them," Bracket concluded.

"Still can't get a signal on your G-fone?"

"Nothing."

"We should alert Josephine that they're out there."

"I'll have to send it manually."

He wrote a message for Josephine:

We're okay. Hold your fire.

He figured he should at least buy the Wodaabe women some time. He set the G-fone down in the dirt, and it began scurrying off into the bush, Bracket hoping that it would draw enough heat from the ground as the temperature began to drop, because its battery was already low. He composed countless other messages in his mind but could think of none that would set Josephine at ease. Because he himself wasn't at ease—the women were no longer in sight.

CHAPTER 26

The five Wodaabe women paced quickly away from the tunnel, melting into the scrubland. Bracket hadn't noticed when Abir and Balewa exchanged glances after he had offered his help. Unlike that loudmouthed man, Wale, who had lied when he assaulted Durel with his cane, Balewa trusted the other two. She found that the white man with the deep voice had delivered on every promise he had made, and he seemed to be the moderating force in their group. But the scientists had not practiced singing with them, and indeed seemed to have no musical ability, meaning that they would not be reliable with a Songstone.

As they pushed through the bush, Balewa reminded the others of their stratagem and the names of the songs they would use to unleash their stones. They had all washed their bodies with water infused with the bark of the *tanni* tree to protect against sorcery, and they consulted the talismans strung around their necks and ankles for courage in the face of danger. The cave had allowed them to rehearse freely with the stones, but the fresh air would present new problems, because there would be no amplification other than their own lungs. She thought this might rattle the other women, who would perhaps lose their focus.

In fact the opposite seemed to be happening. As they plunged deeper into the wilderness, they recalled their days roaming the lands to the north. The vegetation was familiar. The soil under their feet felt similar. They found their old alertness coming back, sensing odors on the wind and hearing the rustle of the grasses. Here Abir noticed a twig bent by a cow; there, Durel spied a pile of goat dung, about three months old. Herders must have moved through here and left.

"We're here for the children," Durel reminded them.

"We're with you," they all replied.

This had been the one condition upon which Durel had agreed to participate, that they were not to become murderers like the militants. They were only going to demand what was theirs by right.

"Let's begin," Balewa said. She wanted the women to use their Songstones well before they came within sight of the Jarumi. Together they began humming in unison, crouching down low, and she was pleased that the aurae surrounded them correctly as they had practiced. They were soon immersed in a tunnel of multicolored light and sound that amplified the fading colors of the foliage around them.

Ahead of her, she caught sight of a flame as a militant lit a cigarette. He was less than fifty paces away.

"Abir," she said.

Abir began to clap softly, humming all the while. The aura strengthened, a blue haze cutting through the light brown earth.

"Durel."

Durel started clapping a slightly different rhythm, and the other women soon added a third and a fourth rhythm, so that all of them were clapping and singing softly to the beat. Balewa would join in last because when she sang no one would be able to speak anymore, and they could indicate only with their eyes where they intended to go. In the cave, they had tried to communicate through lyrics but that required improvisation that made them lose their focus.

Balewa let the chorus build around them, the aurae strengthening until it began crushing back the vegetation. Dust clustered and swirled.

It was time. Now Balewa added her voice to theirs, stringing together the various rhythms with a sensuous harmony. She took a step forward and the women rushed from their cover among the scrubs. They startled a group of men who were busy stoking a fire. One of them raised his gun and Balewa hurled her aura around him. The bullets ricocheted within it, until he fell. His companions rose to their feet but were surrounded before they could discharge their weapons. The militants still couldn't see who they were and shielded their eyes from the spitting dust. To them, it looked as if a small tornado had swarmed from the scrubland. One man hurled something in their direction in desperation, but Abir surrounded it in midair and it disappeared in a white explosion, shaking the ground with the force.

Focus, Balewa thought. *Focus on the music. We are here for the children.*

Next they came across some women and girls locked inside a makeshift cage, where they were guarded on all sides by men and dogs. Many of the girls had only just begun to form breasts, and yet their bellies swelled. *Pregnant. Pregnant like me.*

She split off from the other women to confuse the guards. The men shouldered their rifles more quickly this time and began firing. But they should have looked behind them. Abir flung her aura until these men too tumbled to the ground in agony after being struck by their own bullets. Then Durel, of all people, swept in and crushed their legs with a blast so powerful it stung Balewa's ears.

All about them now, the Jarumi soldiers rushed this way and that in confusion, thinking it was a coordinated attack. One group of men leapt into a truck to escape, but Balewa punctured their tires with a shrill note.

"Tell me where the children are!" she shouted.

"That way," one man said, terrified. "Over there."

The children were kept in a corral made from bramble and bushes, just like those they used to build their *suudu* during the migrations. The young boys and girls were of varying ages, but before the Wodaabe women could search their faces, some women in the corral surrounded them protectively and held them back with their arms. These women didn't seem as frightened as the others they had found being held prisoner earlier. They were all wearing niqabs, covering their arms and faces, instead of the customary hijabs. Suddenly they parted and Latif rose from behind them holding a rifle.

She ducked out of the way as Latif squeezed off several rounds. This time it was Abir who maintained her pulse, belting out a blast that knocked Latif from his feet. Balewa scrambled to her feet to grab Latif's rifle, but one of his wives picked it up and pointed it at her.

She had not expected this, and Abir kept humming while glancing at Balewa for instruction.

Laughing, Latif slowly climbed to his feet. He had wrapped a bandolier around his shoulder, and his eyes were half asleep, glazed over from marijuana smoke.

"She'll kill you if I say so," he said in their Fulfulde dialect.

"We won't let her," Balewa replied.

"You think that you're here to rescue them, don't you? But they don't want to be rescued."

"That's a lie," Balewa said.

"It's God's truth." He motioned with his neck and the girl pulled the trigger. But the Wodaabe were prepared. They launched a dust cloud at the girl until she couldn't see, then they knocked the rifle from her hands with quick bursts of sound. Latif tripped over his own legs as the dust pelted his eyes.

Balewa looked into his long, malnourished face—a face that had once enchanted beauty contests at the Geerewol—and remembered his tobacco-stained teeth when he had forced himself upon her. She thought of the infant kicking in her belly and how it would have the soul of a coward.

"Stand up," she said, as the other women continued to chant and clap around them.

"You can't stop what I've begun," he said. "These children will defend me to the death."

It was true, she realized. She could recognize the loyalty in the children's eyes. They would protect him. These girls must have been his wives, and she realized that the other children also seemed suspicious of their intentions, as if they were the attackers and not the other way around.

"Tell them how you raped me!" she said. "Tell them how you betrayed your own clan!"

Latif's face pulled into a scowl, and he spat in her direction. "You don't even deserve the seed I've put in your filthy womb!"

So he knows, Balewa thought. He knew that she could be the mother of one of his own children yet still thought nothing of killing her. She couldn't will herself to sing again in the face of such selfishness and cruelty. It was as if he had swallowed the very music from the air.

"We know the true way," he went on. "We gave these girls something they never had: money, security, and the comfort of God. What do you offer them? Nothing! Poverty, shame, and hunger. All while the government spends billions of cowries on going into space! We are right here, living on Earth, and no one is providing for us. No one except God. God gives us what we need. God provides them with husbands and dowries and all the food their children can eat."

"God does not order you to kill," Balewa retorted. "God does not order you to steal."

"He takes from the greedy. We're going to take the food from the nonbelievers at the spaceport, and we'll sell the rest. Nothing you can do will stop us."

But Durel had heard enough. "Shut up, Latif," she interrupted. "Give us back our children."

She inspected the children, scanning their faces, searching for any sign of recognition. She shouted out their names: "Mohammed? Tambaya? Boubacar?"

"We sold them a long time ago," Latif scoffed.

"Where? Where did you sell them?"

"You're all apostates! We'll bring all nonbelievers to justice under God's will! We'll serve God with a new generation of true followers! There's nothing you can do to stop us!"

"We've heard enough, Latif," Durel snapped. "I nursed you myself when you were a child, and this is your thanks to us. This is how you treat people from your own clan, who loved and supported you. It's time for you to face justice."

Now Durel led the song with a ferocity that caused Latif to cower before her. He tried to scuttle away like a land crab, plugging his ears to protect himself against the sound. But there was nowhere else to go.

CHAPTER 27

Dusk fell rapidly, and soon it was growing so black that Bracket could barely make out the silhouettes of the bushes stenciling the Sahel. Above them the stars speckled the sky, each one sharp and distinct. This was the sky the Nok had lived under, the stars that caravanserai had followed across the desert, guided to the kingdom by their astrolabes bearing jade and turmeric and cornelian. Here they would have discovered rich music that melted rock itself.

Seeta perked up beside him.

"I can hear them. They're coming back."

The women returned through the bush dragging along Latif, a tall, lanky man who whimpered as he was half marched, half carried to the entrance to the tunnel. They looked weary and their braids were covered with dust from the fight, with globules of blood splashed here and there on their wrappers. Bracket realized as they brought the man closer, with revulsion, that they had crushed one of his ankles.

"Oh no," Seeta observed. "They're alone."

Their children weren't there. He could see the bitter disappointment in their faces. One of them, Abir, buckled over and began crying aloud, her chest heaving. They all grieved together in the starlight.

"Spaceman," Latif said when he saw Bracket, wincing as the women prodded him forward. He motioned with a hand as if launching it into the air. *"Mask-raid."*

"What's that?"

"He's saying *Masquerade*," Seeta explained. "The ship."

So Bello had ignited the imaginations of the Jarumi about space travel too.

Bracket turned to the Wodaabe women. "What will you do with him?"

They pointed toward the tunnel. They would take him back inside.

"And then what?" he asked.

They didn't reply. The bandit cried out from fear as Balewa sang open the entrance and dragged him down below.

When they returned underground, Wale had subdivided the chambers into quadrants, having scratched lines and numbers into the dirt. He was eagerly cataloging what he found in each quadrant: the statues, glyphs, and carvings, even the bones. He pointed to one of the tunnels, which was strewn with rubble and dust.

"It appears that some recent seismic activity weakened the structure of that tunnel considerably," he observed. "The next rocket launch may do even more damage, so we must act quickly." Then, noticing the women: "The children?"

Bracket shook his head. He was the one who had promised the women they would find their stolen children, a promise he should never have made, and he felt partly responsible for the failure, even if they had managed to capture Latif, whose ankle had swollen up like a balloon. Seeta explained to Wale how the women had taken the Jarumi camp with their Songstones, breaking their siege against the spaceport. They had released the rest of the captive women and children, who had set down along the road to Kano.

"It seems the two of you made it out in good stead," Wale said, finally giving them his full attention.

"We're fine," Bracket said.

"Good. I'll need your help maintaining the integrity of this site. There are no radiocarbon dating labs in this country, a situation that I will soon rectify. We can't disturb anything, not until we have preserved samples, especially from quadrants A4 through A10." He ushered them away from those areas. "I humbly ask that you confine your activities to these designated sections."

Wale used his cane to capture images of the quadrants. When he noticed Latif, who was now lying down against the wall, he warned Durel: "You can't go on killing people. It only takes a day to disgrace yourself and you'll feel it for the rest of your lives. That won't bring your families back to you."

"You are free to go," Durel said.

"I'm not going anywhere. I'm going to study this site properly, for the sake of our own history. This discovery deserves careful, responsible documentation."

"Wale," Seeta said, "this isn't up to us. You know what that man did to them."

"He acted like a barbarian. Yes. I understand. But look what they did to Clarence. Did they show him any mercy?"

Bracket now saw that the scientist had dragged his bodyguard into the corner, where his giant frame was turned away from the wall. The man's eyes were closed. It must have been a considerable effort with Wale's paralysis.

"He would have shot them," Seeta said.

"Clarence was defending *me*. Besides, they'll only harm themselves. I've been trying to understand this technology. It's dangerous—dangerous to their enemies and also dangerous to their bodies. Come with me, I'll show you."

He led them down a dark tunnel, which split in two and then split again. He limped to the left for a couple of minutes before it opened to a small chamber with shelves like a catacomb—the same chamber in which Bracket had first arrived with Seeta. The air felt close and heavy. He could still smell the reek of Abdul Haruna's body.

"This is a burial chamber. I've uncovered two of the skeletons. Carefully, of course. You'll see that their legs are folded to the side and their hands rest on their skulls as if they're asleep, a common way of burying the dead among the Nok. But look at this clavicle."

"It's like a bone spur," Bracket said.

"Yes, it's warped. And this skull. That is the cranium itself, you'll see. It's also abnormal."

"It looks like a growth."

"Exactly."

"You're jumping to conclusions," Seeta argued. "You need time to gather more evidence, and then even more time to analyze it. We don't have the tools to understand this place—you said it yourself. You should get some rest. We've been through a lot."

"No, I've said from the beginning that these aren't typical meteorites. I'm not sure what's given them the power they have, but there must be an explanation."

"The carvings amplify the sound," Seeta countered. "So does the architecture of these rooms."

"Yes, but there must be more. They're too powerful. I think the meteorites may have been annealed to isotopes, radioactive isotopes. The charged particles from the Flare reignited the radiation, awakening them, as it were. Every time these women sing, they are probably exposing themselves to more radiation. That's what I believe happened to the Nok. They didn't just disappear. This technology, whatever it is, killed them in the end."

The scientist went to great pains to explain his suspicions to the Wodaabe women, but they seemed not to comprehend or remained unconvinced. And Bracket could understand why. They knew the full power of the Songstones, the energy they had unleashed. They had discovered the strength to shape their own futures. Now Wale wanted to take that strength away from them.

"We need to get going," Bracket said.

"Yes, we should take Clarence's body to his family," Wale agreed, leaning on his cane, suddenly looking old again, exhausted even. They were all tired. "Clarence deserves better. He deserves better than this. No one should be left to die alone here. Not anymore. Not after what we know now."

CHAPTER 28

"How did you do it?" Josephine asked. "We saw light moving near the Jarumi. We captured it in the infrared and UV spectrums, but we saw no bodies, we saw no faces, no weapons. And then you two return here as if everything were perfectly normal. The least you could do is tell me how you chased them away."

"We listened—" Bracket began.

"To our conscience," Seeta chimed in.

"And what conscience is that?" Josephine asked skeptically. "The conscience that had you abandoning your responsibilities right before launch, Dr. Chandrasekhan?"

"Give it up, Josephine," Seeta said, folding her arms. "We're not going to tell you."

They were standing inside the Nest, where Josephine was busy managing the launch from her command chair in the center of the room. She explained that Op-Sec had disarmed the rest of the militants, but nobody could share the specifics of what had happened or why. The militants weren't talking. Neither was Bracket nor Seeta, because they had agreed to keep the Songstones secret for now. The women had been through enough pain already, the scientists figured, and were still reeling from the discovery that the Jarumi had sold off their children like chattel. The Wodaabe had decided to leave Kano altogether to begin their search near Cameroon, where Latif had confessed he had last seen the children.

Besides, it wasn't so easy. Josephine would probably consider the women heroes now because she was in a generous mood, but she might change her opinion of the Wodaabe once she witnessed what they had done to Abdul Haruna and Clarence.

On the main console of the Nest, stretched across the wall, he could see Masha Kornokova suiting up for an EVA walk, preparing to exit from her module so that she could rendezvous with the *Masquerade*. The Naijanauts would no doubt be simulating the rendezvous in Naijapool, which meant it was time for Bracket to get back.

"One more thing," Josephine said, as he and Seeta turned to leave. "Bello's on his way."

"He's safe?" Bracket asked, incredulous.

"He's coming with the NAF. An entire battalion."

"But how?"

"Listened to his conscience probably," she said, and smiled. "Damned if I know. He'll be here at sixteen hundred hours. And he wants to see you, Kwesi. Now, if you please, we have a mission to launch."

The Capstone, as Nurudeen Bello called his offices, was set back from the main compound behind the Nest, surrounded by a moat about two meters deep (it was not filled with water) and ringed with a wire fence behind that. The one-story building was located about fifty paces from the fence. Bello had installed a fountain shaped like an eagle that gurgled clear water. Passing through security, Bracket felt a blast of cool air once he entered the dimly lit vestibule.

There were three rooms inside the building. One served as Bello's office, the second was a vault, and the third was a lounge where the politician could greet visiting dignitaries and investors.

"Come in, Mr. Bracket."

Bello was wearing thick rimless glasses that made his eyeballs seem to pop out. He had on a lightweight gray alpaca suit with a lavender tie, a burst of vivid color against his dark skin. His wide desk was covered with monitors, including one depicting Josephine giving orders in the Nest. He pointed at her as she paced on the screen.

"Josephine tells me," Bello said, "that you rose to the occasion during my absence."

"It was my job to support our mission. We've invested a lot in this space program and it's something I believe in."

Bello chuckled softly to himself, shaking his head. "You sound like a Naijanaut, humble and exactly on message. I thought you were more imaginative than that. You deserve a reward and you'll get one—I can't express my gratitude enough. But is that really how you feel about everything that happened? You were threatened by an intruder in your quarters, according to Op-Sec, and survived an ambush in downtown Kano. And then, by Josephine's account, you personally repelled the Jarumi. Yet somehow you made it out alive with Dr. Chandrasekhan and, I might add, Dr. Wale Olufunmi, one of Africa's foremost archaeologists."

Bracket felt trapped by the voluble politician, who used words so effortlessly to propel himself forward. His movements were slow and measured, but he spoke quickly and eagerly, showing his boundless energy. Bracket, by contrast, was tired of posturing.

"I've been through a hell of a lot, Mr. Bello. I've barely slept and I've seen friends die around me, and frankly I helped save the spaceport because it was the right thing to do. I respect what you've accomplished here, but I think you have some explaining to do yourself—like why you disappeared."

"Now that's more like it, Mr. Bracket. That I can work with."

"Where did you go, Mr. Bello? We thought you had been kidnapped."

Bello raised an eyebrow. "By Senator Kidibe, was it?"

"Well, yes."

"I'm impressed that you figured it out. Kidibe has always been jealous that he hasn't been able to siphon money from the spaceport, like he did as a criminal in the delta region. He knew

I was trying to gather more funds from the Senate for our project, and I suspected he had tapped my Geckofone. He seemed to be one step ahead of me during my negotiations for a budget allocation. So I set a trap for him by making a note on my G-fone that I was going to send a bribe of forty thousand cowries to another senator. A ruse, of course—I had no intention of doing so. Kidibe threatened to expose me for exactly forty thousand—the same amount—so I knew he had infiltrated my device. Now that I was sure he was tracking me, I sent my G-fone with my fiancée to distract him."

"Omotola Taiwo," Bracket said.

"That's right. You've met her—and you did an excellent job with her film, I might add. It nearly forced a vote on the Senate floor if Kidibe hadn't blocked it. I sent Omotola on a diversionary trip to lure away Kidibe and his people. He wasn't going to kidnap me—you're mistaken about that—but he did intend to blackmail me. Extortion is his specialty. By the time he discovered Omotola was traveling by herself, it was too late. Because I had already flown to Yola to convince the Task Force Battalion of the Nigerian Armed Forces to defend the spaceport. They're securing Kano as we speak, watching for stragglers from the Jarumi. But I'll admit that you had made my efforts almost inconsequential by the time I arrived."

Bracket found himself piqued by Bello's scheming when so much had been at risk. "You should have told Josephine, or someone, that you were all right."

"For all I knew, our communications were compromised. There was no easy way for me to tell her when I was in Abuja, not when so much was at stake. And now, thanks to you, I have Kidibe cornered. The Senate will have to approve my request to fund the program beyond the mission."

"I'm glad you're safe," Bracket said, tired of Bello's political games. He lived in a different realm altogether. "I've got to get back to Naijapool to prepare for the launch."

"Always focused on the task at hand. Just like Josephine. I admire that, Mr. Bracket. I'll walk along with you."

Outside the Capstone, warmed by a late-evening breeze, Bello enthusiastically greeted an astronaut as she walked by, taking a moment to congratulate her and wish her luck, even though she was a backup pilot who wouldn't be traveling on the rescue mission. She delighted in the politician's praise, unaware of his far-flung schemes.

"She's not going on the mission," Bracket explained as they continued walking.

"Not on this mission," Bello agreed. "We've got long-term plans for her. I suppose it's time you know why I was *really* in Abuja—before Kidibe intervened, that is. You've proven yourself trustworthy. The rescue mission is hardly worthwhile to build an entire space program around, wouldn't you say? We could have more easily let the Americans or Europeans operate our facilities for the rescue. Or even the Japanese. And, in fact, they even offered."

Bracket contemplated this as Bello smiled and waved at an Indian engineer scurrying from the Nest. He had never questioned Bello's ambition, convinced by his incessant propaganda and visionary thinking. But maybe he should have. "You're talking about proof of concept," he guessed.

"That's it. Proof of concept has value in the market. If we can show that the *Masquerade* can run a successful crewed mission, we can make some cowries off repairing satellites or joy rides for space tourists. But our national ambitions are much greater than that. What is abundant in space that no one else can exploit at the moment? Asteroid mining."

"No one has found a way to make money from that," Bracket objected. "The fuel efficiencies aren't there."

"That's because we've never had a good staging ground to launch missions to capture those resources. And they've never had a country in charge that has thrived on extraction. Nigeria's greatest expertise is oil extraction, and it's been the lynchpin of our economy for decades, for better and for worse. We are experts in monetizing the extraction process."

"I've seen where that money goes," Bracket said. "You only have to look at the potholes on the roads here to know whose pockets have been filled. You'd be no different than Senator Kidibe."

"That was the old mode of operating, Mr. Bracket, one not backed by rigorous contracts and consummate transparency. I'm talking about a new destination, a new launchpad for our ventures: a colossal space station that can be used as a staging ground to accomplish all of those things. The LaGrangian points. It's the place where the gravity of Earth, the moon, and the centripetal forces of the Earth-moon system are balanced. Specifically point L4. The space powers are fixated on L5, so we believe L4 will more than suit our aspirations. We can place hundreds of thousands of tons of objects there and use it to mine the cosmos. It will be a true space station controlled by Africans. The Indians are fully aware of the risks involved, of course. We've got a contract for the next fifty years using their rockets and the *Masquerade* to build the station. They'll take a cut of the profits, but the station will be all ours."

Bracket stepped back to take in the politician, whose limitless optimism continued to fuel his grand vision. It was an ambitious, almost impossible project.

"I think you've lost your mind."

Bello burst out laughing, amused by the thought. "I'm sure you do," he smiled. "I'm sure you do."

They had stopped beneath the bronze replica of the *Masquerade*. Up close, reflected in the spotlights illuminating the statue, Bracket could see the sculptor had mixed silver flecks of mica into the patina coating the thrusters, simulating the ice particles that would form on a real launch.

"So I've shared my crazy secret with you, Mr. Bracket. Now it's time you shared your secret with me. How did you do it? How did you repel the Jarumi? The NAF has reviewed the recordings and found only strange vocalizations, but they can't identify what made them. Was it some new stealth technology? Cybernetics?"

Old technology, Bracket thought. *Not new, but old.*

He watched Bello, trying to determine if, like his other questions, he already knew the answer to this one and was one step ahead in his thinking, laying a trap of sorts. But how could Bracket explain what he'd seen the women do? The elegance of their movements? The power of their voices? Even in the pitched battle, the Wodaabo had refrained from killing anyone, allowing the militants to destroy themselves. And anyway, the scientists had all agreed to keep the Songstones secret until the women had left.

"I can't tell you that."

Bello nodded. "I admire your discretion." He pointed at a stain on a corner of the statue of the *Masquerade.* "See these streaks here? It's blood. Chicken blood, most likely, but possibly blood from a ram. Someone brought it here as an offering during the night, a blessing for the voyage. You see, there's no contradiction between our heritage and our ambition if the conditions are right. That's a myth perpetrated by people who want to keep their privilege. They can thrive together harmoniously."

CHAPTER 29

Thousands of people assembled to watch the launch of the *Masquerade*. Cars lined the entrance road to the spaceport, and merchants were selling binoculars, key chains, fresh fruit, sacks of water, folding chairs, charring strips of *suya*, hot tea from samovars, and plastic masks painted with spaceships to commemorate the launch. A band set up an enormous sound system to belt out catchy Fuji music, spurring people to throw open their arms to dance, the lead singer interjecting the word *Masquerade* into every song, even when it didn't rhyme. Electric *okada* motorcycles busily transported people to the area before zipping off again to collect another fare.

In the spacecraft, the astronauts were on their backs in their molded chairs, running through the final safety checks with Josephine at mission control. The Wodaabe women melted into the teeming crowd, bidding Seeta good-bye as they waited for Max to take them to the border with Cameroon to find their children. The fixer somehow maneuvered his pickup truck through the throngs of onlookers to meet them near the entrance road to the spaceport.

"Looks like you fixed that windshield, Max," Bracket observed.

"A friend fixed it for me."

"You mean friends fix things for you too?"

"All the time, Kwesi. I'm saving to buy a new truck."

Inside the cab of the pickup, he could see that Max had brought his boy with him, an almond-eyed kid about five years old who buried his face in his father's armpit, looking sleepy.

"He wants to see the launch," Max said.

"Might sleep through it," Bracket replied, and laughed.

Police lights flashed as a car moved slowly through the crowd. The Wodaabe women ducked behind Max's pickup truck, but they were mistaken—the police car was merely leading an entourage of mounted horsemen, the riders looking resplendent in their royal-blue-and-crimson turbans. The Emir of Kano's face was obscured by a veil as he passed by with his bodyguards and royal coterie, an impressive display of power. Bracket was surprised to recognize the trader Ibrahim Musa spurring his own horse along too—the man had never spoken of his connection to the royal family. The emir waved to the crowd as he made his way through the procession to the front gates of the spaceport, the *clip-clop* of horses continuing until the caravan disappeared inside the gates.

"You should probably get going, Max," Bracket said.

"All right, *oyibo*." He gently snapped a seat belt around his son, who had fallen asleep.

The Wodaabe women huddled in their wrappers against the swift cold of the Sahel as Max started the ignition. Bracket was turning away from them when Balewa beckoned to him with her finger. He stepped closer and he saw that she was carrying something in her hand: an amulet, no, a rock. A Songstone. She handed it to him. Then she and the other Wodaabe women were riding away as the crowd parted around the truck, on their way now to find their children.

Fingering the Songstone in his pocket, Bracket paced quickly back to Naijapool, where his staff were eagerly awaiting him. Five Naijanauts were resting below in the suit-donning room, and the divers were carefully scrubbing and checking their equipment. For now, they would all be watching the rescue mission from afar. He climbed the stairs to the operations room and joined the others at their posts. Flipping on the various screens, he saw Josephine hooked in to her command chair in the Nest, her movements swift and focused as she manipulated the menus before her. On the comms he heard her checking with the various directors at the station. Another feed showed the *Masquerade* itself, and a different one displayed the astronauts strapped into their chairs, the form-fitting seats upholstered in goatskin, cow leather having been shunned by the Hindu staff. The interior of the spacecraft was painted in bright colors, with patterns borrowed from various cultures across Nigeria.

The countdown began, slow and measured, Josephine pausing long enough to give each director an opportunity to abort the mission if anything indicated a safety hazard. *T-minus...3...2...1...*

And she continued on until you could see the Naijanauts vibrating as the rocket lifted them skyward. Bracket felt the entire building shake with the tremendous energy of the launch. In the corner of the image, the mission clock was inset into the wall: 1:08. The G-forces pinned the astronauts back as they ran through the safety checks. One Naijanaut—a Yoruba man, with a sculpted, taut-skinned face and dark lashes—smiled as they accelerated quickly beyond the sound barrier. 2:34. The feed ran through various angles as the first rocket stage detached. The Yoruba man let out a whoop of joy. Soon they had passed out of view of the naked eye. 5:56. The second rocket detached. And now it was just the *Masquerade* rushing out alone along the blue horizon.

The spark started as a blip, almost like a ghost pixel that hung on the screen for too long. It erupted into a white light that lit up the interior of the craft in a hail of static. The astronauts began jerking violently in their seats. Josephine began bellowing orders: "Seal valve 26-7!"

"Can't do it remotely!"

"Mission commander," she said. "Seal valve 26-7. Manual!"

A young Naijanaut reached out against the colossal forces of gravity to unstrap one of her buckles, which flung backward over the seat. Now she was pushing her shoulder away from her berth and reaching up and . . . there! She had switched the valve and stopped the hissing air just as the *Masquerade* freed itself of the atmosphere.

"Damage report!" Josephine barked.

The crew indicated that two rivets had blown off a starboard-side porthole. The window had remained in place and was properly sealed for the moment, but it had also bent under the friction, losing its structural integrity.

"Engineering—will it survive reentry?"

"No," came the reply.

"Find me a solution! We need to seal that now! Kwesi," she added, her voice oddly calm, "get ready to put your team in the pool. *Masquerade*, follow your workplan. We'll send new orders for reentry in sixty minutes."

On-screen, Masha Kornokova was dangling from a tether in her space suit outside her living module of the station, awaiting the arrival of *The Masquerade*. Through her helmet you could see her face made gaunt from more than a year of rationing and weight loss. Her healthy cheeks were now stretched tight against her jaw.

The astronauts on the rescue crew put on their helmets and depressurized the spaceship, allowing Kornokova to ingress through the cargo bay of the *Masquerade*. One of the Naijanauts unstrapped to welcome her and fasten her into a berth. They could be seen cheering widely, reaching over to pat her on the back, or giving her arm a playful squeeze.

The sight of Kornokova alive and well filled Bracket with elation. Like most staff, he'd seen her alone in the cold recesses of the station for months on end. But there she was, ready to return to Earth.

Except they couldn't return home now—not without risking the spacecraft and everyone's life with it. The lost rivets were a unique design that had no replacements on the station or the spaceship. After scanning a schematic, one of the Indians in the Nest located an extruder in the exposed Kibo module, a 3D printer that had only been used for experiments before the module was damaged by space debris.

"What do we know about the printer?" Josephine asked.

"All we know is that it was custom made for the station by Daihatsu."

"That's it? Can someone get ahold of JAXA?"

The Comms team tried to hail someone from the Japanese space agency, to no avail. "They appear to be offline," they reported.

"I know someone who can help," Bracket chimed in over the comms.

"Who?" Josephine asked.

"Give me five minutes." He hurtled down the steps to the dive equipment room, where he found Santander, whose head jerked to and fro as he was immersed in his newsfeed. "We need your help."

"Three hundred million tune in to watch botched space rescue. I'm not allowed to dive, Kwesi."

"Not to dive." Bracket explained what he needed as Santander removed his glasses and his eyes refocused on the room around him.

"I can find it," the newshound nodded decisively, "but I need full privileges to run a proper search. Let me out of the Loom. I need access to all the international networks. They've got to turn off their firewalls."

"Josephine?" Bracked called in. "Did you catch that?"

"We'll make it happen," she said. "Someone get me Bello."

The politician set to work calling in favors to diplomats and business associates around the world, until the national networks in Nigeria, Kazakhstan, Argentina, Malaysia, Japan, and even China began to lower their firewalls one by one. Freed from all restrictions, the newshound plunged in, scraping the networks at blazing speed, hopping across borders until he found a former Japanese astronaut posting pictures of his pet papillon on a local microblog. Soon the astronaut was explaining the specifications of the extruder from the Kibo module in minute detail, with Santander translating it for Josephine in near real time.

"What's its application?" Josephine asked.

"Machine parts," he replied. "We printed wrenches and hand tools with it."

"Will it be strong enough for reentry?"

"We never tested for that—the machine is designed to work in microgravity."

"I need an answer. Will it be strong enough?"

"In theory, yes. The polymer is rated to seventeen hundred degrees celsius."

"That's our best shot. Run the simulation, Kwesi."

Bracket sprinted to the pool deck. Five minutes later, the Naijanauts and the divers were in the water. Bracket coordinated their simulation from the operations room as Josephine uplinked a modified workplan. Soon she disappeared into her privacy cone. She was fully jacked in now, linked to all the mission directors through haptic feedback that would vibrate as status reports came in.

In the tank, the divers placed a mock-up of the extruder in the Kibo module. A Naijanaut had to enter underwater, then she had to carry the 3D printer back outside the station to the *Masquerade* through the cargo bay, where the crew would bring it to room temperature for it to function properly. The first underwater attempt failed, as the damaged Kibo module didn't allow the astronaut to enter from earthside. So they improvised a hook that allowed the Naijanaut to wrest back the damaged canvas of the module to create enough room for an EVA pack to slip inside.

"Something's inside the module," one of the Naijanauts shouted on the comms.

A silver streak flitted through the water.

"Just a fish," a diver said. "Must have been living in there."

"Ignore it," Bracket ordered. "Won't hurt you."

"How did it survive down here?" the Naijanaut asked.

"Forget about it. Focus."

Bracket was feeding orders back to Josephine, as they continually corrected and refined each maneuver. They ran the simulation four times in a row until they had perfected each twist of the rivet, each hiss of gas from the EVA pack, Bracket's underwater team performing with passion and intense concentration.

And then it was happening two hundred kilometers above them. Already friction was wrenching away the solar panels of the ISS, which would soon begin its deorbital fall to the planet. The silicon wafers rippled under the force. They watched as the Naijanaut in space pushed through the Kibo module, grabbing the 3D printer. And then she was winding herself back along the station, clipping on hook after hook, as Earth slid away beneath her. She passed the extruder through the airlock for the crew inside to print out the rivets. An hour later, three tiny red rivets in hand—one extra, in case one floated away—the Naijanauts spacewalked outside the ship to fix the porthole, bolting it down.

Once the Naijanauts were safely back onboard, the pilot maneuvered to the underside of the station to correct its orbit, pushing the creaking hulk up five full kilometers away from the atmosphere. Now the spacecraft fired its booster to begin the descent back to Earth. The pilot angled the craft so that its tiles would absorb the tremendous heat of reentry, pitching the nose slightly to deflect heat away from the damaged porthole. Soon it was gliding expertly through the atmosphere. They were coming home.

All eyes were on the porthole. They would know soon whether they had secured it. Everyone watched as the cameras began to rattle. It seemed to be holding. But then the rivets! The rivets were becoming pliable, gummy even. A drop began to form, like a red protoplasm reaching out from the glass. Then the comms cut off.

A hush went over the operations room as Josephine ordered all chatter to stop.

In the ensuing silence, Bracket found himself humming a song, an old song pulled from his memory, the song of the Wodaabe and the Nok before them. He felt the Songstone warm in his pocket, thinking: *This could be our lodestar. This is what they need up there.*

And then he heard the cheers erupt as the *Masquerade* returned into view.

"We're okay!" the Naijanauts confirmed over their comms. "We've made it!"

Masha Kornokova, though weak and shaken, was kissing the camera lens, pointing at a rivet, which had solidified as it cooled, dangling from the porthole like a question mark.

"Josephine!" she was shouting, flicking the hardened rivet with her glove. "Josephine, I'm coming home!"

And still Bracket heard the song. He felt it inside him now. There. There was the source of the kingdom. There was the coiled-up, thigh-burning sprint. The rush of air around the brow. The beats surging in the blood. The dream that would sling them forward.

EPILOGUE

Ten years later

The *Masquerade III* slowly approached the River, the colossal space station that was anchored far beyond the Earth-moon system in a gentle equilibrium. Kwesi Bracket watched the liquid plays of light and color flowing through the station as the craft began to decelerate.

The River was made up of two parallel banks that undulated for thirty kilometers in a twisting helix. Between the Banks, barges ferried equipment powered by Noktech, riding on currents of pressure. Lattices of solar arrays branched from towers into the darkness like trees.

Seeta was strapped into a berth beside Bracket, busily reviewing a design for the latest thruster, a miniature version of the propulsion system that had carried them so rapidly from the spaceport in Kano. She was wearing a gold-and-violet sari-top suit that she could cinch open or closed for airflow.

"Have a look," Bracket said, pointing out the porthole.

She picked up her head briefly before returning to the blueprint on her Ivy-fone, which was curled around her upper arm. "I'll relax more when I know these idiots won't blow themselves up. They've confused miniaturization with replication. The physics change at scale. You can't shrink down a design and expect it to work exactly the same."

The space station in the distance was in effect a giant mining machine, where chunks of asteroids were hauled in at the source of the River to be pushed downstream by cometsmiths. By the time the asteroids emerged at the far end, all usable materials had been extracted, stabilized, and prepared for shipment back to Earth. The rest would be jettisoned carefully to the far reach of the system or sent for extrusion.

On approach, the station appeared nearly vertical to their own position in the starship. Bracket and Seeta had envisioned a horizontal approach vector in their original concept, like a seaplane landing on water, but fuel efficiency ruled out such comfort. The *Masquerade III* would follow the optimal path to dock. The varying routes also allowed Bracket a chance to observe the station from different angles each time he made the journey: the soaring telemetry spires, the photon shields, the circular clusters of habitats, and the steady stream of traffic maneuvering through the Banks. Compounding the visual puzzle, the entire helical structure swiveled on its long axis to induce artificial gravity. The twisting motion made his mind reel as he searched for a place to anchor his vision.

"I think I'll take a canoe down to the Compound," he decided.

"Are you feeling nauseous again? That's why I don't watch when we dock. Makes me bloody vomit."

"Might help if you could spin me some music."

"I already battened my equipment away, Kwesi. I've been through three pairs of earbuds because they keep floating off." She squeezed his hand. "Next time I'll remember to leave some out."

"I'd appreciate that. I can't help myself from watching the station. Anyway, I think I'll stop in to say hello to Sybil on the way down to the Compound."

"You just want her to prescribe you some antinausea pills."

"Won't complain if she has them."

Seeta ordered her Ivy-fone to climb onto the wall so she could get a better look at the blueprint specifications displayed on each of its leaves. "You know she's dating someone, right? A nurse."

"She didn't tell me."

"Go easy on him. He's a sweet kid."

"Sweet I can handle. That tends not to be her type."

"She's not a student anymore, Kwesi. She's on her own."

It was true. His daughter had developed a proud independence during the Flare that had won her a medical fellowship at the River without Bracket needing to pull any strings.

They waited as the *Masquerade III* tethered itself to one of the Banks, feeling the subtle shift in rhythm that indicated the spacecraft had docked, and he immediately exited with Seeta to avoid getting stuck in the queue for the airlock—the starship, stretched to its physical limits by Noktech, now accommodated some fifty passengers, most of them scientists, with some prosperous sightseers among them. These would ride down the River in a luxury tourist yacht, stopping at ports along the way, and then either take a countercurrent back to the dock or lift off again from the catchment area at the far end, which was called the Basin.

They were greeted at the elevator by an official crier.

"Presenting Chief Bracket," the young woman announced.

"It's Kwesi." He didn't like the title that Nurudeen Bello had conferred on him.

"My mistake, sir. Presenting Chief Kwesi Bracket." Before he could correct her, she scanned Seeta's biometrics: "Presenting Ambassador of Sound Seeta Chandrasekhan."

"Thank you, young lady."

The Indians had allowed Seeta to choose her own title for herself.

The elevator brought them down to the level of the River, and Bracket felt the added weight of his space suit as the microgravity kicked in. Seeta stepped out of the airlock into a diplomatic shuttle to zoom ahead straight to the Compound without making any stops. He waited to board a canoe tended by a sullen woman with a bright green-and-orange Kente wrapper.

"Where are you going?" she asked.

"Medical."

She had the glazed eyes of someone who'd been chewing synthetic cathinone. Station employees used khat to stave off their appetites on long shifts.

"Medical Port will take an hour. We've got eight more stops."

"I'm not in any hurry."

"Ten cowries."

He flashed his badge. "Diplomat."

She clucked her tongue against her teeth. "Ah, no, no, no. Diplomatic badges only work between eight hundred and eighteen hundred hours Earth time."

"When did that start?"

"Last week."

"No one tells me these things." He fished out a cowrie to place in her purse, which extracted the value into her account. All canoe pilots worked for their wages after Nurudeen Bello had insisted on opening intrastation travel to competition, even if food, medicine, and lodging were free.

After checking the passengers' safety tethers, the pilot began singing softly under her breath. The engine registered her voice and powered the vessel into the current. Soon it was looping back her melodic phrases as she layered on two counter-rhythms. They swiftly joined the flow of passing crafts, all of them tightly surrounded by a bluish spectral field that added to the liquid feel of the River.

Bello messaged him as soon as they pushed off.

"What is it, Nurudeen?" Bracket asked.

"We've got a problem with the Zuni emissary."

"From the Pueblo Confederacy?"

"Yes."

"I'll be there shortly. First I've got to see my daughter."

"I'm sending you a shuttle."

"It's too late. I'm already on a canoe. I'll see you soon."

"Don't dally, Kwesi."

"Never do."

The pilot called out each port for the passengers to dismount: first the Fields, which also included the protein vats; the Pits, which held the recycling facilities; Exploration, for research and development; then the Forges, which contained the extruders that had built the station. Each port was painted in a different color, the Forges looking the most exuberant with their robes of silicate beads woven together in a billowing lattice that traced the path of the sun.

"Next up, the Oracles," the pilot announced.

Bracket felt his stomach beginning to settle in the slow, meandering current. He swiveled his body to watch the Banks slide by and saw a hauler plodding along in the shipping channel with a hunk of ice fifty meters wide in its grappling arms. Behind him, he could hear the dulcet tones of the pilot's voice as she maneuvered the canoe through the River. She wasn't bad, he thought. Wasn't bad at all.

ACKNOWLEDGMENTS

I had a tremendous amount of support in creating this book. My wife, Carolynn, is the most generous editor and insightful reader I could ever have dreamed of. My literary agent, Gary Heidt, has been my advocate for some time, believing in me and constantly encouraging me to do more. Chris Heiser and Olivia Smith at Unnamed Press launched their publishing company with *Nigerians in Space* and patiently helped me develop this sequel into a coherent story. From the beginning, they never insisted that I write a stereotypical novel about an African village with acacia trees. Thank you for that.

And my family continues to believe in me and my strange hobby. Thanks especially to Jide Olukotun, who helped me with Nigerian Pidgin.

I was helped by several scholars. These include Professor Tamara M. Greene, an expert on ancient Harran; Sharon Thibodeau, an expert on astrolabes; Professor Ravi Rau, an expert on quantum physics; and Hilary Matfess, an expert on Boko Haram and a research analyst at the Johns Hopkins School of Advanced International Studies. Dr. Olufemi Agboola generously showed me around the National Space Research and Development Agency in Abuja, Nigeria, after an introduction by Dr. Wole Soboyejo, dean of engineering at Worcester Polytechnic Institute and the former president of the African University of Science and Technology. I also received assistance from the archivists at NASA, who dug up the article about the tracking station in Kano that was the genesis of much of this book. The idea of an ancient chamber that resonated with music first came to me through Antoine Seronde, who studied the temples of Egypt for acoustic resonance decades ago. I was like a kid in a candy shop (or a sea lion in a pool) at the Neutral Buoyancy Lab in Houston, where I went on a tour guided by a high school kid at the space center. Nigeria should have high school kids giving tours of its space facilities too.

I'd also like to thank the reviewers who read *Nigerians in Space* and praised it, or lent their critical eye to the story so that I could write this one better. This includes Tade Ipadeola, president of PEN Nigeria. And finally, thank you to the independent bookstores that have carried *Nigerians in Space* and coaxed readers into buying it.

Any honest author writing today owes a great debt to Wikipedia. So do I—it fulfills the promise of the open Internet. Along those lines, I'd like to thank my colleagues at the organization Access Now, including Gustaf Björksten, who provided insights into some of the technology described in the story. (The technical errors are my own.)

The following sources are listed more for your interest and further reading. This is not an exhaustive list—there are many more great works (and people) that inspired me to create this story.

El-Rufai, Nasir Ahmed, *The Accidental Public Servant* (Ibadan, Nigeria: Safari Books, 2013).

Gibbs, Sharon, with George Saliba, *Planispheric Astrolabes from the National Museum of American History* (Washington, D.C.: Smithsonian Institution Press, 1984).

Krause, Bernie, *The Great Animal Orchestra: Finding the Origins of Music in the World's Wild Places* (New York: Little, Brown, 2012).

Mann, Charles C., *1491: New Revelations of the Americas before Columbus*, 2nd ed. (New York: Vintage, 2011).

Nuwer, Rachel, "Solar Sleuths," *Scientific American,* July 2016.

Ojo, G.J. Afolabi, *Yoruba Culture: A Geographical Analysis* (London: University of London Press, 1966).

Onukaba, Adinoyi Ojo, *Atiku: The Story of Atiku Abubakar* (Abuja, Nigeria: African Legacy Press, 2006).

Popper, Nathaniel, *Digital Gold: Bitcoin and the Inside Story of the Misfits and Millionaires Trying to Reinvent Money* (New York: HarperCollins, 2015).

Saro-Wiwa, Noo, *Looking for Transwonderland: Travels in Nigeria* (Berkeley, CA: Soft Skull Press, 2012).

Smith, Mike, *Boko Haram: Inside Nigeria's Unholy War* (London: I.B. Tauris, 2015).

Soluri, Michael, *Infinite Worlds: The People and Places of Space Exploration* (New York: Simon & Schuster, 2014).

Tanner, Henry, "African Tracking Station Set Up in Desolate Area Near Aging City," *New York Times,* February 21, 1962.

Tsiao, Sunny, *"Read You Loud and Clear!" The Story of NASA's Spaceflight Tracking and Data Network* (Washington, D.C.: NASA, 2008).

Tyson, Neil deGrasse, *Space Chronicles: Facing the Ultimate Frontier,* ed. Avis Lang (New York: W. W. Norton, 2012).

van Offelen, Marion, and Carol Beckwith, *Nomads of Niger* (New York: Harry N. Abrams, 1983).

DEJI BRYCE OLUKOTUN is the author of two novels, *Nigerians in Space* and *After the Flare*, and his fiction has appeared in three different book collections. He works in the field of digital rights on issues such as internet shutdowns, cybersecurity, and online censorship, and he is also a Future Tense Fellow at the New America Foundation. Previously, he defended writers around the world at PEN America with support from the Ford Foundation. His work has been featured in Electric Literature, Quartz, VICE, Slate, *The Los Angeles Times*, *The Los Angeles Review of Books*, *The Wall Street Journal*, National Public Radio, *The Atlantic*, and *Guernica*. He lives in Brooklyn, NY.

@unnamedpress

facebook.com/theunnamedpress

unnamedpress.tumblr.com

www.unnamedpress.com

@unnamedpress